Being Dracula's Widow
A novel
By Faith Marlow

Published by

Crushing Hearts and Black Butterfly Publishing, LLC.

Novi, Michigan 48374

Cover art by:
Rue Volley
Edited by:
Elizabeth A. Lance

This is a work of fiction. All of the characters, organizations and events portrayed in this novel are a product of the author's imagination. Any resemblance to persons, living or dead, actual events, or organizations is entirely coincidental.

Scottie, this is for you, with much love and appreciation. Being the spouse of an author is not an easy job but you handle it all in style. Thank you. I hope you are ready to do it all again.

Part One:

Life after Death

Faith Marlow

Chapter One

"Valeria! Valeria, I am afraid!" Ilona's scream sliced through Valeria's heart like a thunderclap, despite being no louder than a whisper. Terror swept over her, not for her own sake, but for Ilona. The sound of the old slayer's boots against the dirt and stone floor of the crypts sounded like the tolling of church bells after a funeral, deep and hollow. "Valeria, please!" Ilona cried out as the slayer placed his hateful stake upon her heart and lifted his hammer high overhead.

"I will do it, Ilona, I swear! I swear it!" Valeria screamed to the terrified woman, her friend, her lover. Every fiber of her body wanted to rush to her rescue, to tear out the slayer's throat and hold Ilona close and safe against her as he died at their feet, but she could not move, not even lift a hand to help her. The hammer thundered down upon the stake, Ilona gasped and gurgled as it shattered through her chest like a battering ram. Another echoing impact rattled Valeria's bones when the ruthless slayer struck the stake once more and pierced Ilona's gentle heart. She gritted her teeth as she listened to Ilona die, to her lament for her fleeting life and for the son she had waited so long for.

"Ilona!" she screamed, her squinted eyes flooded by bloody tears. She felt like the weight of the world was pushing down on her, the breath squeezed from her chest. Time passed with slow cruelty as a labored gasp refilled her lungs and her eyes popped open, a fine mist of sorrow settled on her face like dew, flung from her lashes.

Terror filled her heart as the slayer looked down upon her, Fleur and Ilona's blood caught in the wrinkles of his face. She feared death in that moment with the same intensity she had felt when she gazed down from the battlement of Castle Dracula on the last night of her human life over four centuries ago. Only now she feared not for herself, but for Emil,

Ilona's beloved son, who would no doubt die a cold and lonely death should she not find a way to survive.

"Aunt Veevee."

A quiet voice and a light touch on her shoulder woke her from her nightmare with a shock. The face above her started to change from the vengeful slayer's puzzled stare to the intently concerned face of a young boy. Still caught within the spell of the dream, Valeria continued to cry, reliving the emotions of that terrible day with chilling realism.

"Aunt Veevee, did you have the dream again?"

Valeria snubbed and shook her head in agreement before covering her face with her hands. Slowly she rolled to sit on the side of the bed, propping her elbows on her knees while wiping her eyes. "I am sorry, Emil. I did not mean to frighten you."

"You didn't frighten me, I just hate seeing you so sad," he replied. He shuffled around nervously for a moment as he waited for her to compose herself before finally excusing himself from her room.

Ten years had passed since the deadly encounter with the slayer on that frigid winter night. Ten years since the restless Fleur had found her death at the end of his stake and knife. Ten years after Valeria had promised her beloved Ilona that she would stop at nothing to protect her son in her absence. She could still hear her cry in her dreams as clearly as the moment she died. And after four centuries of marriage, she had spent a decade without him, without Vlad.

The grief caused by his absence puzzled her the most. The cold grief of Ilona's absence was no surprise. It was only natural to long for her companionship and gentle presence. She had been loyal and loving when he had not, present in his absence, a wife when she had no husband. Vlad was an unfaithful, deceptive, and cruel man, a terrible husband more often than not, but she had loved him and in his own misguided way, she knew he had loved her as well. In a dark and strange way, he had loved all three of his wives. Even when he abandoned them, she knew he would always come back, a constant in a world that was always changing. Without him somewhere in the background, she felt completely alone. It was like she was surrounded by a tomb of ice.

Emil had become her light in the darkness, her purpose for existing. During the same ten years, he had given her much happiness and it had been remarkable watching him change. Every day she could see he had grown a fraction taller, a measure smarter, while she remained unchanged. He understood it and it had made no difference. He loved her, his Aunt Veevee, and she loved him dearly, not only as a nephew, but as a son. But with the joy came an inevitable sadness, a pain with the happiness, bittersweet. He was growing up, becoming a man and she could not hide him away from the world forever. She knew one day sooner than she would like, she would have to let him go to live his life in the world of the living. For her, the span of his years would pass in the blink of an eye and then he would die, taking with him the last of happiness that remained in her life from her days at Castle Dracula. She knew she would live to see his children's children die. It seemed immortality had more to do with death than living.

The front door shut with a groan and a clack and Emil came back inside with an armful of firewood, his black hair full of snow. He shook it out, shaggy and damp, as he stuffed the grate with wood. He had left her to recover from her reoccurring nightmare, knowing she was reliving the last moments of his mother's life in her mind yet again. He remembered little of Ilona, save her long black hair that reminded him of spilled ink and her chilling embrace that felt identical to Valeria's. His mother and aunt shared the same snowy white complexion and the same curious eyes that flickered red in the light and as far as he could understand, had shared the same husband.

He had no memory of Vlad, but knew from Valeria's stories that he was a complicated and difficult man. He knew he was not his father, just as he knew Ilona was not his true mother, and neither Fleur nor Valeria were his true aunts. However it was not a painful knowledge, as it would have been far more difficult to believe he was their blood born child. He did not speak of his birth parents, knowing only that Ilona had taken him in after their death. He did not dare ask more about them for fear of upsetting Valeria and for fear of what he might learn.

Despite their seclusion, he had had a nurturing and pleasant childhood in his aunt's house, always well provided for and much loved. Although he had lacked the companionship of other children, he knew that in many ways he had lived a privileged life. He had never known hunger or want. He could read and write in four languages, Romanian, Hungarian, German, and English. He had studied mathematics and science. In addition to his studies and despite his young age, he was an accomplished hunter with a rifle and knew how to preserve meat. Valeria's gift to Emil had been that of confidence, the knowledge that he was prepared for whatever life decided to put in his path. She had prepared him for a life without her and as he grew older, that realization became more evident to him. Valeria lived in mortal fear for their lives, every minute of every day.

Valeria finally entered the main room of their small home. She leaned against the wall and watched as he carefully fed the fire, remembering how she had placed him in front of the stove to warm him that night. He was so small, so cold and hungry, so confused by their absence. She remembered his tiny arms around her neck and how his little voice, so full of concern and love, helped to draw her from the stupor induced by Vlad's death. He did not complain when she told him they had to leave Castle Dracula, did not cry when he had to leave most of his belongings behind, and did not fear her when she explained that to survive she had to drink the blood of the living. She credited Ilona with his pleasant disposition. Time had passed so quickly.

"Are you feeling better?" he asked, dusting the snow and chips of bark from his heavy coat.

"Yes, and thank you for fetching the firewood," she answered, walking to him to receive her morning hug. It was a habit that had lingered from when he was very young. As a small child, the soundness of her sleep troubled him when he woke earlier than her. Many days she had heard him call her name and felt him shake her arm to wake her, but the affliction of her sleep made it impossible for her to make any noticeable movements or produce any audible sounds to comfort him. Now he slept nearly as late as she and stayed awake late into the night before finally giving in to sleep. She looked out the window to gauge the time. "Did I sleep late?"

"Yes ma'am," he answered, pulling the watch from his trouser pocket. "It is nearly half past one o'clock. You struggled within your dream for better than an hour."

Valeria sat at the quaint table in the corner close to the fire, still groggy. Emil sat across from her in their other chair. "When did you start taking care of me instead of the other way around?"

"Around the time you started looking less like my mother and more like my sister," Emil replied with a smile, garnering a critical grin from Valeria.

"Fair enough, I suppose," Valeria responded. Her expression changed from playful to serious, seizing the opportunity to inquire upon his thoughts of the future. "But you cannot watch over me forever. Have you given any thought of your future, of a trade?"

Emil rubbed the back of his neck, put off by her interrogations. "You worry too much, Aunt. I am but thirteen, there is plenty of time for such talk."

"No Emil, this is exactly the time you must be thinking of these things. You do not have a father's footsteps to follow into a trade or business and many young lads start apprenticeships at eleven or twelve, sometimes younger." Valeria preached passionately, but he was less than enthusiastic. She knew that years that seemed like an eternity away for him would pass her by like days, every day as only a few hours. She worried one day she would wake and discover that he was no longer be a boy, but a man who lacked the skills he needed to survive in an unforgiving world, should she no longer be able to watch over him. So she had become part mother and part headmistress, providing extensive instructions in the areas she believed would serve him best in a quickly evolving world. She had to live up to Ilona's expectations and time seemed to be slipping through her fingers.

"Are you so eager to be rid of me?" Emil fired back. He instantly dropped his head, regretful of what he had said in frustration.

Valeria gasped and covered her mouth with her hands, as though she hoped to grab the words and take them back. "Oh Emil, I am sorry." She quickly stood and rushed to him, standing before him with arms outstretched. "Please forgive me. Nothing could be further than the truth."

The human boy looked up to his vampire guardian, his motherly protector, with relief and accepted her gesture. He had never sassed her, never had a frustrated word for her until that moment. "I am sorry, Aunt Veevee. It was wicked of me to speak to you in such a way."

"No Emil, it was I that was wrong. I forget sometimes that time passes differently for you and I. It's only because I want to do what is best for you, what your mother would have wanted for you. I am so deathly afraid I will fail her…and you."

"I know you want good things for me, Aunt. I will think on it, I promise," Emil agreed, contemplating his transition from child to adult, from their secret life to the outside world. A budding fear and uncertainty began to bloom within his heart.

***

By the time Valeria returned from hunting, Emil had already fallen asleep. She slipped into the house without a sound and laid another log on the fire. Emil shifted in his sleep, as though his subconscious was aware of her of her presence. If their house had been larger, he would have had his own bedroom with a large fireplace and lined with shelves of books. Instead he slept on a simple rope and straw bed in the main

8

room of their house, the warmest room. Valeria stayed in the small second room, having no need for the warmth of the fire.

She had hidden in the woods with him in the tiny hunting lodge since leaving Castle Dracula. She discovered it only days after Vlad's death and quickly began making repairs, working from sunset to sunrise until it was fit for a child. Long abandoned, the seclusion meant safety from any slayers or curious villagers that might be looking for her. The little house had become her sanctuary, but she knew the time to move on was quickly approaching. If Emil stayed there much longer, he would grow up to be a reclusive mountain man. That was not the life she wanted for him or what Ilona would have wanted for him. She would have wanted him to meet friends and find love. Then if he should choose to raise crops and children for the rest of his life, he would be provided with farmland and animals to tend. No matter what he chose for himself, Valeria would see to it that he had it. With enough cunning and careful charms, she would find a way to set him on the path to any life he wished for. Ilona would have done no less.

She felt guilty for pressuring him earlier. How could a boy who knew so little of the world be expected to make such an important decision about his future? He had never been to a city, or even a village of respectable size. It was then that she realized that he had known more vampires in his young life than humans, and most of them were now dead. She had hidden him away long enough. Tomorrow she would decide the city and in a month they would be living in a new home.

Chapter Two

Three weeks and two days later, just after three o' clock on a chilly afternoon in early March, Valeria and Emil stood in front of a boutique in downtown Brasov. They were wearing their finest work clothes, gazing through the window at the latest fashions the twentieth century had to offer. Until that day, Emil had never seen more than four people in one place, but now he suddenly found himself in the heart of a crowded, bustling city surrounded by hundreds, if not a thousand strangers. Valeria was quite amazed how well he was handling himself, refraining from the tell-tale rubbernecking of a visitor. She was so impressed by his performance that she decided that she would speak with him about studying acting or taking on an apprenticeship at one of the great acting companies in Paris or Prague, or perhaps even London although her past association with the city had made it an unfavorable destination for her.

With only a nod from Valeria, he strode calmly and straight backed into the shop, the bell over the door announcing his arrival as he entered. He understood her situation and knew he would need the proprietor to provide an invitation before she could enter. She waited outside; carefully standing away from the large picture window, fearing a passerby might notice her lack of reflection.

"Excuse me sir but do you have time available to speak with my aunt concerning a purchase?" Emil asked as he motioned outside, laying the bait. The man peeked around Emil to look through the window for a glance, but Valeria was out of eyeshot. "She has particular tastes."

"Of course lad, I am sure our shop can meet her expectations," he answered with the wide crocodile smile of a salesman, stopping short of a true invitation to enter.

"So she can come inside now, to speak with you?" Emil stammered awkwardly.

"Yes boy!" the man spat with a cross look, his bushy brows knitted over his pockmarked nose. "Go fetch the lady! Never keep a customer waiting!"

Emil dashed outside and nodded it was acceptable for her to enter, informing her as though she did not possess the ability to hear their conversation. He politely held the door open for her and followed two steps behind her, as he had been instructed was proper. They both agreed it was rubbish, but did so as to not stand out any more than they certainly were going to despite their best efforts. Humans were almost magnetically drawn to Valeria, like a moth to the flame. Often they would walk away from her, questioning themselves how she was different, but unable to put their finger on just how. Women were often jealous of her unnatural beauty and men would become smitten after only a glance.

The shopkeeper stared at Valeria a moment, his face bent by perplexity, before he noticed himself and politely bowed. For his sake, she pretended she did not notice and nodded in return, a thin grin on her sealed lips. "How...how might I help the lady today?"

"Yes sir. Recently my nephew, whom you have already met, and I have had a stroke of good fortune. We have come into some money, not a considerable amount of cash, mind you, but favorable to us just the same. Until now we have been but simple farmers, laborers of the land, as I am sure you can see by our dress, but no longer. We wish to start again here in Brasov and we will need proper clothing." She explained in half truths, her voice melodic and low like a lullaby.

"Yes ma'am. Yes you will," he answered, slowly shaking his head in agreement as the last waves of her words washed over him. "What did you...did you have in mind?"

12

"I don't know. What is smart these days?" she asked, allowing a smidge of her pearly smile to shine through her lips in a beguiling grin. "Can you show me?"

He nodded slowly again. "Yes…yes ma'am," he answered, catching himself in an unblinking stare. He awkwardly sprinted toward a mannequin on display and pulled it toward her. "This is the latest fashion ma'am, a shirtwaist blouse," he said, turning the form so she could see the pouter front and tailored lines. "And this stylish skirt is very popular with ladies of high regard, floor length of course." He pulled the bottom of the skirt out to better show its trumpet-like shape.

"Of course, I will take four skirts and six blouses and three sets of undergarments," she answered nodding her head, which he mimicked. "I will need to see your selection of fabrics when we have finished."

"A corset?" he asked.

"Of course," she returned coolly. "And I would like for you to measure Emil for two shirts, two pairs of trousers, and a suit befitting a young man. He will need undergarments as well."

"Certainly, ma'am." The man smiled widely, the anticipation of such a sizable purchase knocking loose the binds of her charms. She watched him intently as he scurried around the shop and then as he pulled the measuring tape taunt along Emil's arms and legs, taking a pencil from behind his ear to note his dimensions on a small pad. Occasionally he would look at her and pause, briefly glued in place by the power of her gaze, before returning to his work. "Might I impose upon the lady for some measurements?"

Valeria nodded cordially, but inwardly she was concerned he might become alarmed by her lack of warmth. He wrapped the yellowed measuring tape around her waist, hips and bust, carefully noting the measurements in between, before measuring her length from waist to the floor. Finally he stretched it down her arm to the edge of her sleeve, pressing the end of the tape against the back of her hand.

"Dear God, woman! You have the coldest hands I have ever known!" he blurted out, before sucking his lips over his toothless gums to shut his mouth. His eyes wide, he was immediately afraid he had insulted her, thereby endangering her business. He bowed his head. "My apologies, ma'am."

Emil suddenly ruffled, his forehead wadded tight. "As right you should, insulting the lady in such a manner!" His untamed hair and burgeoning yet sporadic beard outlined his face in such a manner that he resembled an angry cat.

Valeria quickly pulled him to her side, wrapped her arm through his in an unassumingly strong grip. The man crinkled his nose in disapproval of his youthful reprimand. "Poor blood circulation, I am afraid, quite anemic as well. I take no offense, sir. Please excuse my nephew. He is terribly protective of his sickly aunt."

"Right then…" he answered, still put off. Emil shifted uncomfortably from foot to foot. "When will you need your order completed?"

"Can you have it finished in three days?" she asked.

"Ma'am, an order of this size, with all the alterations, usually takes no less than a week," he responded, as though he was informing her of something she should have already known.

She focused her eyes into his, looking behind the iris to the mind within. "Three days and you will be rewarded handsomely, a bonus of thirty percent."

"I look forward to seeing you in three days, ma'am, and you too young sir," he answered, stretching out his hand to shake hers, the hand he had only moments ago recoiled from. Emil stuffed his hands in his pockets and dropped his head, intending to have no part of his duality. The shopkeeper pulled his hand back and rubbed them together, chilled more from Emil's rejection that Valeria's grasp. "Right then…"

"Until Friday…" Valeria said, gracefully nodding her head in his direction. She turned and left, Emil following just behind her.

"M… Ma'am, I apologize, but I do not recall your name," he stuttered, grabbing his pencil and pad again. "What name should I place the order under?"

She felt her stomach drop, despite having given her alias to several clerks during the process of purchasing their house and its furnishings, signing it on countless papers. She had left her true name behind her, locked away with her secrets in Castle Dracula. Her false name reminder her how much things had changed, how alone she and Emil were. The shopkeeper looked at her patiently, still under the affects of her charms.

"Miss Albescu," she responded, hoping he had not heard the uncertainty wavering in her voice. She turned and quickly started for the door, carefully keeping her speed in check. "Valeria Albescu ," she said over her shoulder without looking back.

***

As soon as they were out of earshot of the shopkeeper, Emil ran in front of her to stop her. "Why did you allow that man to talk to you like that?" Emil questioned, confused by her submissiveness. "Why did you tell him you would give him more money after that?"

"Because I wanted our clothes to be done by Friday," she answered plainly. "Not everything has to be complicated. Some things just work out by themselves."

"Do we even have that kind of money?"

"No, not even half of it." She smiled, quickly dropping her head to avoid being seen. He chuckled and stuck out his arm, feeling rather vindicated. She looped through his elbow as they walked down the street, unconcerned to those who looked on or questioned. "You know if you take on an apprenticeship and your employer speaks harshly with you, you mustn't speak back."

"I know… I am just not accustomed to it, that's all," he replied, sighing heavily. Valeria petted his hand in consolation. "You have spoiled me, I am afraid."

"It would seem so."

Valeria sat in a chair by the window, watching the moon on her faithful patrol across the sky, like she had so many nights. Occasionally a shooting star would make it past her perimeter, but more often than not they all stayed where they belonged under her silent watch.

She listened to Emil's breathing through the wall of his new bedroom, listening for it to change into the slow, rhythmic pace of sleep before leaving to hunt. She scratched her scalp through her golden locks with both hands, almost like she was trying to massage her brain. She worried she had been too lax with him, that she had kept him hidden for too long to fully integrate now. He was comfortable with her, but had no patience for the rules and appearances of man's world. That, she feared, would be a problem. The all too familiar fear of failure was creeping into her heart again, fear of failing at her most important task, fear of failing Ilona. She sighed deeply and her body relaxed into a pillar of glittering mist, into the breath of the moon, and slipped out the cracked window.

A thin layer of smoke hovered over Brasov like a halo. She skimmed over the snow covered rooftops, leaving a trail of snow- dust behind her if she flew too low. It was offensively cold, which made finding an easy target stumbling down the street or into a dark alley impossible. She circled the heart of town again before coming to rest briefly atop the Trumpeter's Tower of the Town Hall. She had instantly fallen in love with the tower, had felt a strange kinship to it simply because it was older than her. It helped her to feel less like an artifact of an ancient time and more like an important part of present life, as the tower had endured many things over its long life and continued to be of importance. She wondered what had happened to Castle Dracula since she and Emil abandoned it, but the growl of her belly and the fire in her throat quickly refocused her attentions.

She had not fed since arriving in Brasov over three weeks ago. The urge to seek out a meal was now impossible to ignore, but caution had to be her biggest concern. Her strange and alluring presence drew enough attention to her and Emil while they were out and about in town. One mistake could endanger them both. People were no longer as quick to believe superstition, or as easy to fool. The late nineteenth century, and surely the twentieth to follow, was an age of scientific methods and cynicisms. It was harder now than ever for her to blend, to hide in plain sight.

High atop her perch, her mist shrouded body lingered against the cold tiles of the roof and listened as the giant clock's gears turned, ticking away the seconds and minutes with ruthless precision. The hollow clunks of the moving hand seemed to heighten her frustrations, remind her of the quickly approaching dawn. With a huff, she descended into the streets and quickly began to check the alleys and doorways, almost teleporting through the abandoned, snow drift lined streets. Her mind sporadically jumped between every store and city building she had been granted access to since arriving in the city, most of which were now dark and empty until morning, all but one.

A soured taste developed in her mouth as she remembered the homely, toothless tailor. She had known from the beginning she would be able to find a meal there, only having to wait until the aging man had fallen asleep to ply her trade, but his shop had still been the last place she had chosen to look. His ruddy complexion combined with his bloodshot eyes and the scent of cheap ale on his breath and skin announced his longstanding friendship with the bottle louder than if he was screaming it from the rooftop of the shop. After Fleur's unfortunate encounter with the intoxicated slayer, she had shunned hosts who were fond of drink, but tonight she had no other choice.

The shop was sealed tight, windows and doors shuttered and locked against the cold Romanian winter. The chimney puffed a steady plume of grey smoke, a sizzling fire blocking her entry through the hearth. Silent and swift, her shimmering shadow skirted the foundation in search of a crack or a loose rock, any point of entry she could exploit. Luck finally turned in her favor when she discovered the smallest of

17

holes gnawed through the wall, hidden behind the rubbish bin. Condensing into a thin stream, she poured through the mouse's secret door and into the shop.

Once inside, Valeria settled on the floor and against the wall like a thick, low-lying fog. She could hear him snoring noisily, could already smell the cheap beer on his breath. If drinking from a handsome young man was like having a goblet of the most expensive of wine and a lady of high society was a decadent desert, surely she would be having her vegetables tonight.

A dozing housecat's ear turned in her direction as she passed her, heading upstairs to the living quarters above the shop. A lantern at the top of the stairs shone dimly through its soot stained glass chimney, its pale light stretching across the floor. Just outside the halo of light, the slumbering tailor slept soundly in his nightshirt and cap, his blankets pulled tightly against his ear. She paused for a moment, choosing to remain in relative safety of her mist form. As he lay, he was inaccessible and although she had not received the warning call of the approaching morning, she knew it was only a couple hours away at most. Valeria groaned inwardly, knowing if had gone to bed drunk it could be some time before he moved enough that she could get her teeth on him without disturbing him. He could remain motionless until after dawn.

The fire burning in her throat was straining her patience, pushing her to test her limitations. She flattened herself into a thin cloud of haze and smoke and slid quietly under the bed. Moving over and around the cobwebs, shoes, and handful of empty liquor bottles, she scanned the edge of the blanket for a gap. His heart pounded in her ears, like a dinner bell, anticipation bristled up her amorphous spine. Every sense was heightened, every nerve was on edge as she compressed into a ribbon of dust and breath and crept beneath the bedding. With all her concentration, she gently settled her molecules into a thin layer, almost absorbing herself into the woolen blanket. Her vision jumped from the bend of his throat to his wrist, trying to decide which was the most accessible. With a loud snort he flipped onto his back and the decision was made. Before she disturbed him any further, she traveled up the wrinkles, hills and valleys of his nightshirt and settled around his open collar.

Warmed by the mountain of blankets, the tailor's skin was clammy with sweat, peppered with the scent of booze leaking through his pores. She wanted to shudder, to burst out from the blankets, and shoot out the window like an arrow before his smell could settle on her. Instead she allowed her face to lightly materialize from the fog; fearfully sharp teeth brandished and sank quick and deep into his flesh. As soon as the blood began to bubble up and pour into her mouth, she forgot the staleness of his breath and his offensive body odor. The first drink was quickly followed by another and the searing heat from her belly was stoked even hotter, demanding the next indulgent drink. A third mouthful of life and then a fourth was necessary before she began to feel a hint of rejuvenation, before the scalding heat was reduced to a slow burn. The man settled into a comatose deep sleep, the toxins of her kiss replacing his missing blood with apathy. Five and she could feel his energy pass from him and out through the fibers and cells of her dismantled body, bringing her back to life one molecule at time. Six and the gnawing hunger was abating, allowing her to smell and taste his skin again. Her forehead knitted, lines indicated by thicker concentrations of her misty form. She released his neck and slid out from under the bedding like a waterfall, a sheet of haze and luminous matter caught in the light of the lantern. Her shimmering silver- white fog was now stained by the slightest hint of red, a rosy hue like the shades of pink within a sunset. Instead of exiting through the way she entered, she condensed against the window and pushed against the sash and cracked it just enough to slide through. She carefully closed it behind her so he would not be alarmed when he woke, to confirm that anything he might remember had certainly been a dream.

As soon as she returned home, she glided through the window and returned to her physical body. She tiptoed through the setting area, past

Emil's door, and into her room, quickly closing the door behind her. Her garments fell to the ground as she evaporated out in an arching trail of fog, materializing whole and perfect in time for them to crumple into a pile at her feet. She was not bothered by the chilled water in the wash basin or the lack of heat or light in her room as she lathered up a sponge in fragrant soap and scrubbed hastily. The new day was approaching and the last thing she wanted was to wake up with the tailor's stale odor still lingering hours later. At least Emil would get a good laugh when he learned with whom she had had dinner with.

Chapter Three

A month after her evening visit to the tailor, Valeria huddled against the wind as she walked down the frozen street, pulling the collar of her wool coat high and covering her face with her scarf. Between the scarf and her rounded, Russian-style brown rabbit fur hat, all that was visible of her face was her icy, metallic blue eyes. She was not, cold but she needed others to believe she was.

Over the last two weeks, she had thoroughly enjoyed her new clothing, a fond memory of finery from long ago that would no doubt now be rotten and moth eaten. She had forgotten how wonderful good clothing felt, how every inch of her skin noticed the texture of the fabric, the direction of the weave, how she had enjoyed listening to it rustle as she walked. But as proud as she was of her new fashions, seeing Emil nicely dressed again made her the most proud. She had never believed that Ilona would have approved of their survival in the wilderness, living hand to mouth and toiling the earth, but she believed she would have approved of her reasons, her almost obsessive need to protect him. However Ilona had intended Emil to have bigger and better things and finally Valeria could see her dreams starting to come into fruition.

Against the will of the blustering snow, she arrived at the printing house where Emil had chosen to begin an apprenticeship. She shook the snow from her hat and coat quickly and silently closing the door against the winter air. She tucked her fur topped gloves into her coat pocket and stood quietly by the fire for some time to acclimate her temperature before approaching those inside. She desperately calculated her actions around these humans in particular, determined to draw no attention to herself for Emil's sake.

She was proud that after only a couple short weeks, Emil was well on his way to learning his chosen profession and relieved that Mihai, the master printer, no longer looked strangely at her. It had taken some convincing on her part, carefully chosen words to make the skeptical man believe that she was truly his young aunt. Her intricate web of lies detailed the most unfortunate situation, spun around the falsity that she was not yet ten years old when her unfortunate older sister had died in childbirth. His father was to have died of pneumonia when he four and now that her own parents had passed away as well, Emil was her responsibility until he was grown, his only remaining family. The fact that she claimed his lineage to Transylvania on his father's side and Hungary on his mother's positioned Emil in a fortunate bracket of Brasov's population. Despite being a stranger in the city, it was a place that along with some carefully placed charms would ensure Emil a chance at success in the highly biased and corrupt economic scene.

"Sorry Ma'am," Mihai said as he rounded the corner wiping his hand on his apron, surprised to find her there. "I never hear the door."

"It is quite all right." She smiled. "I try to not disturb you."

He paused for a moment, seemingly forgetting himself as Valeria tightened the reins of her deception. "Emil," he shouted as he walked away, rubbing his eyes. "It's time to go. Tomorrow is another day."

As she bundled up in coat and hat again, content that Mihai would not be shaking her hand tonight, Emil rushed to the door. When he saw her, his countenance slightly sank. She knew why, but said nothing. He shouted over the clanking gears and spinning belts. "Goodnight, Mihai."

Emil walked at a hurried pace, desperately trying to put distance between himself and his hovering aunt. He pulled the collar of his coat up to his ears, bent over to let the stiff winter wind blow over his head and down his back. She wanted to call out to him, to race to catch him, maybe even outpace him, but she decided to allow him his space. She was in no hurry for the confrontation she knew was impending.

Once inside the house, Emil was purposely silent, making as little sound as possible as he removed his snow covered shoes and neatly hung his coat and hat. The bottom of his trousers were wet from the slush, so he sat close to the fire to prop his feet on a small stool near the hearth. Valeria sat in front of the fire as well, hoping to start and finish the conversation as quickly and painlessly as possible.

He sat with his arms crossed tightly over his chest, his eyes darting between her and the fire. She could hear his teeth grind, see the muscles of his jaw constrict and clench in frustration.

"Aunt Veevee, I…"

"I know. I know you don't like it when I meet you at the shop, but…"

"I asked you not to. I can find my way home perfectly well without you holding my hand."

"I know. I know you can it's just… I worry about you. I promised…"

"I know all about your promise to my mother and if she was here, she would tell you that I am old enough to walk home without you! How am I supposed to be taken seriously at work when my *auntie* has to walk me home at night?" he stated, taking his arms from his chest to grasp the armrests of the chair, digging his fingernails into the upholstery. "It was you who insisted I take on an apprenticeship, that I needed to think of my future. How can I do that if you never allow me to think for myself?"

"I am sorry, Emil. I don't mean to offend you," Valeria conceded, taking one of his hands in both of hers. "I *must* worry about you. It's my job."

"For all the talk of my mother and your promises, I know so little about her. I hardly remember what she looked like." He sighed and leaned his head against the back of the chair, allowing some of his tiredness to catch him. "It seems like she has been gone forever, like she was only a dream."

"It often seems like just yesterday you were small and your mother was here, happier than I had ever seen her," Valeria confessed while still holding his hand, which was now the size of hers. "I assume that is why I do not talk of her more. The pain is still so new for me."

"Time passes much differently for you, doesn't it?" Emil asked, feeling comfortable enough to venture some questions.

"Yes, very differently than it did when I was human ," she said, her eyes drifting as though she was looking back through the ages, back to a time when her touch would not have chilled his hand. "Now it passes both very slowly and very quickly, which ever will distress me most. It has been so very long since I laid eyes on my own mother, but yet you seem to grow twice as fast as you should."

"Tell me about my mother, Valeria. I don't want to forget her," he pleaded, letting go of her hand so she could move her chair closer to his. He pushed the stool toward her so her feet could share it. "Truly tell me about her, not just clouded words and riddles. How did you meet her? Where did you live?"

Valeria pulled her bottom lip into her mouth, tugging at it gently with her teeth. She knew sooner or later he would ask. One day he would need to know the details that she had kept hidden because of their confusing nature or because of the feelings of loneliness and pain they rekindled. She would tell him now regardless.

"Well you may not believe it, but the first time I met your mother, I did not like her in the least. In fact I hated her, not because of whom she was, but because of the circumstances that had brought her into my life. I actually vowed to kill her."

"Kill her?" Emil said, almost shouting from the shock. "Why?"

"It's quite complicated."

"Please, Aunt. I know so little about her, about you, or her husband. He was your husband as well, was he not?"

"I said it was complicated ," she responded, her voice tinted by sarcasm.

"Please try, Aunt Veevee. I feel like I was just dropped on this Earth, like I fell from the sky like a shooting star. I know so little about how I came to be a part of this family." His eyes pleaded as he implored to her, piercing her quiet heart. "I deserve to know something."

"Indeed you do, so I will try," Valeria conceded, burying her face into her hands as she rubbed her eyes. She felt she lacked the parental tact necessary to explain such a dark and twisted tale to one so innocent. "I do not know even where to start."

"When were you born?"

"In the year 1440, I was the second daughter of Lord Stefan Karajan of Romania. I was married May nineteenth 1460 to a Transylvanian Count and moved to the castle where you lived as a young child with your mother and I, and Fleur," she explained, giving as brief an overview as she could and hoped he would not ask her the last name of her now very famous husband. Vlad had left behind quite an impression in the minds and hearts of the Romanian people.

"This Count, was he…" Emil did not how to continue.

"A vampire?" she interjected, helping him. "Not at first, but yes. It was he who bound me to this life, all of us to this life."

"How?" he questioned, his curiosity stretching past her level of comfort as her mind recalled in a blink a multitude of passionate nights, heated encounters, rapturous pain.

She shut her eyes for a moment to clear her mind. "An exchange of blood by bite, but I am afraid this is all I can tell you," she stated shortly, leaving no room for further questions. "Upon my death, I transformed into the creature you see before you, neither alive nor dead."

"How did you die?" Emil asked, deciding to push the envelope a measure more.

"I jumped," she confessed, the response coming easier than she had anticipated, like she was reciting the death of a character in a story

25

instead of her own demise. Her voice was dry and her eyes distant. The pit of her stomach still dropped when she thought of it, a sensation similar to falling in a dream. "The castle came under attack and my husband abandoned me to the invaders. I jumped so they could not take me captive."

"I am sorry, Aunt. I do not mean to cause you pain," he whispered, wringing his hands.

"No, it is all right. I cannot tell you your mother's story without telling my own. Our lives were intertwined too tightly to separate," she reassured, continuing the story despite the heartache because she believed, as he did, that he had a right to know his family secrets. "After my death, Vlad ended up in Hungary, where he was given your mother's hand in marriage by the King. She was a daughter of royalty, you know, a cousin to the King himself. They eventually returned to Romania and to the castle, which is where we met. She was great with child and believed I was dead."

"Is that why you hated her, because she was married to your husband?"

"Yes, for the most part, but I hated him even more for it. I knew from the beginning she had been deceived."

"What changed? How did you go from wanting to kill her to…" His uncertainty stopped him again.

"To loving her?" she asked boldly. "It did not happen overnight, but eventually we became friends. Vlad left her, after both she and the infant died in birth, just as he had left me. I could have easily killed her then, but instead I was compelled to help her, to ease her suffering. As greatly as I had suffered, I knew her pain was far worse. But over centuries our relationship blossomed, evolved. We were kindred spirits, the only people on the entire Earth that understood the other, that ever could. Not even Fleur understood this."

"You talk as though you loved her… as you would love a wife, I suppose." He was obviously confused.

"I told you, it was complicated." A small laugh highlighted her response. "But yes, for a while just before the end. When our husband felt it necessary to take his third wife, we turned against him and to each other."

"Aunt Fleur?" he asked. His forehead pinched with pondering.

"Yes, Emil. Our relationship with your Aunt Fleur was troubled at best. If it had not been for your mother's gentle nature and convincing, I would have killed her countless times." She watched Emil's eyes grow wide. "She was a difficult woman, especially when she was young to this life. But before the end, we made amends with Fleur, largely because of you."

"Me?"

"Yes. Vlad was gone, again, this time to London where he quickly began to chase necks and skirts with abandon. Ilona wanted to insure a stable home for you and she asked that both I and Fleur contribute to your upbringing, to help her protect you from those that would kill our kind." Valeria took her nephew's hands in hers and held them, just tight enough to feel his beautiful pulse below the surface of his fingers. "You brought peace to our home, to our lives, and joy. You brought unspeakable joy to your mother. You became her rising and setting sun, the light of her life. She loved nothing more than you, not even Vlad."

"I know I was born from a human woman. What happened to my human family?" he asked quietly, afraid of hurting her by asking.

Valeria felt the words stick in her throat, a dry knot of deceit. She could not bring herself to tell him of his birth mother's horrible death by the hungry wolves, how she had cried out with her broken mother's heart for the return of her child. She could not bear to tell him that she and Ilona had heard her cries and then watched her die, never once offering to return him to her or intervene on her behalf. "Vlad returned with you after a night of hunting. Your human parents were dead and you were left alone. You would have surely died if he had not found you when he did and brought you to Ilona," she lied as carefully and gently as she could. She rubbed the tops of his hands methodically and

27

rhythmically, her voice low and steady. Despite her outward calm, she was sick at her stomach, in her heart. She had promised herself that she would never use her ability to influence his mind, to make him believe a lie no matter how painful. She was revolted by her weakness, by how easily he was deceived, and how eager he was to believe her. "Ilona was overwhelmed with joy and fell in love with you from the moment she laid eyes on you. She promised that very night she would do whatever it took to protect you and I promised I would help her."

Slowly Valeria allowed her influence over Emil to wither, gently so he would be none the wiser. He paused for a moment as though to think and yawned. If she was lucky, he would contribute his momentary lack of concentration to his fatigue and think little of it. She acted as though nothing had happened, like she had not noticed his pause.

"Aunt Veevee..." he whispered, so quietly his words barely created sound. "Tell me how she died."

Valeria dropped her head and she squint her eyes. She felt a ripple of old fear chase up her back, heard Ilona's and Fleur's death cries in her mind. Most days, she could keep the images that haunted her dreams repressed from invading her waking hours, but Emil's question had riled them, brought them to the surface. So much happened so fast that night that it was difficult to know where to begin.

"Do you remember anything of that night?" she questioned, deciding to start there if he did.

"I remember Mother's hair brushing over my face when she told me goodnight. She stopped in the doorway to tell me she loved me and then she was gone. She seemed so sad, like she knew something was going to happen."

"She was afraid, Emil. Afraid that what happened would indeed come to pass."

"How did she know?"

"We knew slayers were close. Our less than faithful husband had been careless with his cavorting in England. He chose another man's wife for his latest bride, but he and his companions were set against it.

They chased Vlad back to Transylvania and followed him as he traveled toward our castle." Valeria paused a moment to catch her breath. She had spoken to no one about the events of that night, had not even confessed her trauma to the silent pages of a journal. She had struggled and suffered in silence for ten years, confiding in nothing or no one. She had vehemently shielded Emil from it for a decade, but now she was spewing her secrets like a fountain. It felt as though she was committing a wrong, breaking a promise, but she continued the purge. "We had decided, Fleur, your mother and I, that we would not accept another into our family. We vowed to kill this new woman and anyone that protected her to teach Vlad a hard lesson, and to protect you."

"You were going to kill her because of me? Why?"

"To protect you, Emil, it was too great a risk to have a young, delicious smelling, helpless human in the house with a new vampire."

"Did you ever want to eat me, did Mother?"

"No never, neither of us. However Aunt Fleur had different ideas when she first met you. She thought you were a midnight snack!" Valeria added, hoping to lighten the air with her joshing.

"Aunt Fleur?" Emil exclaimed, clutching his throat. "What did Mother do?"

"She protected you like a mother lion, dared her to touch you, as did I," Valeria stated proudly. "We would have stopped at nothing to keep you safe. I still feel the same."

"So what happened? Did you kill the other woman?"

"No. The old slayer that was with her was too wily and the dawn came too quickly. Our slumber overtook us before we could attack them. The last thing your mother did was race up the stairs to check on you, one last look before falling into her deep sleep." Valeria swallowed hard and bit at her lip, looking toward the fire, but not at it, her eyes drawn to an invisible point in time. "It was the last thing she did, checking in on you. You were still asleep."

"Did they find you?"

"Yes, Emil. Sadly the old man found us before sunset, before our powers were returned to us. Had it not been so, we would have torn him to ribbons for invading our home, for threatening your safety, but as it was, we were powerless. We could only watch as he came for us, first Fleur, then your mother, and finally me."

"What did he do?" Emil pushed further, desperate to finally understand the nightmare that woke Valeria so often.

"Must you know, Emil? Must you know every detail?" Valeria said, almost moaned and rolled her head to look at the ceiling, as if she was asking for mercy. "It will be nothing but pain for you."

"Please Aunt Veevee, I need to know what happened to her," Emil begged, eyes filled with earnest tears. He had never asked anything of her, had never questioned her actions or choices. Now he would not be denied.

Valeria sighed, knowing she could not talk him out of it. "He went to Fleur first. None of us could move. We could barely speak and even then it was so low that only we could hear it. He placed a wooden stake over her heart and raised his hammer high. I couldn't see it happening, nothing but the hammer rising, but I could hear it. She screamed pitifully, so loud I will never forget it. I think it was burned into my brain." Valeria felt a cool, blood tainted tear roll down her cheek. "He went to your mother next. She was terrified." Valeria's voice broke, shuttered under her emotions. "She didn't beg for her life or cry for mercy, instead she said only *please, Valeria please.* I knew what she meant."

"She was asking you to take care of me."

"Yes Emil, with her last words. She begged that I would take care of you, look after you in her absence. I swore to her I would, promised on my life I would."

"How did you survive?" Emil asked, quickly wiping tears from his eyes so she would not seem them.

"To this day, I am not sure. I could not speak loud enough for him to hear, had nothing to offer him. I looked up at him, his face splattered with their blood, and begged him with my eyes and my mind. I pleaded with every fiber, every particle, to let me live, not for myself, but for an innocent that I had sworn to protect. He looked at me strangely for a moment before putting the lid back on my tomb, sealed it with a portion of a Sacred Wafer and then made his escape. As soon as I was able, I came to you, hoping in my weakness you had not frozen to death. I praised the name of God for the first time in centuries when I found you, alive and whole."

"I remember you taking me to the kitchen, warming me by the fire and feeding me," Emil added. Valeria nodded her head in silent agreement, composing herself. "Then I remember something happening to you. You fell down like you were ill."

"That was when they found Vlad. They killed him just moments before sunset. If they had been mere seconds later, I would have joined him and we would have smeared the snow red with them. But, it was not to be," she said ruefully. She reached out and ruffled his black, shaggy hair. "I stayed with you instead. I did not try to pursue them because to do so would have broken my promise. I took you away from that castle as soon as I found a safe place, away from prying eyes and curious slayers. It was all I knew to do."

"Thank you, Aunt, for all that you have done for me. I will try not to complain the next time you walk me home."

"You don't have to thank me, Emil. You saved me as well." Valeria reached out to her enlightened nephew and held him in her arms, warm, perfect, and safe. "And from now on, I will trust you to find your own way home."

Part Two:
Life after the Lie

Chapter Four

Time flowed over Valeria like a river around a stone, rounding her keen edges. She had changed, her fortitude weakened and dulled by the guilt of her lie, eroded by it. A part of her wanted Emil to figure out the truth, that she had used her mesmerizing powers to warp his perception, just so she could confess to him in a half truth, but he had never spoken of his human family again since that night. For three years she had longed to be discovered and yet thankful every day that she had not been.

She sparsely fed, instead allowing starvation to age her just as Vlad had before leaving for England. But she did not allow decades of decay to catch up with her as he had, only the equivalent of a few years. It had been just enough to keep the people of Brasov from being suspicious. On the rare nights she did feed, she would often pass over Emil walking to work beneath the dim light of the streetlamps as she was heading home, gliding high overhead with the smog and smoke so he would remain unaware of her presence. Emil had grown to love Brasov, had learned to thrive in it, and she refused to allow her condition to make him leave another home.

Under Mihai's supervision, Emil had grown to be a useful and profitable apprentice. Every night he came home with his hands stained with ink, his heart full of pride, ready to return the next morning before dawn just to see the next copy of *Gazeta de Transilvania* come into existence for the literate Romanian speaking populace of Brasov to enjoy. The *Gazeta de Transilvania* was the collective voice of a people, whether they could read its words or not it spoke loud and brave, for them.

Emil had quickly grown attached to Mihai and looked to him as a mentor, a father figure to emulate. He was an ordinary man who had earned his title with much labor and many sleepless nights. He had an ordinary family, a wife and four young children who waited anxiously at the door of their ordinary home for his return every night. None of them possessed supernatural powers or even believed in the existence of vampires in such a modern day. They were the face of a new Romania; one that had shook off generations of superstition and greeted the new century with scientific hopes and logical dreams. The new Romania looked to end the social injustices suffered by the ethnically diverse population by means of literacy and political reform. She believed this was what drew Emil to Mihai. Before coming to Brasov, Emil had lived his entire life in the vacuum of a hidden existence, oppressed by supernatural threats and fears. But Mihai lived in the clearly visible world of man, his knowledge of Valeria's unearthly world relegated to stories intended to scare naughty children, a life of black and white.

Valeria was intimidated, jealous, yet happy for Emil simultaneously. It was why they moved to the city, for Emil to create a life for himself aside from her. She was proud that he had accomplished so much so quickly and pleased that he had chosen such good and honest folk to associate with. She had watched Mihai unawares, scanning his behavior from a crow's perch, and found him to be honest in his business and upright in his life. He even donated a portion of his hard earned wages to care for the orphans and widows. She attributed Mihai's perfection to her loss of appetite, but she knew the truth deep in her heart. Emil no longer needed her, but she still needed him. He was the last tenuous tie that remained to her family, to her old life that died over a decade ago. Even if he had chosen to hide away with her in the darkness and shun the outside world, eventually either by accident, disease, or by the simple passage of time, he would leave her. One day Emil would die and with him the rest of her world, but she would continue to exist. One day, there would be nothing left but her.

***

The night Emil came home with a borrowed book, Valeria knew her time was up, even before he had said a word. She could feel the change in his energy, could hear his heart pounding like sledgehammer behind his ribs. His cheeks and ears were red, his jaw clenched, eyes narrowed. She had never seen him so angry, not in all their years together. She instantly knew his anger was directed toward her, could feel the heat of his fury boiling against her. She held her breath and her tongue.

"I just finished the most interesting of books today, Aunt." He tossed the book onto the table, gliding in its smooth cover to a stop just in front of her. Her icy white fingers trembled as they traced the single word of its title. "It's about a Transylvanian Count and his three most peculiar wives." Valeria felt the air in the room turn stale and drop to the ground like dead flies. "Do you know why the Count and his wives are so peculiar?"

Valeria shook her head, afraid to look at him, to look into his raging eyes. Her eyes were locked to the name on the cover, her last name. Dracula.

"The Count and his wives are vampires. Quite a coincidence, don't you think?"

She shook her head in agreement, knowing their secrets had somehow been laid bare within the pages of the book that now seemed to be burning a hole through her dining room table.

"However the book is not written by them, but formed from the accounts of several individuals. One man, a solicitor named Jonathan Harker from England, was in Transylvania on business. While he stayed with the Count in his mountaintop castle, he witnessed many unusual events, but one stood out to me as certainly the most unfortunate." He paused for a moment, gritting his teeth while he waited for a reaction from her, when he received none he continued. The sound reminded her of the stone wheel grinding against grain in a mill. "This man, Harker, saw the Count return to the castle on two separate occasions with a bag that obvious held something living within it, although he never actually saw the contents of the bag for himself. A few hours after he returned on the second occasion, a woman approached the castle gate and begged for the return of her child. You see, the Count had stolen the child while wearing Harker's clothing and so it was he whom she did beseech for her child's return. Harker said nothing, did nothing but look upon her in her anguish. The book then says the Count called down ferocious wolves from the surrounding mountains and they devoured the woman, leaving nothing behind. Is any of this sounding familiar to you, Aunt?"

Valeria's heart raced from its normal undetectable pace to one that rivaled a healthy human rhythm. Her hands felt clammy and a shiver shook her insides. She looked at the name of the author, Stoker. It was unfamiliar to her. She felt faint, almost motion sick. Who was this Stoker that he should have access to these accounts?

"Aunt?" Her name sounded like it curdled as it passed over his lips. She looked up and for the first time, their eyes locked. Valeria saw rage, but Emil saw fear. "Is there anything you would like to clarify as to how I came to be a member of your family?"

She did not know how to respond, what to say or even how to begin. She could hear his pulse increase in intensity as he grew tired of her stalling.

"Valeria!" he demanded.

"I… I don't know what to say, Emil."

"Does that book speak the truth?" he shouted. His grasp on his composure almost weakening.

"I haven't read it…"

"I told you what it said, almost word for word. It is on page sixty-five; you can read it for yourself if you like!"

Valeria opened the book, terrified what of lies and what truths it had intertwined within it. She read the page, which was marked by a dog-eared fold on the corner and then covered her face with her hands, collapsing backward into the chair behind her. The room would not stop spinning. Emil's strained breathing and furious heartbeat filled it to the brim. Her lie now stood between them like a gigantic icicle, pierced through Emil's life and trust.

"The truth, Valeria!"

"You were the second child he brought to the castle. The first was a boy not much older than an infant, too small and weak. He smothered before he arrived. Vlad had forbidden us to hunt for the duration of the solicitor's stay. For days he brought us nothing and we had begun to slip out when he was occupied with Harker to hunt for ourselves. One night, shortly after the death of the first child, he returned from hunting. He was dressed in Harker's clothing and with him was a bag. Your mother…"

"She was not my mother!" Emil interrupted, his eyes flashed with purest rage.

"Ilona." Valeria changed her words quickly to stave off his fury, if for just a few moments longer. "Ilona was heartbroken from the death of the first child and when she saw the bag, she hoped with a mother's heart that this child could be saved. Vlad untied the bag and she saw you for the first time, holding a bite wound on your neck."

"That monster fed from me?" Emil shouted, outraged and disgusted by a vampire for the first time in his life.

"Yes, taking just enough blood from you to weaken you. I assume so you would not struggle within the bag. He intended you to arrive alive."

"Why, so you and the others could kill me?"

"Yes, I think so. He meant to break us, to humiliate us by forcing us to feed on a helpless child. It was the most cruel thing to do to Ilona, knowing how her heart bled for a child of her own. To kill a child would have destroyed her. But instead of killing you, Ilona instantly loved you, took you in as her own child. He later took credit in giving you to her, almost as though he had fathered you."

"Did he kill my father?"

"I do not know."

"Brothers, sisters, did I have any?"

"I don't know, Emil."

"My mother, is that truly how she died, devoured by a pack of wolves?"

"Yes," Valeria answered, unable to lift her head to look at him.

"Did you see it?" His anger simmered off to a slow burn. Valeria could say nothing, pinkish tears dripped from her nose to her skirt. She heard his fingernails dig into the finish of the table before he clenched his fist. He leaned over it and slammed his wadded fist down on the table, bouncing the book off its surface. "Valeria! Did you see my mother die?"

"Yes," she whispered. "But it…"

"You saw her there, at the gate crying for me and you did nothing to help her? Ilona, the endearing mother, did nothing to help her?" The fires of his anger rekindled even hotter than before. They reminded her of how Vlad's eyes had flashed with the fury of hellfire toward her so many times.

"It happened so fast, Emil. By the time we heard her at the gate, he was already calling them. We didn't know what he was doing!"

"And you just stood back and watched as my mother was eaten alive?"

"There was nothing we could do, Emil! What should we have done, pushed you back into her arms and between the wolves jaws?" Valeria cried out, desperate to sooth the tempest that was once her nephew, her son. "Should we have pulled her away from them and left her without an arm or a leg or her face? She was sick, weak, you could hear it in her voice as she cried. Even if there had been a way to save her, if he had allowed us to save her and return you, she would not have survived. He would have gone back and slaughtered you both the next night! All we could do was keep you safe and try to give you a better life, a life she would have wanted for you."

"A better life?" Emil snarled, heavy with arrogance and resentment. "Three years ago, I knew no one other than you. I was hidden away, like I was walled up in a tomb, trapped in a tomb with you!"

"I know it has not been a perfect life, or even a good life, but it has been all I have known to do! I had to hide you, protect you!"

"From what, protect me from what?"

"Slayers! Cowards that would kill me and then kill you, simply because you live with me, because I love you. They would do all that and more in the name of God, to earn His favor!" she pleaded, reached her hands out to him.

"I think you hid me away because you were afraid. You were afraid I would leave you if I knew what the world was and then you would be alone."

"I was afraid, Emil. I'm still afraid, terrified that I will do wrong by you, fail you somehow." Valeria wiped her eyes and found the pinkish tears were more concentrated. They left red streaks from her eyes to the edge of her jaw, as if they were bleeding raw. She quickly wiped her hands on her dress, hoping it would not offend Emil further. "I know I have made mistakes, but I only meant to protect you."

"Why? Because you promised that vampire whore you called my mother you would?" The expression on Emil's face was not the boy she had grown to love as her own child. She could barely recognize him behind his mask of unbridled fury. His words gouged within her heart and before she knew what she was doing, she found herself standing before him, staring him eye to eye.

Valeria slapped him across the cheek. He stumbled backward to catch his balance, desperately hoping not to fall. "Because I love you, as she loved you, like a son! Insolent boy! Speak of me however you wish, call me whatever you like, but do not speak of her with such disrespect!" She stood before him undaunted by his outrage and looked into his eyes, fearing neither his words nor any physical retaliation. She saw fear in his eyes toward her for the first time as well, as he truly understood that she was no mere human he had offended, but a skilled killer, a seasoned hunter of prey, a lioness. "She would have fed herself to those wolves if it meant saving you, only for her wounds to heal and do it again night after night if that was what it meant to keep you safe! There was nothing she would not have done for you, no sacrifice was too great! For the first time in thirteen years, I am relieved she is dead because your hateful words would have killed her tonight! I would never wish that burden upon her or you."

She walked away from Emil to seek solace in the glowing embers of the fire. Her hands trembled and she clenched them into fists to steady them as she wrapped her arms around her waist, supporting her churning stomach. She had forgotten her nerves were capable of being rattled so thoroughly. She closed her eyes, hoping the dark would settle her and keep her from vomiting. They were closed only a moment when they instinctively popped open, wide with alarm. It was as if the entire room had been sat on its end. The fire was no longer warm and inviting and the entire house felt cold, unwelcoming. A shiver raced her spine. She quickly turned to Emil, who was now sitting at the table with his chin on his chest. His demeanor had somehow changed the entire atmosphere of their home.

"Valeria, you promised you would protect me, safely raise me to adulthood. That debt has been paid. Your promise has been fulfilled and you should feel no shame in my upbringing. I believe you meant to do right by me and I assume, given the situation, you have," Emil whispered, still looking at his lap.

"Emil, please…"

"However I feel that our time together should come to an end…"

"Emil, I'm sorry I shouted at you. I'm sorry I struck you. Please…please don't do this," Valeria interrupted, only able to strain out the softest of whispered from her grief constricted throat.

"Valeria you are no longer welcome in this house," he said flatly. Each word felt like he was pounding another nail into her coffin, squeezing another breath of life from her chest. She whimpered quietly, crying so intensely that she was shuddered, no energy left for words.

"Emil…"

"Get out and do not return."

As soon as his words passed over his lips, she was instantly compelled to leave the house. She felt like she was drowning in the river again, her body forcing her outside. It was unnatural, unstoppable. She desperately tried to refuse her feet to move, but she had to walk toward the door, reflexively, as though she had held her breath so long her lungs were forcing outside to take a breath. She walked outside and stood at the foot of the stairs, looking helplessly back at the doorway where he stood. She was frozen there, unable to return, but unwilling to leave.

"You will find your belongings here on the stairs tomorrow evening just after sunset. If you do not take them I will call a truck to pick them up the next morning."

"Emil, please… I love you," She called up to him, desperately hoping he would reconsider his rash banishment after seeing her alone on the street and allow her back inside his house, back inside his life, but he did not. He turned away from her and closed the door without looking back.

Time seemed to stop as she stood alone in dark of the frigid February night, staring at the door like a dog that had been turned out by its master, confused and waiting for the door to reopen. Unlike a dog, she knew it would not open for her, not tonight, perhaps not ever. The threshold was the ends of the world for her, the edge of the flat map that sailors dared not passed for fear of dropping off into oblivion. If she was set on fire, she could not enter that house to save her life. He was every bit as far from her within its walls as Ilona and Vlad were from her in the afterlife. She was simply a ghost, a shadowy figure glimpsed through shuttered windows by dim candlelight, an apparition, dust and fog, a memory.

Chapter Five

Valeria waited until the cover of dark to fetch the steamer trunk filled with her personal belongings from the front landing of her former home. The house was entirely dark. The drapes had been drawn over every window, not even the dim flicker of a single candle escaped. She could hear Emil's heartbeat, immediately recognizing the slow and steady cadence of his sleeping rhythm that she had so thoroughly memorized over the years. Surrounded by a slumbering city, his heartbeat was as clear and recognizable as his voice and it was effortless for her to pick it out of the crowd. By the sound she knew he had been in a deep sleep for a few hours.

She climbed the steps silently, the soles of her shoes refusing to break the perfect silence of the frozen night. A light haze of frost had already formed on the tooled leather exterior and brass fixtures of the trunk, like the fine fuzz on a peach. She bent and grabbed the strap handles and hoisted the heavy trunk up and let it rest against her legs as she carried it away. The size and construction of the trunk would have made it too heavy and unwieldy for a woman of her frame to carry alone, even if it had been empty. But filled to the brim, its weight had had doubled and would have given two strong men a struggle maneuvering it down the stairs.

She quickly turned into the narrow alley between Emil's house and their neighbor's and sat the trunk on the ground, listening for any signs of activity from the street or nearby houses. If anyone was to witness her carrying such an impossible load alone, it would destroy the fragile reputation that Emil was just beginning to build. Despite her best efforts, she had become one of the most recognizable women in Brasov. She had dined and had tea with most of the eligible bachelors in the town, all to maintain appearances, and had managed to spoil all of their interest in her by revealing she had been divorced or by confiding that she would never be able to bare children. Sometimes a mix of the two tales was necessary to extinguish their interests, or a bit of mild convincing charms, but she had never done anything so extreme it would harm Emil's social standing and regardless of his current feelings for her, she never would. She could never purposely harm him, which is why she knew she had to leave Brasov immediately.

By banishing her from their home, he had effectively revoked her welcome to the entire city. If they were to be seen apart, after having been so close, questions and rumors would quickly abound. Her thoughts immediately settled on the only place she knew to go, her refuge in the thick of the forest, but attempting the journey of such distance so late in the night would be foolish. She would use the remainder of the night to secure a safe place, where she and her trunk would not draw attention to themselves, to wait out the day. She lifted the trunk once more and slipped out of the city through the closest gate. Trumpeter's Tower maintained its silent vigil over town square. Just before he was out of earshot, Valeria heard Emil's linen sheets rustle as he changed position in his sleep.

***

Without a human companion to slow her, Valeria skimmed above the forest with what remained of her life tightly drawn within her shimmer. Despite being lighter than air, she felt heavy and damp like low lying fog just before daybreak. For most of the journey, she chose not to use her vision, but instead rely on her sense of direction. She sought to span the distance between two heartaches, flying as a crow from Brasov toward Castle Dracula and the nearby cabin.

She had taken flight as soon as the sky had sufficiently darkened enough to conceal her. Thankfully the moon had been hidden behind a cottony blanket of snow laden clouds. Winter still held the countryside under his frozen thumb and below her nothing dared to move. Heavy snow had fallen recently and the dismal conditions had been to her benefit, since she had not had to concern herself too greatly with being discovered by a prowling hunter while she slept in what she considered close proximity to the city. If it had been spring or summer, she would have been pushed much deeper into the forest, but as it was, both she and the trunk were completely concealed during her vulnerable hours in a casket of snow. Her clothes and hair had frozen into place, her eyelashes incased in ice, and her skin was bluish and hard as her body had begun to freeze. She recalled the time she, Vlad, and Ilona had spent in Russia so many years ago as she felt the spiky crystals of ice form inside her. In so many ways she had learned that being unnaturally strong and unable to die did not mean she did not feel pain. Although her tolerance was much higher, she was very much capable of feeling pain and when her threshold was finally surpassed, it came with unrelenting intensity. She would have to build a fire to stop the freezing process when she arrived or she would have to wait until spring to thaw.

The cold wind sweeping down from the Carpathians mixed with her grief, and she felt as though her particles would fall to the forest below like sleet if she did not arrive at her destination soon. She and her trunk would leave a crater in Earth like a comet, a fallen guardian angel with no one left in her charge to protect. Together they would shatter and she cared not if the pieces were ever gathered together again.

She wished she had chosen the middle tomb instead of Ilona that tragic night the old slayer darkened their door. She wished she had died and Ilona had survived. If Ilona had lived, she would have known exactly what to say to Emil, how to soothe his raging heart. Instead it had been her, hot-headed and sharp- tongued Valeria, that had failed at all that she had ever sought to achieve and everyone she had ever loved.

The landscape blurred with speed, the passage of time, and instantly frozen tears. If it had not been for the quickening in her senses, she would have passed the tiny cabin completely. It lay beneath a blanket of snow, silent and cold, without even as much as the tracks of a stray deer or hare to break the cloak of white until her freshly materialized feet broke the ice crusted surface. She sat the trunk down and she rubbed her nose and face vigorously as the dead weight of the luggage sank through the layers of snow to the frozen ground beneath. The heavy drift against the cabin's side could not hide its presence, even though it nearly reached the roofline on two sides and to the window sills on the remaining two. She lifted the trunk before it was utterly swallowed by the snow and slowly walked toward the structure that no longer felt like home or the sanctuary she had pined for, but like just another tomb. She treaded so gently that despite the extra weight of the trunk, which suddenly felt light against the thousand pounds of guilt that yoked her shoulders, she left no footprints behind. She longed to be invisible, to simply disappear into the snow, into the frigid underworld of Cocytus and exist no longer, leave no trail for Dante and Virgil to follow.

But exist she did, and she was certain that no amount of ice and snow would kill her, but only compound her misery. She had to get inside and warm herself, if only to a degree above freezing. She dropped the trunk just to the right of the door, against the rough split log wall and instantly faded into mists, spiraling upward toward the long cold chimney. Pouring down its soot coated throat and into the hearth below, Valeria felt like she had entered one of the forgotten pyramid tombs of Egypt.

The cabin had remained untouched, just as they had left it. She chose to walk through it in the flesh instead of merely floating through like a bank of fog. Her fingers touched almost every surface, cold and forgotten, still unaware that she had returned to give it purpose again. Remnants of Emil's energy and scent that was still present after more than three years gouged at her raw nerves. The grip of an invisible, icy hand threatened to squeeze her heart until it burst. She was certain that no human had so much as crossed the threshold in her absence. She wondered if something of her had lingered behind that humans could sense that had deterred them from venturing too close, an uncertain threat or hidden danger like the mouth of cave that could be hiding a stash of gold and a slumbering dragon. Did it feel cursed, like a house that had been purged of its inhabitants by the plague?

She carefully opened the door, hoping the wall of snow outside was frozen enough to support itself and not fall into the tiny cabin like an avalanche. She reached into the wall of snow and slowly pulled the trunk's handle toward her. The drift gave way just enough for her to pull it inside without collapsing. Within hours the clouds would drop their load and the wind would rearrange the snow she had displaced, quickly hiding her arrival. Her small fire would cause little smoke, draw no attention. She did not need to keep it as warm as she once had.

After a lengthy ordeal starting the fire from the supplies she and Emil had left behind, she finally opened the trunk. She had waited until now to open it, unwilling to accept the rejection fully until she had done all she had to do, until she could give into the grief fully and mourn however dreadfully she wanted. Slowly unbuckling the straps and lifting the lid, she found that he had tied the key to a shirt through a buttonhole with a length of twine, ensuring she could lock it later. Beneath the neatly folded layers of clothing, she found two pairs of shoes, a variety of toiletries, and several books. Bram Stoker's tell-all was not among them.

As she repacked the trunk's contents, she saw the corner of a note sticking out of the narrow document compartment inside the lid. It was plain paper, but carefully folded to almost measured proportions. She opened the note and found written in Emil's hand only two words.

Begin again

***

49

Chapter Six

Valeria listened to the snow blow against the small windows of the cabin, knowing it was settling higher against the walls. She had chosen to stay inside, despite having not fed in almost a month. Not even the scalding gnaw in her belly could drive her out into the blizzard conditions that rattled at her door. She had just begun to feel the blood slowly migrating through her veins again after having nearly frozen as solid as a rock. Perhaps the conditions would be more favorable for hunting tomorrow night. She was in no hurry, had all the time in the world.

A sudden knock on her door jolted her to her feet. She had been laying silently on the small bed close to the fire, listening to the snowstorm bury her alive, and had heard no one approach, could sense no rhythm of a heartbeat. She instantly bristled, crouched low to the ground and strained to hear anything other than the unrelenting wind and snow. The knock came again, with more urgency. No pleas for help. No heartbeat.

"Who's there?" she shouted, her hand bracing the sliding lock of the door in place.

No answer.

Certain that any human, even the best slayer, would have already been betrayed by their heartbeat, she disengaged the lock and yanked the door open. She sprang up, prepared to tear out the throat of any young vampire foolish to trifle with her, but stopped in her tracks.

51

"Valeria, is this how you greet all your guests?" Vlad stood before her solid and flawless, the snow clinging to his hair and coat.

Valeria stumbled backward, her mouth agape. Count Dracula of Transylvania, the husband she had loved and lost, stood before her in a whirlwind of white. She had no doubt it was him, she could feel him, smell him.

"Vlad..." she whispered with her hands clasped over her chest to steady her heart. She finally dared to reach out to him with one hand, to see if her fingertips would make contact with him or if he would simply disappear into the shadow of memory. He remained motionless, only smiling, following her movements with his eyes as she dared to touch the back of his hand and inspected the spaces between his fingers with the slightest of touch.

A blast of arctic wind bombarded her with frozen breath, her fingers ventured to his face. She ignored the gust of snow as it blew against her, cutting through her dress, pelting her face with tiny crystals of ice as her hair billowed behind her. He closed his eyes as she passed over his thick eyebrows and across the tips of his lashes, down his nose, and outlined his lips. He looked just as he did before his fascination with England had consumed him and he began to don the disguise of an elderly man. He was perfect, like he had never left her.

"How?" she questioned skeptically, recoiling from him slightly. "I felt it when you died. How is it you live now?"

"Please Valeria, may I come inside? I am nearly frozen to the core," he asked, his eyes searching through her mind and soul for the answer her lips were hesitant to ask. "Please. I will explain everything to you, I promise."

She could feel his influence over her; his plead washing against her like the tide upon the shore, gently nudging her his way. She could not resist him, had no want within her to deny his request. "Of course, come in."

She watched as he shook the snow from his hair and removed his ice encased coat and boots, setting them neatly and carefully by the door.

He looked around the small space of the cabin, taking in the all the details of the utilitarian structure. "This is certainly not a castle. Why are you living here like a peasant when you should be relaxing in luxury with servants to stoke your fire?"

"Things changed after you…left. The castle wasn't safe anymore. If one slayer had discovered our secret, more were sure to follow. I could not risk Emil's safety."

"Emil, Ilona's son, where is he?" Vlad turned his head to finely tune his hearing for a heartbeat.

"He's not here. He is grown now, making a life for himself in Brasov." She followed him toward the fireplace, standing almost close enough to touch him, but not quite. The logic in her mind forcing her to be cautious, denying her heart's urging to wrap her arms around him and hide her face in his chest, to breathe him in. "He no longer requires my smothering protection, so I returned here, only hours ago."

Vlad watched her as she stared into the fire, refusing to break its hold on her. Her chest rose and fell quickly, not out of necessity, but out of reaction to his presence and to the pain she was desperately trying to hide from him.

"Valeria…" he said, taking her hand in his. Her delicate hand easily remembered the shape of his and responded. "Always so strong, always so desperate to hide the truth. Beautiful. Stoic, like a marble goddess of Rome."

She could feel tears collecting in her eyes. A crack had sprung in the dam that had held her emotions in check. As the trickle swept past her defenses and raced down her cheeks, she could feel the pressure of the pent up pain and fear pushing against the weaknesses in it. He slowly pulled her to him, allowing her to come on her own instead of forcing her too quickly. Finally he surrounded her in the shroud of his chilled embrace, taking her in. His face leaned against her head as his hands squeezed up and down the length of her arm, and followed her spine with the fingertips of his other hand.

"I thought you were dead!" She finally gushed, her body instantly swept up in a rush of emotion, shuttering like a ship's sail in a gale. "I thought I would never see you again!"

"Death could not keep me from you, my dearest Valeria, my dearest bride." His voice filled the empty places of her heart, gave breath back to her lungs. He brushed his fingers through her hair, smoothing it against her back, curling it around his fingers. "I am a part of you, and you a part of me. We are eternal, inseparable like the moon and stars. Life and death has no hold on us, no dominion over us."

"Ilona and Fleur are dead. I could not save them." She wept, as though she needed to confess her failure to him.

"I know. I have mourned them, as you have." He lifted her chin to see her face, wiping the hair that had stuck to her face with tears. "It is not your fault, Valeria. You did all you could for them, and for Emil. You must forgive yourself."

"I lost everything I loved, everything that mattered in my life," she said, trying to calm herself to steady her voice.

"Dearest Valeria, this is a time for rejoicing, not sorrows. We are together again and no power on this Earth will take you from me again." He gently held her face in his hands, her features cold and perfect beneath his thumb as he wiped the last tear from his cheek. "So long I have waited to hold you in my arms again."

Valeria could feel his energy, his magnetic pull, drawing her face closer to his. She had forgotten the power of his embrace, how simply looking into his dark, bottomless eyes she could forget everything. She relinquished, allowed herself to be overwhelmed by his voice, his appeal. A ripple of excitement blossomed in her bosom. Electricity coursed through her arms, down her body, and filled her cheeks with warmth. Then in an instant, like a lighting strike, she felt life rush back into her body when his lips touched hers. She realized she had allowed herself to forget the taste of his kiss, the sensation of his tongue darting past her lips.

She quickly forgot herself in the excitement of the moment, longing to be closer to the man that she had given up for dead. She briefly shimmered and her body reduced to the mists in structure while retaining her silhouette, a pillar of stars. She instantly returned to her flesh, her dress crumbling in a pile at her feet. She grabbed his shirt at the buttons and yanked it from his shoulders, the buttons popping loose and falling to the floor, settling between the gaps in the rough lumber planks. His chest was perfect, unblemished, bearing no mark of the slayer's knife at his heart. She greedily ran her hands up his chest and around his neck, pulling his lips to hers again as he freed his arms from the remained of his shirt.

Beside them the bed called out to them and she backed him toward it. She walked on her tiptoes; her arms wrapped around his neck as their kisses changed from their lips to their necks, with the most tender of nibbles, and then back again. With a playful smile she pushed him backward and he leaned deeply backward and stumbled as though she had overpowered him, pulling her down with him. She could feel the energy spark as her breasts pushed against his skin, consciously noting every moment of their reunion. She anticipated lying atop him, feeling the muscles of his chest ripple and move beneath her as his hands roamed across her body, returning to familiar places. As he fell backward, his eyes locked with hers and for a moment time seemed to freeze, the world comprised of nothing beyond the boundaries of his dark iris. She felt the weight of his body change, his expression turned blank, and she fell through him to the cold bed below. She instantly sat up to her knees in the center of the bed, searching the room for what corner he had chosen to hide away in. She was surrounded by a haze of grey, thin, nothing like the blend of light and cloud she transformed into, but powdery. Instantly her heart sank and her throat constricted. She was surrounded by dust, covered in it, as it swirled around her and floated toward the ceiling. To her horror, Vlad was gone and nothing, but his ashes remained with her.

Valeria grabbed her hair with both hands and screamed out, looking vaguely at the ceiling yet crying up to the heavens above her. She felt tears roll from her eyes and down her cheeks and she struggled with what she knew was true. Vlad was dead.

Like she had been slapped, Valeria woke from her dream. Her eyes were opened wide as tears effortless rolled from them. She snubbed and gasped, trying to catch her breath, trying to escape from her nightmare. Everything about it had felt entirely real. She had felt him beneath her hands, smelled him, and tasted him. His voice had sounded perfectly, chillingly accurate. She struggled to sit upright on the edge of the bed. It was not covered in his ashes. She still wore her dress. The fire was cold in the hearth. She slowly crept to the window and wiped the frost from the thick glass. It was midday; the snow had finished its assault sometime during the night and early morning while she slept. Cold, heavy hearted, and still slumber drunk, she finally accepted Vlad had never been there.

In her mind she saw the cold and unforgiving face of the old slayer, stained with the blood of Ilona and Fleur. That old bastard had taken everything from her! Her sister wives were dead, Vlad was dead, and Emil had been turned against her. She felt her face contort into a snarl, her gut clench. No doubt his loose lips had spilled her secrets to this Bram Stoker, and no doubt he had earned a wealthy payment for it! Her blood boiled at the prospect of his prospering at her misfortune yet again. If that damned book had not been written and published, Emil would have remained blissfully unaware of his human mother's unfortunate end! She would be resting in her comfortable home in Brasov instead of a musty old cabin in the wilderness. He deserved to die for what he had done, to atone for the sins he had committed, like he had judged Vlad, Ilona, and Fleur!

She figured that Harker had some part to play in the mess, but her thoughts centered on the slayer, even though she still did not know his name. Learning it would be simple enough. Harker had come to

Transylvania from England and the directions to the locations they had visited, names of people they knew, and a list of habits and techniques used against them had collected and bound. All that stood between her and the slayer's throat was obtaining a copy of Stoker's book. Through Stoker and his novel, she would have her revenge and sate her consuming hate with slayer blood.

Part Three:
Exhuming the Past

Chapter Seven

Valeria sat on the bank of the Danube, at its origin in the south of the Black Forest, watching the smaller Breg and Brigach rivers intertwine and give birth to the blue river of legend in art, song, and lore. She'd left her heavy trunk behind at the cabin, exchanging it for a small knapsack, bedroll, and blanket. Instead of carrying a supply of Transylvanian earth, the sack held a fresh dress, shoes, coat and a few toiletries to scrub away the journey before facing human eyes.

It seemed with Vlad's death, Valeria was no longer bound to Transylvania. The stipulation of Vlad's curse had been in order for the blood he consumed to be beneficial, he had to sleep upon soil of his homeland, a means of limiting humanity's exposure. They had sidestepped this by carrying crates of Transylvanian soil with them as they traveled across Europe, but now since she was without a master, she was no longer tied to his homeland. She could slumber in whatever country she chose and still benefit from the rejuvenating effects of its inhabitants.

Despite not having to worry with a crate of dirt, the journey had taken longer than she had hoped. Even though she had covered inhuman amount of ground every night, it had taken nearly a month of nights to transverse the length of the Danube, a watery line drawn across the width of Europe. Sustenance had been scarce, kept behind tightly locked doors and windows from the bitter cold, but it helped that the river passed through several substantial cities on its race toward the

Black Sea. It was the large expanses of wilderness between the cities that had proven to be the greatest hunting challenge, but had in turn provided plenty of places to hide away the days. Exerting so much energy on quick travel required fuel for the undead fire- warm crimson fuel, metallic and sticky on parched lips.

Now stretched before her was the country of France, Fleur's beloved Paris, and passage to England. But she was in desperate need of a meal. Just as a starving human body cannibalizes itself in times of starvation, a vampire's body would consume itself until nothing remained, but a dry husk, a cocoon. Although she was not near that level of desperation, she was tired of the screams of hunger from her belly and the scratchy thirst in her throat. She needed to be in peak condition while traveling, not only to expedite her travels, but in the event she should she meet the unlikely adversary, a risk which multiplied whenever she hunted in a city. She had learned to never take safety for granted, or assume it existed at all.

A short distance from the river nursery was the German city of old, Donaueschingen. The city was an important hub for railway travelers, which increased her chances at acquiring a meal even on such a frigid night, but it also increased her risks of being discovered. She had spent weeks acquiring invitations and learning the layout of Brasov before taking her first drink, but she would be walking into Donaueschingen blind and thirsty.

The delicious scent of living blood lured her to the railway station, hot and congested with travelers arriving in the pre-dawn hours. The usual rabble of miscreants and destitute stood around flaming barrels, huddled close to defend themselves and each other from the slicing winter cold. Without a coat and covered in dirt, she blended effortlessly into the shadows. She slumped against a wall, far enough from the flame to keep most of her features hidden. She knew it would only be a matter of time before one of the regulars singled her out for interrogation. She pretended to shiver and held her bag close to her, as if she had something to protect.

A little over an hour, two hours before dawn, a rough looking man in a tattered wool coat and a beaver skin hat entered the back of the alley. He was broad shouldered and least six feet tall, loud- mouthed, and reeked of cheep booze. She watched the people around her cower, even smaller than they already were. She stood against the wall, purposely trying to draw his attention from his usual victims and onto her. She didn't know if he was a landlord, a pimp, loan shark, or some combination of the three, but he was in need of a lesson in humility.

"Who said you could stand in my alley?" the man huffed, standing over Valeria. He used his voice and stature to try to make her feel smaller, lower than him, less than him.

She understood and spoke perfect German, but she chose to keep silent.

"You have to pay the toll to stand in my alley," he barked, attempting to yank the satchel from her arms. She held firm.

"Give it to him, missy. It's not worth your pretty face," an old beggar woman pleaded, afraid to raise her head when she spoke.

Valeria held even tighter. She could hear his heart rate increasing with anger and the sick rush of excitement he got from abusing the homeless and helpless. She raised her eyes to look the thug in the face and glared at him, still silent, taunting him.

"You should have listened. She knows her place," he spat and slugged Valeria, breaking her jaw. He expected her to hit the ground unconscious, to take the satchel from her without any objections from those close by.

Instead she raised her head, her broken jaw hanging to the left. The onlookers gasped, amazed that she had not crumbled to the ground. She released her right hand from the bag and straightened her jaw, wiggling it around to realign the broken bones. Having almost instantly healed, she flashed her attacker a wide and sinister smile.

The man stammered backwards, not stopping until his back slammed against the opposite wall. His eyes were wide with fear, his lip began to quiver. To her surprise the beggars and their companions did not run screaming in fear, but stepped backward far enough to block the entry of the alley from view of the restless street. Their abuser looked to them, hoping to find some sort of pity in their ranks, but did not. She quickly leapt upon him, wrapping her legs tightly around his waist and her arms around his neck, still clutching her satchel, and yanked his head to the side. She stretched her mouth wide and sank her razor sharp incisors into his flesh. His terrified heart beat faster and faster, pumping blood into her mouth from his severed artery almost faster than she could swallow it. He was unable to breathe, much less scream. She held firm and his legs buckled beneath him. He crumbled, sliding down the wall he had backed himself against. She would not leave him alive to prey on the weak again.

Like a lioness choking the life from a gazelle, the thug's arms and legs slowed in their struggle, and then stopped altogether. The resistance left his body and his eyes fixed, glazed. She felt the warning within call out for her to stop, that to continue would cost her victim his life, but she ignored it. Within her mind, a memory of the old slayer flashed. She rumbled a deep growl and suctioned the life sustaining fluid from his throat with even greater ferocity. His heart beat once, twice more and then stopped. His last breath curled from his lips and he died in her grasp, denied even a shred of mercy. Everyone who witnessed her act was thankful, relieved that he was dead. Valeria felt no remorse.

Covered in blood, she stood and looked at the humans who dared to look back at her. They were not afraid of her as they had been the man she had just slain. They remained silent, as they had through the ordeal, but thanked her with their brave eyes, eyes that stared into hers without hesitation. She nodded, wiped the blood from her mouth with the back of her hand and picked her satchel up from the ground. She grabbed the remains of her meal from the ground and slung him over her shoulder.

She hunkered down and leapt skyward, landing on the roof of the building she had just stood beside. She would stash his body in a part of the city where he would have no business being, on the wealthy side of town where no one would be accused and no investigation held. His death would not make the newspaper and his body would be buried somewhere outside of town, in the potter's field with the undesirables he had subjugated in life.

Valeria was almost frightened by how deliriously easy it had been to take his life, to ignore the voice in her mind that begged her to stop, how she had not been intimidated or discouraged by the human spectators that helped to hide her crime. Feeding openly before humans, for the first time in over four centuries, had been liberating, exhilarating. She had seen no goodness in his eyes, had felt no soul within him. He tasted of greed, corruption, and cruelty, curdled from the inside out. Instead of guilt over the life she had ended, she thought of the slayer and how much more delicious his blood would be than what she had just had, a vintage libation of sweet revenge. But in order to have her vengeance, she would have to find him, his name still a mystery. Thanks to Emil and the book who bore her husband's name, his identity and much more would soon be revealed.

Chapter Eight

Freshly fed, washed, and clothed in the dress she had carefully carried across Europe, Valeria stood in a Paris bookstore holding a copy of the book that had destroyed what had remained of her ruined life, Bram Stoker's *Dracula*. She felt like her forsaken surname screamed a red lettered proclamation to the humans around her; *she is one of them; she is not like you; she is a predator, a killer, cold as ice.*

She looked over her shoulder, expecting to see every single person within eyeshot of the bookstore to be staring at her, held in fear like a gazelle in the presence of lioness, but they were not. They continued with their human lives in blessed ignorance of their differences and the existence of her kind continued to live only in the realm of bogeymen, old wives' tales, and newly published fiction.

However the shopkeeper behind the counter looked at her dubiously, but for different reasons. Just below the surface of her pudgy face and beneath her sagging eyelids, her envy of Valeria's porcelain beauty was almost palpable, like needles piercing her flawless skin. She laid the book, a leather bound journal, and a handful of odds and ends on the table, but the woman said nothing. Valeria reached into her dress pocket and retrieved a few of the remaining gold coins she had taken from Vlad's stash before leaving the castle and placed them on the counter by the book. She knew their value surpassed the price of her purchase, but the woman had to agree to her offer. She glared at Valeria again and slowly took one of the coins and gnashed it between her teeth. Convinced of its authenticity, she greedily snatched the coins, wrapped the book in brown paper and tied it with twine before placing all her items in a small paper sack. She pushed the bundle toward her.

"Merci beaucoup, Madame," Valeria said, her French heavily accented by her native Romanian.

The resentful woman grunted in her direction, not giving her the respect of a correctly spoken response. Valeria wondered if the woman's opinion had been formed because she was more perceptive than she had appeared, keen to her unnatural advantages and proclivities, or maybe she just didn't like Romanians. Perhaps she was simply xenophobic, untrusting of all the damned foreigners running about ruining her beautiful city. But no matter how slim the chance, it was the possible that she was privy to some sort of information or ability that made Valeria stand out against all the other shoppers. The slayers of Palermo and Fleur's vivisection at their hands vividly flashed in her memory. She should make her time in Paris short.

The glare of the late winter sun over city's rooftops irritated her eyes. It would be a few more weeks before spring would deliver Paris into a wash of green, trees sparkling like emeralds against an urban grey blanket. She wished she could tarry there, watch the magnificent city change with the seasons perched atop the grand Eiffel Tower, but more than that, she wished that Fleur could see her city again. She had loved Paris more than anything, loved it the way Vlad had loved Transylvania, and had always longed to return to it. Gazing at the grand tower, Valeria imagined Fleur had lent a measure of her spirit to The Iron Lady. She was bold, defiant, and unapologetically Parisian, just like Fleur.

***

Valeria sat in the quiet solitude and security of her quaint inn room, the entire space lit by the oil lamp on the table beside her. The establishment she had chosen, unlike most of Paris, was not wired for electricity. It was newfangled technology that had created a mass of overhead wires that resembled the intricate weavings of a bird's nest. The night would never be entirely dark again, which for her meant a whole new assortment of disadvantages that she did not intend to dwell on tonight. For her journey into the past, she had purposely chosen the oil lamp to guide her way instead of the electric bulb. It seemed only appropriate.

She held in her hands the chronicle of her destruction, knew the end of the book before turning the first page. She was certain that reading it would open old wounds, cause them to fester and ooze, but it was her roadmap to resolution, the lancing necessary to relieve the infection in her wounded heart. Soon she would better understand the relationship between Vlad and Jonathan Harker, between the solicitor and the slayer, and hopefully gain some insight as to how Stoker fit into the puzzle.

Her fingertip traced the engraved word again, Dracula, red lettering against a mustard cover. She opened the cover, but hesitated to turn even the first page. She feared what she might learn, despite knowing any truths found therein could only be half-believed, skewed to make a better fiction. Still, she could not shake the nervous twinge in the pit of her stomach, afraid she would learn something that would further taint her husband's image. If much more ruinous exploits were discovered, the silver lining that had trimmed her relationship with Vlad would be so thoroughly tarnished it would be unrecognizable.

Her mind drifted, her eyes stared unblinking, out of focus, at the letters of the title page. She remembered how the cruel, icy cold hand of betrayal had felt as it strangled her last hope from her the night she leapt from the battlement of Castle Dracula. It was the unforgiving burden of truth that had weighed down upon her, a stone around her neck that had effortlessly pulled her beneath the frigid river waters. But not even that abandonment or enduring the murder of her lover, nor suffering the shame of his wife collecting or countless accumulated years of absence had been enough to loosen Vlad's grip on her heart.

She loved him until the day he died, for better or worse, from worse to unimaginable. She loved him still.

Losing Vlad had been an exorcism and an amputation. For the first time in centuries, her mind was free of his influence, which meant she was free to live as she pleased, but it also meant she now suffered the complete brunt of his absence without the soothing poison that had often lessened the impact in the past. Soon she would learn how the end had begun, assuming she had the courage to turn the first page. She held the book open with one hand and rubbed her eyes and between her brows with the fingertips of the other, wishing she could physically soothe the whispers of doubt and anxiety in her mind.

Chapter 1: Jonathan Harker's Journal.

The book was a collection of journal entries? Although she had not known what to expect, it certainly had not been that. The small passage she had read in Emil's presence had not been enough to reveal its anatomy. She had not been aware the solicitor had also been fond of recording his days in a journal as she, Ilona, and Fleur had done. Quickly flipping through the pages, she saw that each of the contributing sources had been that of journals and diaries, with the addition a handful of letters, telegraphs, and newspaper headings added in for good measure.

She read intently, scanning each page carefully yet quickly. She only required a fraction of the time needed for even the quickest human reader to glean its vital information. On page fifty- five, she read Harker's side of the encounter in which she had come so close to biting him that her fangs had already indented the sensitive flesh of his neck. She recalled how his heartbeat had intensified from a walk, to a skip, to a breakneck run. If Vlad had not caught her at that exact moment, with Ilona and Fleur urging her on, he would had found Harker drained dry, a husk with a smile on his face. The story would have changed course, the future altered. Vlad would not have met Harker's beloved, would not have chosen her to be the fourth Mrs. Dracula. The slayer would not have come to her aid and it was conceivable that Vlad, Ilona, and Fleur

70

would all still be alive. Valeria sighed and cursed her hesitation. She now knew Vlad's intended, Harker's fiancée, name was Wilhelmina Murray, Mina for short.

On page sixty- four, Harker revealed that he had once again been tempted by the brides of Dracula. It was the night they had appeared to him as a swirling maelstrom of stardust and frost, hoping to gain entry to his room by the window. Meanwhile, Vlad was roaming the countryside, preparing to steal a young boy from his home, a gift to his hungry wives. Surely he had not anticipated Ilona would lay her claim to him, adopt him for her own. Only a few hours later, Emil's mother would be devoured by wolves at the castle gate. The secret, the lie, and the fallout would be years in the making. She rubbed the space between her eyes again, holding her place with the other hand. She was just as helpless now to stop her death as she had been that frigid winter night.

It was on page one hundred forty- four that her eyes first read the name, Abraham Van Helsing, of Amsterdam. His council had been requested by a man by the name of Dr. John Seward, to view his patient Miss Lucy Westenra, a dear friend of Mina's. Help would come too late to save Miss Lucy and she found herself at the end of Van Helsing's stake just as Ilona and Fleur had, killed not by the old man, but instead by her lover, Arthur, at his insistence. By page two hundred sixty- five, Abraham Van Helsing was guilty of being an accessory to murder. Arthur had even thanked him for it, such a disgusting and weak man!

Valeria pushed the book away from her, open and face down on the table. Arthur made her sick and Van Helsing all the sicker! What perverse enjoyment had the old man felt as he watched Lucy's betrothed hammer a stake into her heart? Had it truly been necessary for him to do it? Any one of the men present could have ended her life. She was neither more dead by his hand, nor would she had been less dead by the hand of another. Yes, she had been cruel, had murdered innocent children in her bloodlust, but had her actions been her fault? If Vlad had protected her, taught her how to skillfully hunt as he had Fleur, would they have discovered her so easily? Why did he leave Lucy, starved and

71

impulsive, to hunt on her own after what they had been through with Fleur? She could only assume it was for the same reason he had allowed her to learn the new ways of her life alone. Why had he entrusted Ilona's schooling to her when she had vowed to kill her only days before? Had he figured on Ilona teaching herself as she had done? Had he ever cared if any of them lived or died?

Valeria felt tension rising through her shoulders, tightening the muscles in the back of her neck, her jaw firmly clenched. On page two hundred eighty- five, Van Helsing praised Mina's intelligence, proclaiming she had "a man's brain…and a woman's heart". She sneered. His sexist remark further infuriated her, added another measure of hate to him. Why would Mina tolerate such belittling? She was certain if it had not been for Mina Harker, the happy band of murderers would had muddled around London so long that Vlad would had escaped safely back to Transylvania. She was nothing if not smart, patient, and prudent, all the inspiration her testosterone fueled avengers needed to sail across the ocean to defend her honor, yet without her guidance they would have been as directionless as a blind dog in a slaughterhouse.

Mrs. Harker noted in her diary on the first day of October that she had dreamt the most unusual dreams the night before, a rolling fog invaded her bedroom and a pale face emerged from the shadows. Valeria had no doubt whose face she had saw, whose dark eyes she had peered into, not in a dream, but under the hypnotic charm of her own womanizing husband. She knew all too well the power of his eyes, the poisoning apathy of his kiss. Mina fared no better against his wiles than she, Ilona, or Fleur had. She herself had dismissed her early visitations by her transformed lover as dreams, foretold by rolling fog beneath the castle. He had played the same game with Mina as he had played with her centuries before.

Valeria learned that while Vlad traveled over the ocean to return to Transylvania, his pursuers chose to go by land. She remembered how she could sense his presence growing nearer, how she had been vaguely aware of his influence over Mina to a much lesser degree. It was like she had dreamt of her once, but had mostly forgotten upon waking, the details lost in the recesses of her consciousness. Unfortunately after Vlad's death, that fragile bond had been severed. If it still held, it would make her search for those who had wronged her and her family so much simpler. She did not enjoy detective work, searching a book of half-truths for a lead, wading through the heartache. If she had still been connected to Mina, finding them would be no different that following a map, their locations marked with a blood red X.

To her surprise, she felt a twinge of envy poke her heart. Harker had been so sincerely worried for Mina's safety, while Vlad had always seemed to be the opposite. He had always been so certain, or simply assumed, that she, Ilona, and Fleur could survive and thrive perfectly fine without him for years at a time. Harker's heart was broken when he had to leave his stricken beloved for just a few days. She thought of Serghei, her hot-blooded blacksmith. Her senses were overwhelmed by the memory of his scent, of fire and iron fresh on his skin. He had worried for her safety every time she left him. Sleep well, love, was always his farewell as she raced the dawn to the castle. Is that the difference in a human heart and that of an undead man's? Can only a human heart burn with such passion and intensity? No, for she too had felt the engulfing flames of passion consume her own heart. Had Vlad been incapable of worry, or had he simply not cared enough to be concerned?

Valeria felt a lump in her throat start to form as she read Van Helsing's account of the encounter he and Mina had with her and her sister wives, the night she had intended to kill them, but had instead been chased back to the castle by the threatening sun. They had been so close, just an arm's length away. If it had not been for their protective circle, both the slayer and his charge would have been eliminated. Why had Vlad chosen to stay sealed up in a box of dirt? Why had he not erupted out of that faux-grave and stained the snow red with the blood of those who would be his death? He could have slipped out, thin as fog, and met up with them, ran away with them. It was almost like he had given up.

It was on page four hundred forty-four she realized it had been Vlad himself that had told Van Helsing where to find his slumbering wives. His need of sleeping in dirt, his negligence in hiding that need, and his arrogance that none would figure his peculiarity out had been the death of Ilona and Fleur and had damn near killed her, as well as Emil by association. If he had only dusted his mattresses like they had done during their travels across Europe, Van Helsing would have gone into the Castle first, would have had to have searched it in entirety to be certain they were not within before moving to the crypts. It was possible that it would have bought them enough time to at least awaken from their death sleep, to at least have had a chance. Three strong, young mortal women could have overpowered one old man, even one as clever as Van Helsing. They would have at least had an advantage.

Valeria rubbed her eyes and the bridge of her nose yet again and cleared her throat. She knew what lay ahead in next few pages. A small, fragile voice within her begged her to put the book down, to skip ahead at least. It said she could not endure it again. The dreams were bad enough without adding even more fuel to the fire. For a moment she was confident if she continued to read she would die, just as the book had claimed. Struck dead, her fractured and cracked heart would finally break into irreconcilable pieces and scatter like dust in the breeze. But she knew she had to ignore that little, pleading voice. She had to allow her heart to break once more so Ilona and Fleur's death would not be in vain. It was the only way she would be able to hold their murderer accountable. She pressed on.

"Bastard!" Valeria spoke aloud to herself, throwing the book down on the table. She stomped about the room, fists wadded at her sides, arms and back straight as boards, the grinding of her teeth audible in the room next door. Had he truly believed that he had done Ilona and Fleur a service by killing them, by giving them the "full sleep of death", or is it only what he had told himself so he could look at his reflection in the mirror and not see it stained with their blood! He had called Valeria, "the fair one" and had stated she was "radiantly beautiful" and "exquisitely voluptuous"! It made her skin crawl, left a sour taste in her mouth. She had believed he had seen sincerity in her heart that night, had known that she too was bound by the same bonds of protection to the life of an innocent. Was it so, or had he spared her because he had been so taken by her beauty, so aroused by her, that he did not have the heart to destroy her? The thought that he would have found Ilona so inferior that he had found her easier to kill infuriated her. No! Not her beautiful, gentle Ilona. She had been perfect. Loving, peaceful, she had been radiant, like a precious jewel, like the night's brightest star. He mentioned precious little of their screams, their anguish as he butchered them. How they begged with their eyes to spare their lives, how they had done nothing to anyone to deserve such indignant deaths. Either Van Helsing had neglected to record it or Stoker had chosen to omit it. To do so would have meant his heroes were nothing more than murderers, more cold blooded than her fellow vampire wives.

Fearing she would not be able to hold her emotions in check much longer, she trimmed the wick of the oil lamp and settled back into her chair. She placed her hands on the book once more and steadied herself, calmed her nerves. She knew dawn was closing in and she hoped to have at least a few minutes to clear her mind before falling asleep. She was terrified of the dreams that would surely follow if she didn't. She would be forced to relive it all again with chilling reality, trapped within the merciless dream world from which she was powerless to awaken until noon released her. She knew the worst pain, the greatest hurt, was yet to be read because in the book, Vlad was still alive.

As she read of how Vlad's pursuers had encircled his convoy like vultures, she remembered her frantic race to Emil. Like a film playing in her mind, she could feel her hand gliding against the cold stone wall as she sped up the stairs. She could still feel the hatchet in her hand as she chopped at the door to his room, the impact reverberating through her bones. She remembered how good it had felt to pull little Emil into her arms, cold and hungry, but alive, miraculously alive. He had never felt more alive than he had in that moment, like the essence of humanity had condensed into him. He was the purest form of life in all of God's creation, huddled in her arms.

She could still remember how she had felt life rush back into her when the color started to return to his cheeks as he warmed by the stove. At that time, she did not know that Harker and his companions were fighting their way through the gypsies, breaking Vlad's defenses. Mina saw the box lid pried open, dirt scattered across Vlad's chest as he lay there, motionless. Were his last moments of life fleeted away in shock that his brave Szgany had been so easily and so quickly defeated? Surely he had believed that his horsemen would have gladly given their own lives in defense of their master.

As if she were caught in the midst of a hallucination, the darkly lit inn room was replaced by the equally dark, cold kitchen of her former home. She gasped, tried to catch her breath, closed her eyes and opened them, but the false world persisted. As far as her senses were concerned, she was present in that moment in her past, but her eyes could still see the words before her enough to allow her mind to somehow process them, changing the color and shape of her memory. She could see young Emil perched by the stove, waiting patiently for food. Then like a flash of lightning, she caught a glimpse of Vlad. He was dressed in fine clothes, handsome and dark, despite his countenance being twisted by rage and betrayal, his eyes practically glowing in the sun's failing light. Then the glint of steel obscured him from her view, a large knife sliced across his throat and left a wide, crimson gash in its wake. She dropped the food she had prepared for Emil. The bowl exploded into shards at her feet the moment it impacted the stone floor. A wounded man, his shirt stained in blood, plunged his bowie knife into Vlad's heart. In the kitchen, she fell to her knees, but in the inn room, she remained motionless in her chair, almost catatonic.

Her eyes wide, refusing to blink, glued to the book in her lap. Four centuries of marriage raced through her mind. She could hear Emil at her side, shaking her and calling her name. She could not answer him, only cry out to the heavens above, wail like a lost child. He was dead! Those ruthless bastards had done the impossible, the unimaginable! She watched in horror as Vlad's body withered into ash, just as Ilona and Fleur had done. Emil wrapped his arms and legs around her, but she was unable to hold him, unable to move her arms. Her lungs too constricted to draw breath, she heaved instead of sobbing. Tears of blood streaked her face, dripped onto her dress, her vision veiled by a film of red. She could hear Emil desperately calling her name between her gasps for air, drowning on grief. In the present for a moment, she could feel her chest seizing, fluttering beneath her blouse like a trapped bird. She knew she was crying, could feel the tears roll off her lashes. She was not sure if the strained wails and whimpers were from her past or if she was actually giving voice to them in the present.

Again her vision was moved to the events of the book, hovering above Vlad's empty box, could see their knives lying in his ashes. The Szgany were gone, the wolves had stopped their serenade. She looked down upon the man who had pierced her lover's heart, watched as he bid his farewells to his beloved company. He felt he was dying a hero, a martyr to the cause of righteousness. He looked to Mina, proud he had contributed to lifting her curse, smiled and died. The last beams of sunlight on the final day of Vlad, Ilona, and Fleur's life were flickering out behind the Carpathian Mountains, like a spent candle.

"Gallant gentleman, my ass!" Valeria huffed and hastily wiped her eyes, the spell of her past finally broken. She cursed him even though she could not honestly deny that he had been just as Stoker claimed, a gallant gentleman. He had sacrificed himself in service of another, a woman who was not his wife or sister. He had done what was needed to save her because it was the right thing to do, to save Mina from becoming like her. That realization brought her hand up to her eyes and forehead again, this time vigorously rubbing them, chasing away the first signs of slumber. In less than an hour, she would die to the world of man and become a prisoner to her own mind, her imagination let loose to wreak havoc upon her in the open expanse of her dreams.

She snubbed and took her handkerchief from her skirt pocket, wiping her eyes again as well as her nose. She skimmed the last pages of the novel, exhausted and fed up with it. She learned that seven years after that day, the band of heroes returned to Transylvania, to Castle Dracula. Of course, the great Van Helsing neglected to mention he had returned to remedy his failure, that he had come back to kill her if she had been fool enough to stay there. She had been right to run away with Emil. She learned that the Harkers were blessed with a child, a son named Quincey in honor of their fallen friend.

The final words, written by Harker, but spoken by Van Helsing, stuck in her mind. "Later on he will understand how some men so loved her, that they did dare much for her sake." She read the sentence over and over, no less than five times. She hoped young Quincey would understand when Emil had not. The events they had experienced defied understanding. Despite being murderers, despite having broken her home, they had been blessed by marriage, happiness, children, and the gift of life. Together they had taken more from her than was their right, more than they had fully understood, just as Vlad had taken more from her, from Ilona and Fleur, than had been his right to do. Everything was gone, desolate. For over four hundred years, those she had encountered had taken from her without hesitation, without remorse, without consequence. She decided it was time to take something back.

She walked to the bed and lay down, gazing out the cracked drapes at the outside world coming to life as she died to sleep. She wrapped her empty arms around herself, huddled into a ball. Dear God, how she wished Vlad was with her! She had hated him, had even tried to kill him once, but her love for him had been greater than her hate in the end. Alone and hollow, she would gladly forfeit her extraordinarily long life to have him lie beside her one more time, one last time, just until she was asleep. As always when she thought of Vlad, reminisces of Ilona were never far behind. She could still smell the soft scent of her hair, fresh in her mind. She had awoken so many days to find it stretched across her pillow, just close enough that when she rolled over she would find the black ribbons beneath her nose, like the fingers of a river stretching forth to join the sea. Ilona had always been fond of the earthy, spicy scent of lavender, a warmer shade of gray. As the sun clawed over the horizon, Valeria broke into sobs, once, twice, and was then quiet, overtaken by the dawn. Had more sensitive creatures been present, they would have known that her mourning had continued on into her slumber, too quiet to be heard by human ears.

***

Trapped within the contorted world of a dream, Valeria stood outside the walls of a proud castle, surrounded by formidable defenses. Targoviste. She recognized the intimidating structure of centuries past not because she had ever laid eyes on it, but because Vlad had described it so vividly to her. He had been exceedingly proud of his capital fortress with its soaring proud tower, thick walls and two encompassing hedges of sharpened pikes jutting from the earth. However, she was not within their protection, but outside in the barren field surrounding it. The ground looked scorched and ruddy, like a fierce burn, bloody red beneath, but charred black, and crumbling on top. The handfuls of trees so desperate to attempt existence in such a desolate environment were shabby, gnarled and leafless. The sky was shades of dark purple and blue, accented with slashes of red glow, resembling an injury that had not only lacerated the flesh, but had met it with enough impact to bruise and sand away the top layer of skin as well, exposing the wounded dermis below. She could sense Vlad was close, in the tower perhaps, but she could not see him. He shadowed her footsteps with his eyes, his intent gaze weighing heavy upon her. She could hear the withered grass crunch beneath her slippers with each step. Although the castle was precisely as she had imagined, the land had died and she could not understand what had caused such withering.

As she walked the parched landscape, she was relieved to feel the first drops of rain. Hopefully it would bring the land back to life, lush and green as it should be. The rain fell faster, large drops that splattered as they landed. She could feel her saturated hair and clothing, cold and heavy sticking to her skin, soaked slippers encased her feet. She looked and saw she had stepped into a puddle, not of water, but of blood. She gasped because she could see her frightened reflection clearly in its surface, something that she had not seen since she had been reborn. She tried to back away from it, but only managed to step into another similar puddle. It was then she looked at her dress and skin, soaked in the same sticky crimson instead of cleansing rainwater. She looked to the wounded sky for some sort of explanation, but most of her field of view was blocked. In the same moment she had realized she was covered in blood, thousands upon thousands of stakes had sprung from the ground, each displaying their grizzly trophy.

Men and women, young and old, even children surrounded her upon their stakes. They groaned and gasped, already taken down into such levels of agony that tears served no use for them any longer. Women dangled in the air like discarded marionettes, supported by the hateful spikes erupting from their chest or abdomen, some still trying to clutch upon their bosoms their infants that had already succumbed to the hateful spikes. One man had the additional misfortune of hanging with his face toward the ground, able to witness his innards spilling from his belly as the impalement rent an ever-enlarging hole in his body. As gravity and his own weight torturously pulled him further down, he tried to no avail to take his dangling mass of organs into his hands, to pull them back within himself, but he could not reach. The pole had shattered his spine and rendered him paralyzed from ribcage down. Crows and other carrion feasting birds circled overhead, calling to one another with laughing, riotous caws to join the macabre banquet.

Valeria felt tears of pity, terror, and disgust well up within her eyes. She looked to the castle, but could not find a breach in the defending walls to allow her access. The windows and doors had faded into its red brick exterior, completely invisible. She no longer sensed Vlad's presence in the tower. He had abandoned Targoviste, like he had abandoned her, like Ilona and Fleur in ruins. She was instantly compelled to find a way out of the maze of suffering humanity. She rushed between the poles, stained shiny, brackish red from the blood soaking into the porous wood. She knew why the forest had been cut down. She knew why the grass refused to grow, why the sun no longer shone over Count Dracula's capital city. It had become the gates of Hell, the first encampment of Satan's minions set on overtaking God's creation.

The arms and legs of the dead and dying pummeled her as she desperately tried to find her way through, tangling their desperate fingers in her hair, grabbing her sleeves. She would surely go mad if she did not escape! Finally she found a break in the sea of death, a small clearing between the forest of trees before her and the forest of humanity behind her. Only three pikes stood there, in a row. She instantly knew their victims. Bile and blood retched out of her stomach. What she saw brought her to knees, had finally overwhelmed her. Ilona and Fleur hung on their oversized stakes, naked and exposed, the sharpened ends bursting through their chests, through their hearts. From the gore soaked ground she looked up at them, gritting her teeth, holding on the last scraps of her sanity. She could see their bodies had wilted, dead long before she arrived in Hell. She bawled great, swollen tears of blood for them. Dry, hoarse laments unfurled effortlessly from her lips without her cognizance, without the logic of words to define her grief. The only measure of pity she had received was the knowledge they were already dead, that she could not have possibly saved them. She knew without doubt that if she had seen them in such a horrific manner while they still lived, it would have cleaved her psyche, reduced her to a raving lunatic. She did not know how her mind still processed what she saw, heard, smelled, and tasted on the air. She pulled herself to her feet and feebly tried to walk away from the nightmare once more, but regardless of direction, not matter how many times she tried to turn around, she could only walk into a post of death. Unlike the others, it was always empty and the maddening fear that pounded in her ears like thunder told her why. It was her stake and she was powerless to escape it!

With the understanding of her fate, she found herself flung into the air, her back split by the wickedly sharp point of her stake. She felt it pass through her lungs, stopping her breath, burst through her ribcage, and out her ripped and tattered flesh. She screamed in agony. Pain like she had never known electrocuted her body, traveling down her veins. She screamed again, screamed for Vlad to save her. Where had he gone? Why had he killed so many? What manner of devil had come into possession of his body and chosen to kill his wives with the same calloused cruelty as his enemies? What kind of monster could condone such atrocities? How could she have ever loved such a man?

Finally the merciful noon day sun released Valeria from her nightmare. She lay upon the bed, pulling her hair in utter distress, screaming louder than she could ever remember screaming. She tried to scream so loud that Vlad, even if he was trapped in the midst of Hell, would have to hear her cry. She understood what her dream had symbolized. Truly Van Helsing had ended Ilona and Fleur's lives and nearly her own, but Vlad had already killed each of them. They shared the same cause of death, a broken heart.

She curled herself into a tight knot, knees against her chest. She hid her face beneath her hands, rubbing eyes that were overfilled with tears. They rolled with ease from the corners, stinging like they had been mixed with soap. The nightmare had only reflected what was within her, what she carried in her heart. She was alone. All that she had known and loved was gone. The very man she had loved more than her own life was the same man she had hated with a fire hotter than any furnace. He had been the reason for all her misfortune, but had undeniably brought her happiness. It was this duality within her heart that had manifested in her dream. That which she had loved had killed her. Loving Vlad had broken her and had destroyed Ilona and Fleur.

Ilona... A wave of grief washed over her, a tinge of nausea. A deep sob unfurled from her chest. She dropped her forehead to touch her knees, tightly wrapping her arms around her legs to make herself as small as possible. She wanted to curl up within herself, tighter and smaller until she disappeared. The sight of her decomposing corpse impaled beside Fleur flashed in her mind. In life as in the dream, death had found Ilona and Fleur before her. As much as the memory of the sight sickened her, it terrified her. It felt like an omen, a portent of her death. In the fourteen years after Vlad's death, she had never felt more alone, more vulnerable.

She cried for a while longer, not the uncontrollable bursts of grief she had shed upon waking, but a quieter, cleansing lament. She cried for what she had once had and lost. She cried for what she had dreamed to have that was no longer possible. She cried for the life she had believed to be hers on her wedding night and for the life she had received after her husband's fangs first pierced her flesh. She cried for the future Ilona had envisioned for Emil, for her part in his life. She cried because she was no longer welcomed in his life, unwelcomed anywhere. She cried for a little longer and then she stopped. There was no number of tears that would ever undo the hurt she had suffered. The tears would not heal her, would not save her. As always, she would save herself.

Begin again...

She set her jaw and hastily packed her few belongings, anxious to leave Paris. The dream had galvanized her, like a length of steel that had been pounded, folded, heated, and pounded again into a new shape, and finally shocked by a bath of cold water to cement the reformation. Just as a sword begins as a rough chunk of metal, she had been formed into a weapon, given a sharpened edge. She had been broken, tempered, and forged into something stronger, something with a purpose.

Her internal compass had been set northeast. An invisible, almost straight, line had been drawn in her mind. It began in Paris, through Brussels, and ended in Amsterdam on the doorstep of Abraham Van Helsing. He had lived long enough! She grabbed her bag and hastily headed to the door, but she stopped unexpectedly, even to herself, frozen in place.

She turned and looked at the small room, empty and showing its age. The quiet of the room, and the building in which it was a part of was so silent, so still, that it seemed to be sapping her strength out through her feet. She dropped her bag on the bed and sat down beside it, her head in her hands. She was tired, not refreshed by her sleep because she had forgotten to feed for so many nights, driven forward only by her pain. She was unable to continue.

Part Four:
The Diversion in Paris

Chapter Nine

Valeria waited impatiently for the sun to fall behind the skyline, most of which was hidden by the rows of tenement housing, hostels, and inns in the small Parisian neighborhood she had chosen the night before. The last rays of daylight stung her eyes, still tender from the river of tears unleashed by her hateful dream. To be still allowed her time to think. She preferred action and movement over contemplation, and had done so quite successfully until yesterday. But sit she had, left with the fallout of the nightmare and returning thoughts of isolation, betrayal, and heartache beyond measure, all drudged up by that damn book. Subconsciously, she scratched the varnish from the chair arm with her fingernail, watching the light fade through the crack in the drapes.

She was alone. For the first time in countless years she was utterly alone. Her mind raced to Emil, how he had evicted her so easily from his life and the knife of betrayal twisted in her back once more. She would not think of Emil tonight. She would think of none of it, not Vlad, Van Helsing, or even dearest Ilona. As the sliver of daylight retreated back across the floor, out through the crack in the drapes, she decided that she would extend her stay in Paris. A light breeze teased the edges of the drapes, pursing them open slightly and allowing them to close, like parting lips. The air was cool and moist, like the city was doused in the same fine sweat that would shimmer across the skin of an exhausted lover. The coming night smelled delicious.

***

Diary of Countess Valeria Karajan- Dracula

27 March 1899- I have returned to journaling, for I am in desperate need of companionship. My journal has long been a faithful friend, a keeper of secrets, and very often a priest. I know I will have plenty to confess once I find Van Helsing. He will not live past the day I cross his threshold. However I can stand no more of this rampaging. My falling out with Emil has finished what was left of me, and the shell that does remain must be refilled or I will shatter into a thousand pieces at the lightest harm. The dream of the field at Targoviste has shown me this, how vulnerable I am. I must live for more than revenge or I will be consumed. Van Helsing will have his day soon enough, as will the others, but for now I must try to live a time for myself. I have forgotten how.

Only now, as I watch the sun set over Fleur's city have I taken time to open this fine leather bound volume, purchased from the suspicious shop lady on my first day in Paris along with Stoker's damned book. Damn him and his book! Damn it all! I will speak with the innkeeper's wife as I leave tonight. I will be staying longer than I had expected in Paris.

***

A blast of cool air swept a few stray strands of hair across Valeria's face as she left the inn on the east side of Paris, cool, but not cold, at least not to her. Many people were trafficking about the streets, either going to or from work in one of the many factories, shops and bakeries that dotted the city. The air was crisp and clean, the scent of their blood unadulterated, warm, metallic, and salty. She drew her bottom lip into her mouth and traced it with her tongue, tasting the residual flavor from air. A jolt of excitement struck within her core, quickly followed by the anxious hunger she had known before to make her decisions impulsive and dangerous. It was the hunger that allowed her to act in a moment and only think of it again after awaking the next afternoon with a satisfied appetite, and a stained conscious. She tucked the wisps of blonde behind her ear and fell into the flow of warmly dressed pedestrians, thankful she had brought her coat from Romania.

The inns with taverns beneath them were easy enough to spot, raucous laughter and the clanking of glass against wooden tables. She could smell the ale from twice the distance a human nose would be able to detect it, even more so when it was carried in the blood of a drunken patron. The establishment she had chosen to stay in was not such a place, and even if it had been she would never be so foolish to look for any type of meal there. She had chosen it for her hideaway, for the solitude, and because she knew the elderly owners were most likely as deaf as stones and just as attentive. Any quirks in her behavior would be overlooked as long as she had money. She ducked into the next tavern she found without having to cross the street, which was thick with mud and horse manure. She did not wish to dirty her dress.

She chose a table toward the back of the tavern, close to the fireplace. It would warm her skin to the touch and give the illusion of color to her cheeks. She browsed the people around her with the selective eye of a picky shopper at the vegetable market, too soft, too young, too old, or too ripe. She nodded, making a mental note as she scanned the room. She would need to acquire some more clothes, maybe some shoes and a nice parasol, perhaps even a hat. Wearing a hat seemed a very Parisian thing to do. The burn from her stomach crept up her throat, but she refused to give in too easily. The last thing she wanted for dinner was a slobbering old drunk or a homeless waif. This catch needed to be fresh, young, preferably handsome and energetic. Blood was not the only thing she craved.

She had been a widow for almost fourteen years. Nearly fourteen years of celibacy, longer still from the last time she had made love with her husband. Ilona's hand had been the last tender touch she had known, the last heartbeat she had felt so gently against her chest, like a butterfly in a cage. To think of them was to think of love, lost love, her broken heart, but it was not love she sought tonight. She would choose carefully, methodically, because whomever she chose to share her bed might not live to see morning, but she would give them a night worth dying for. She closed her eyes briefly, hoping to clear her mind of their memory. The lack of blood was making it difficult to concentrate, trying her patience.

With a hunter's eye, Valeria scanned the room again. It was alive with the sound of heartbeats, breathing, laughing, and even singing. She listened to the whispered plans of two men in the farthest corner from as they plotted to steal the money kept under the bar. She listened as a worrisome man discussed payment for services with the prostitute perched on a stool near the bar. An extra coin insured she would keep her silence concerning their encounter. The human noise was intoxicating. She had denied herself even the most mundane of interactions with humans for so long. She had told herself it had been for Emil's protection, but she had used it as a shield to hide herself from the world, doubly so since she had left Brasov. The world seemed like a much more dangerous place than it had before. She had lost her confidence, her security, the night Vlad died. She intended to reclaim it.

Her eye finally settled on a young man, no older than his mid-twenties. He was tanned to a warm golden brown and he carried the dusty, salty scent of a hard day's work. He conversed and laughed with two friends riotously, drinking as if he may never see another drop. He was a laborer, of that there was no doubt, but she could not determine what kind of work it was simply by scent. Because of her time with dear Serghei, she would never forget the scent of a blacksmith. Emil carried the scent of Mihai's print shop home every night. The scent of blood lingered on a butcher long after the shop was closed. A fisherman always smelled of his briny catch. One of his associates raucously bounced a woman with large breasts on his knee, her dress unbuttoned to reveal the tightly laced corset beneath.

Valeria watched and listened. They called him Lamond. Blonde, golden warm and alive, as different from her husband as possible. She would have him. She settled in to let the course of their evening play out. She had waited for fourteen years; a couple more hours would be of no significance.

Minutes passed into hours, one drink at a time. The friend and his busty companion giggled away into the dark street, cheeks flushed by ale and arousal. The other was thrown out with two other offenders for too much horseplay, two broken chairs, several shattered glasses, and sent to sober up elsewhere. Lamond was left with his drink, alone at the table in the mostly empty bar. He looked lonesome, watching the ale wash around the sides of his glass as he agitated it. He took a drink, but held it in his cheeks for a moment before swallowing it. The party was certainly over. Valeria felt her heartbeat quicken. She needed him to be alone, needed a moment of his undivided attention to lay her charming trap.

She focused her thoughts, every ounce of her mental energy, toward Lamond. The room around her seemed quieted, sounds muffled and movements slowed. As her will soaked into his subconscious, he felt the sensation that someone was watching him. He raised his head from the nearly empty glass and their eyes connected. He froze briefly, surprised that he had not noticed such a beautiful woman before that moment and amazed she was looking at him with obvious interest. The world has stopped now for him as well. She permitted a grin to curl the corner of her mouth, but carefully kept her lips together and her teeth hidden. He looked around, disbelief evident on his face that she was looking at him, and chuckled. He stood, wobbled slightly, and then walked to her table and sat across from her.

Lamond looked blearily at his new admirer with a measure of confusion and mistrust. He could tell by the way this mystery woman simply held herself in the chair that she was not the average tavern patron. The tilt of her head, the straightness in her back, the way her long fingers loosely interlocked, all indicated that this was a woman of means, of higher social rank than he or anyone else for at least a mile in any direction. So why was she in a dirty tavern, unbuttoning his shirt with her eyes? He could only think of one reason, which was plenty enough.

"Bonsoir, Mademoiselle," he said, slightly lowering his head before extending his hand for hers. She slid her fingers over his and waited for his lips to touch the top of her hand before responding.

"Bonsoir, Lamond," she replied as his lips lifted from her hand. She could feel his warm breath on her skin, raising the fine, almost invisible, hairs on end.

He lifted his eyes, looking over the arch of her wrist, before slowly raising his head and releasing her hand. Valeria felt her heart leap. Despite the cheap ale, his scent was enlivening, intoxicating, rousing. The animal, the predator inside her, wanted to drag him over the table and lunge into his throat. She wanted to drink mouthfuls of his life and then kiss him with his blood still in her mouth. She took a deep breath and suppressed the darkest aspect of her nature while the lighter shades of shadow still ran free. She grinned at him instead.

"How is it the lady knows my name, a lowly man such as I?" Lamond questioned, sliding his chair closer. Valeria paused, considering her French.

"I noticed you with your friends. I asked the bartender your name. Your friends, they have left already?"

"Lousy drunks..." He chuckled, his affection for them evident in his insincere insult. "Sleeping it off already, no doubt. Where are your friends tonight, Mademoiselle?"

Valeria propped against the table on her elbow, head in her hand. "Alas, Lamond. I have no friends, no family, aside from this glass." She picked up the glass of ale and looked at him through the empty top half. "As good a reason as any to drink, would you not agree?"

"As good as any…" Lamond agreed, pulling his seat even closer. His leg was against hers, his warmth radiating through his clothes almost as warm as the fire. He propped against the table in similar fashion, the firelight reflecting in his glassy eyes and rosy cheeks. "If the Mademoiselle would allow, I would be a very, very good friend. If only I knew her name."

"Valeria," she said quickly, flinching inwardly that she had been foolish enough to tell him her true name and not one of her many aliases. She would have to mind her head and not allow herself to become charmed. Lamond was as smooth as a snake slithering under silk, and potentially just as dangerous.

He took her hand again and kissed it once more, but instead of a polite peck, he opened his mouth wider to drag his bottom lip slowly across her skin to meet the upper. "It is very nice to meet you," he whispered.

***

After bursting into Lamond's room, he pushed the door closed by backing Valeria against it. He locked both of his hands in hers and pressed them against the door just over her head as he covered the side of her neck in kisses. She could feel the cool air settle against her skin on the lightly moist path that followed his lips over her collarbone, across the fullness of her breasts and back up the other side of her neck. She squint her eyes closed, holding her breath, biting her bottom lip unconsciously. Within her, static electricity was racing through her veins. Lava hot excitement ignited her muscles and burned through them like lit fuses, racing toward her powder keg heart that was beating with the fervor of a human heart, exploding with life for the first time in years.

She pulled his face up to hers, her hands on his cheeks. His light stubble scratched the inside of her palms, his breath warm on her face, laced with ale. She looked long and deep into his eyes, able to feel the cadence of his pulse from his carotid artery under his jaw. She could see the reflection of her hypnotic gaze reflected back toward her. Although she doubted the need to subdue his will to secure his desire, when the time came to make her bite, she wanted to know he was helpless to resist. To feed without struggle required an unresponsive or sleeping victim or someone who was more than happy to submit. Pleased with what she saw, she combed her fingers into his mess of golden hair and kissed him long and deep, her tongue darting quickly between his lips so he would not find her wickedly sharp teeth too soon.

Valeria could feel the blood moving faster through her veins, warming her cheeks, breath quickened. She could not think beyond the moment, could not plan or worry. For the first time in years she existed for the moment, cared nothing for consequences, responsibilities, or promises. She was living simply for the sake of being alive. She grabbed his shirt by the collar and yanked, a quick straight rip raced down his chest to his belt. His eyes widened, inhaled deeply and grabbed the shirt by its ends and finished tearing it off, tossing it across the room. She hastily unbuttoned her dress far enough that she could slide her arms out of the sleeves, resisting the impulse to will her body into mist form and simply glide out of all her fabric trappings. With a little insistence from Lamond and a torn button, her dress slipped over her hips and she kicked her shoes off as she stepped out of its puddle. Falling back into each other again, another rush of feverous kisses and they both busied themselves with the latches of Valeria's corset.

"Damn these things!" Lamond laughed as he dropped to his knees and anxiously worked the last hook and eye latch free. With his chin resting on her navel, he watched her chest rise and fall rapidly as he slid his hands under her thin chemise top to feel the slender curves of her waist, the small of her back, up her spine, and around to cup each breast. Rising to his feet, he peeled the chemise over her head and hoisted her into the air, her legs quickly wrapped around his waist and locked at the ankles. His chest was as hot as a furnace against hers, heart beating like a drum, reverberating into her and filling the quiet of her heart's hideaway with the sound of his life. He carried her the short distance to the simple rope and straw bed and laid her down upon a thick wool blanket.

Valeria folded her arms behind her head and draped her legs loosely behind his boots, watching the subtle changes of his expression as pulled her drawers over her hips and down her legs. She pulled her knees closer to her so he could take the undergarment from her ankles and then quickly rose to pull his pants down from his waist. She pulled him against her, standing on their knees in the center of the creaking bed, almost too quickly for his slowed reaction time to follow. Another frenzy of kisses swept over her shoulders, visiting each breast and nipple and the valley between them. She leaned against his arm that was supporting her back, finding the best position for him to continue, unable to decide if she would release fully to his embrace and follow, or push him backwards and take control. For a second, she considered the cracks in the ceiling and the light that shone through them from above and wondered if the inhabitants above could hear them.

A breeze of lingering winter air slipped through the crack between the wall and the small window. It blew across her lover and delivered his scent to her, pure and concentrated, just as a shimmer of sweat finer than dew broke across his back. It was the scent of a human, alive with blood almost hot enough to boil. Her decision had been made for her. She shifted her weight and flipped him onto his back with simple ease and crawled up him, skimming the length of his body from waist to neck with the tip of her nose, kissing, tasting, as she went. She was ravenous with desire and hunger and the promise of fulfillment for both cravings lay beneath her, more than willing to oblige. Sitting across his waist and arching her back like a cat, she leaned forward and kissed him and then leaned backward to allow the tip of his erect manhood to just touch her glistening labia, another kiss and another touch, the

95

contact electrifying. He grabbed two handfuls of the blanket and held tight, almost insane with anticipation, another kiss, another touch, back and forth. She had forgotten how gratifying it could be to have a lover under her control and relished having him at her mercy. Another kiss, and she leaned back just far enough to allow him past her threshold before pulling away for another quick kiss. His tongue darted between her lips and scraped the keen point of her fang, drawing the smallest drop of blood.

The taste of Lamond's blood filled her mouth, her shark-like sensitivity able to detect its smallest presence. It was the last straw, the final nudge that pushed her greedy senses over the edge. She sat back and finally allowed him to fully enter her, surrounding him with her cool constrictive pleasure. She rubbed up his chest and down his stomach with wide open hands, feeling the muscles tense just below the surface of his flesh. Valeria closed her eyes and tried to solely concentrate on the thrilling sensation of a human man, the fragile strength, the eagerness to please, the almost scalding heat massaging her most sensitive and abandoned place. But the clawing, burning thirst from her stomach demanded satisfaction as well and it threatened to cut short the pleasures of their flesh. In the past, after many encounters with Serghei, she would allow herself a quick drink during their lovemaking, certain that she would be able to refrain from killing him. She had made no such promises to herself concerning Lamond. It would be a shame to kill him before both of them were spent and nothing would sober him faster than seeing his own blood rushing from his punctured wrist or soaking into the bed from his pierced throat.

She dug the fingernails of her left hand into the frame of the bed and interlocked her right by hand with his left, securing it above his head. As she rocked back and forth, she could hear his heartbeat increasing and for a moment she thought his heart might burst, nearly panting for breath. He grabbed hold of her waist with his available hand and kept time with her motion, pushing and pulling her accordingly. When he attempted to free the hand she was clutching for the other side, he caught his first glimpse of her unworldly strength. She held his hand fast against the bed. He looked to her with a brush of disbelief, amazed a woman of such diminutive stature was capable of overpowering him. She looked deep into his eyes, reasserting her power over him with another hypnotic gaze and an extra measure of vigor to her grinding hips. Combined, it was enough to put Lamond's intoxicated mind at ease and return him to her full control without further question.

"You will feel no pain, no fear in this, Lamond," she said in quiet, calm tones, despite the heat and pace of their movements. "You will feel only pleasure from my touch, from my kiss. Do you understand?"

"Yes," he answered breathlessly, nodding his head obediently. "Yes."

Feeling the subtle sensations of her own climax approaching, she leaned close to him and kissed him once more, a kiss good-bye. Her lips raced down his neck and under the square of his jaw, drawing the lobe of his ear between her teeth to devilishly nibble. She could sense his energies concentrate at his loins, feel him lightly tremble beneath her. Only in the last moments of his life did she notice the exquisite green of his eyes. Regardless of how many more centuries she would live or how many lovers she would embrace, she knew she would remember Lamond's eyes, even if she forgot his name. Suddenly perfect pleasure unfurled within her, blooming from her core and racing through her extremities with soft quickening. Lamond answered her impassioned moan with his own aching groan, followed by an eruption of hot life that only heightened her pleasure. Overwhelmed beyond the limits of her self control, Valeria finally released the darkness of her nature. She freed the predator from her restraints and she bit quick and hard into the pounding artery of his throat. The taste of his blood, saturated with pheromones, quickly filled her mouth, the anticoagulants in her saliva ensuring a steady flow as long as his heart held out. She wrapped her arms tightly around him, ensuring his subjection should her charms not hold long enough for her to finish her drink. To her surprise, he caressed her as she drained the life from him, as her hips rose and fell on him until he became too flaccid to continue.

One mouthful after another, Valeria took Lamond's essence into herself until his heart ceased to beat. She wiped her mouth with her hand and sucked the residue from her fingers. Looking down at her exhausted lover, she felt a quick stab of guilt. He had appeared to be a well liked, hard working man in the prime of his life who had had the unfortunate luck to catch her eye. She had been greedy to take his life, but such was the risk of going too long without feeding, without tending to her desires. A man had lost his life in order to give hers back. She gently closed his eyes, hiding the beautiful verdant irises, now vacant. She wiped the blood from his wound and turned his head to the side to conceal it before gently covering his still warm body with the blanket. He looked to be sleeping, enjoying a most pleasant dream. She quietly gathered her clothes and dressed before allowing her body to shift into shimmering mists and slipping out the cracked window.

Chapter Ten

28 March 1899- This evening, I walked to Lamond's apartment, but I was unable to get close. The street was filled with people, smoke hung thick and black in the air. The building was wrapped in flames! The firefighters struggled diligently and the fire was extinguished without great harm to the surrounding structures, but was itself destroyed. Three lives were lost to the fire. Lamond was counted among the casualties and the elderly couple who lived above him.

I was selfish to take Lamond's life, so very selfish.

***

5 April 1899- Over a week has passed and still I am overwhelmed with guilt for Lamond's death. I knew better, but it is as if I feel his piercing green eyes watching me. I have seen his eyes in many dreams, the first thing I think of when I awake and the last on my mind when I fall asleep. I will not wait so long to feed my carnal desires again! This has never happened before in all my years and I am quite unnerved by it. I fear the only way to stop it will be to leave Paris and I am weary yet of travel.

By and large, the climate of Paris agreed with me, neither too hot nor too cold, but perhaps a little damp as this is the rainy season. It will be a splendid spring, I am certain. But even all the rain is not totally disagreeable. It provides plenty of cloud cover from the brilliant sun, which could draw attention to my complexion, and it provides one more reason to use a parasol.

I have fallen in love with Fleur's city. I feel a sense of closeness to her now, one that I did not have while she lived. I understand now why she so longed to return, as I am in no rush to leave. The City of Lights has shone well on my soul, as long as Lamond forgives me and haunts me no more.

***

9 April 1899- I know what I have seen! My eyes have not deceived me and I am not insane. Lamond lives, I am certain of it! Walking with my guilt, as I have every night since his death, I have allowed it to guide me like a compass. I passed the tavern where I found him, but he was not inside it but on the roof, peering from around the chimney! I could feel his presence even before I saw him, before I saw those eyes gleaming in the dim streetlight. I only saw him for a moment but I know, without doubt, that it was Lamond. I do not understand how, but he is a vampire! The dawn was coming too quickly tonight or I would have pursued him. Tomorrow I will search for him, although I do not know what I will do or say when I find him. I must find him. His actions are my responsibility and I have much to apologize for.

***

Again Valeria sat in the chair in front of the window in her room, watching the setting sun. She picked incessantly at the varnish of the chair arm, having scraped it clean all around the rounded end. She gnawed at the index finger knuckle of her other hand, impatient for her powers to return to her. She felt as though she would come apart from the inside out. She stood and began to pace back and forth through the dim light. Finally the sun's hold on the day and her powers were relinquished as it slid behind the horizon. She felt the tingling rush cascade across her body, so familiar and warm. It seemed to stir her blood, to fill her body with the energy the sun had just begrudgingly given up. She stopped in her tracks and stood completely still, knowing that Lamond had just felt the same invigorating wash of abilities return to him. She felt for him across the expanse of the city, searching for the signature of his energy with her mind's eye. She felt a vague notion of his presence and she immediately rushed outside and into the street.

She had no way of knowing how he would react. Would it be anger, fear, or distrust? He had more than enough reason to hate her, more than enough reason to want her dead. Would he attack her or run and hide as he did the first night she saw him? She could feel him in the distance, but he seemed to be hidden, almost buried. Following the Seine, she came to the construction site of the Gare d' Orsay, the grand train station being built for the Universal Exposition the next year. The site was dark and empty, the workers having already left in search of the warmth and comfort of home and family. Valeria could sense her orphan in the bowels of the construction, deep within the labyrinth of service tunnels and bays.

She could feel him pulling away from her, repelled like the matching ends of two magnets. When she was certain she was out of human view, she forsook her physical body for her incorporeal form in hopes that it would make Lamond less aware of her. Thin as smoke, Valeria curled through cracks, down pipes, and extruded herself through crevices until she was only a few feet from him. The inhuman, animalistic aspect of her psyche reveled in watching him without his knowledge, stalking him from gap in the unfinished wall, while her kinder, human nature wished not to frighten him. She was overwhelmed with sadness and guilt at the sight of him.

Lamond, ashen and dirty, was huddled in the corner of a small utility closet, door locked from the inside. She could tell by his scent and the rhythm of his heart that he had not fed for several days, if ever. His senses were heightened by his starvation. He could hear and smell every hot blooded thing in the vicinity with a heartbeat, every rat, every

101

stray dog, every man, woman, and child. He wrapped his hands over his ears, squeezing tight to block the cacophony. Valeria slid from the crack, allowing her body to reincorporate. Even with her back to the wall, she was still only a few feet from him.

"Lamond..." she spoke gently, as if waking a child from slumber. He jerked and began to claw back into the corner as if he were a frightened animal, eyes wide and screaming. "Lamond, please do not be afraid," she said only marginally louder, but her voice filled the entire room. She wanted to go to him, take his hands in hers or pull him into her arms, but she feared he would injure himself should she approach. He was too blood deprived to heal.

"Stay back!" he shouted, his hands held in front of him between them. The dark circles around his eyes hollowed them, like emeralds dropped into a well. "Stay away from me!"

"Lamond, I am not here to hurt you. I want to help you," Valeria pleaded, crouching to the ground first, but choosing to sit on the ground instead, wedged in the corner as far as she could get from him.

"You did this to me! It's your fault I am like this!" She watched his countenance change from fear to fury in a flash. "It's your fault I killed Thayer!" he roared and charged toward her. He grabbed at her throat with both hands, teeth snapping like a rabid dog. She stood and held him at length, looking into his face without fear of his barrage. He clawed at her hands, scratching long ribbons of flesh from her hands, arms, and one across her face. He roared and screamed in anger and frustration.

"I am so very sorry this happened, Lamond." She spoke in her most soothing tones, hoping a measure of her charms may still affect him. "Please, calm yourself so we can speak. I can help you. I *want* to help you, Lamond."

He watched puzzled, as the claw marks on her face faded from bloody red to smooth marble once more. He dropped his hands to his sides and waited for her to release him, finally accepting he was overpowered and would be able to do no harm to her. She let him go and he retreated to his corner, waiting for her explanation.

"I did not intend for this to happen. I was careless and somehow you tasted my blood." Her mind replayed at high speed the heated events of that night, beginning with biting her lip in exquisite anticipation as he lavished her neck and the fullness of her breasts with warm kisses, pressed firmly against his apartment door by his sweltering body. "Do you remember that night?"

"You were at the tavern… Andre left, and then Thayer left with Bridgette… I spilled my ale on you." His face was dimly illuminated by the recollection. "We talked…and then I took you to my apartment. We fucked like there was no tomorrow."

To her surprise, she felt her cheeks flush. "Yes…yes we did. Do you remember what happened next?"

"You bit me…" She watched him struggle with what he understood and what he knew to be true. "I felt myself getting weak, but I didn't want you to stop. I wanted you to take my last drop, kill me, but just not stop." He shook his head, ran his fingers through his hair before pulling it. "Then everything went black. Did I die?"

Valeria nodded, but kept quiet, allowing him to search through his thoughts on his own. Despite the time that had elapsed since he had turned, she knew the lack of blood would fog his memory and muddle with his reasoning. By the time she leapt to her death from the ledge of Castle Dracula, she was already aware of her husband's strange affliction, understood the symptoms of vampirism. When she returned to life, soaked and nearly frozen to the lakeshore, she knew she had become as her husband, a bloodthirsty vampire. She could only imagine what Lamond must have thought.

"I heard Thayer's voice, felt him shaking me. I could hear his heart in my brain, like a drum. I could smell…his blood, smell it under his skin… Oh God!" He shuddered, like a leaf hanging on to a branch, but only just. "Blood was everywhere! I panicked! I put him in my bed and poured lamp oil everywhere and lit it. I didn't think about Doreen and Renaud upstairs!"

Lamond crumpled into the corner like a rag, exhausted from his recollections and their accompanying shame. He hid his face in his hands and sobbed, gasping for air his lungs no longer needed. Valeria crept to him on hands and knees, slowly and carefully. She placed a hand on his leg, hoping to provide some sort of comfort.

"Lamond, when was the last time you fed? Was it Thayer?"

"I cannot eat! I am starving, but it comes back up! Water even comes back up!"

She watched helplessly as her accidental neophyte spiraled downward in darkest despair.

"I want to kill someone so I can drink their blood until I burst! I have tried rats, dogs, cats, but it does not take it away! I can smell them; hear them no matter where I hide!"

Valeria bit into her wrist and quickly pressed it against his mouth before he could resist, knowing her secondhand meal would be better than nothing. He latched on like a suckling infant, pulling the nourishment from her wrist as fast as it would flow. Suddenly he jerked away from her, wiping at his mouth with both his hands, spitting and gagging.

"You cannot live on rats and strays. It will not satisfy you." She wiped her arm on the underneath of her dress. "Human blood is what you need, what you must have. The thirst will have its way and then you *will* kill again. You have to maintain, dance the line between injury and death for those you chose to bite or you will kill them, no matter how much you want to spare them. I waited too long and you paid for that with your life."

"I am not like you! You are a monster! A succubus from the pits of Hell!"

"I have been called worse..." she replied calmly. "But you do not have to be a murderer. I can show you, if you allow me. Please Lamond, let me give you this small measure of your humanity back. I do not ask for your forgiveness. I do not deserve it, but please let me teach you what has taken me years to learn."

Lamond rubbed at his neck, trying desperately to push a swallow down his parched throat. The blood he had taken from her had cleared his mind, but had done little to quench his thirst. He knew he needed more.

"Please Lamond, I will do whatever I can to help you. If you wish for death instead of this existence, I will end your life tonight as quickly and painlessly as possible. But if you want to live, you have to know how to survive in a civilized world instead of behaving like an animal. There are slayers who kill our kind and will hunt you down if you are too reckless. The death they deal would not be so merciful."

Lamond thought deeply of her offer to end his life and her invitation to become her protégé. He thought of his lost life and the new one he had been born into. He was not yet ready to die, not again.

"Teach me."

Chapter Eleven

23 April 1899- It seems Lamond is beginning to accept his new nature. With my guidance, he has fed several times now and has shown great self control. So far he has only fed after me, reluctant to select a host. His confidence will grow with time. Fortunately, he now has time in abundance. He has inquired very little of me, my past or how I was reborn and I do not know how long he will accompany me. Lamond has assisted investigators with their case. He told them that Thayer arrived at his house, still quite ill from his partying the night before. Lamond encouraged him to lie down and left him sleeping with a lamp burning nearby while he went out. When he returned, the building was in flames. I do not know how much, if any, of his prior life he hopes to regain, or if he believes he will be able to stay in Paris. He does not trouble me for details, so I show him the same courtesy.

For now, he is content to stay with me but I will not force it nor will I turn him away. It has been awkward in the least, living with a stranger in such small confines. We have come into this backwards, still reluctant to reveal too much of ourselves to one another after already knowing each other so intimately. The night we met was fed by impulse, lust. I was not looking to enter into a relationship and neither was he. Now I am left to wonder if he feels bound to me like I felt bound to Vlad or if his choice to stay with me was of his own will. He has revealed no intentions and he has made no romantic advancements and neither have I. However, he is my responsibility, no matter what he decides. His choices, his kills, will be on my hands as well as his. It is penance for the sins I committed against him.

***

27 April 1899- Helping Lamond to learn how to survive as a vampire in such modern times reminds me of Ilona's early days as she learned to feed and manage her new, baser impulses. She was such a timid creature to become a hunter, like an actress who is reserved in her personal life only to portray a larger than life character on the stage. Fortunately for Lamond, he is bolder and I do not believe it will be much longer before he does not requires my company when he feeds.

I am not grieved by this, as I have already stayed in Paris much longer than I had intended. I have great business to attend to in Amsterdam, however I will tarry in Paris long enough to see the spring resurrection, regardless if Lamond has need of me or not.

***

18 May 1899- The confines of hovel life have finally became too claustrophobic and I have made arrangements. I enjoy a measure of privacy and there is none to be had here, living with a man who is little more than a stranger. The furnishings will be in the new apartment in two days. When I leave Paris for Amsterdam, I will inform Lamond that the apartment and its contents are his to do with as he pleases. Until then I will help him to understand his new abilities so when it becomes time for him to relocate, as he surely will be forced to do eventually, he will have the ability to provide well for himself.

A new home in the west of Paris means clothing befitting a resident of that assondrement. I will see to that tomorrow, for myself and Lamond.

***

24 May 1899- Tonight will be another first experience for Lamond. He will be accompanying me to the opera for the first performance of *Cendrillion* at the beautiful Opéra-Comique, the *Salle Favart* as it is sometimes called. The theater will be quite a sight to see in itself, considering it has been open for less than half a year after being destroyed by fire, for the third time. The Parisians are certainly a resilient sort.

This will be the first opera I have attended in many, many years so I am just as excited as he, perhaps more. I find it particularly saddening that he has was born, raised, and died in Paris, yet never had the opportunity to attend the opera until after his death, in his unlife. If there was ever a city upon this wide Earth in which to attend the opera, it would no doubt be Paris. Ilona, Vlad and I attended often during the early days of our stay here, as well as frequenting theaters and symphonies, before Fleur. It would have been ghastly to attend any sort of performance with her. She was such a dramatic. Her hat would have been so large that no one would have been able to see around it, just to insure she was the center of everyone's attention, her breast nearly falling out of her dress to make sure she had Vlad's attention.

***

Lamond and Valeria quietly took their seats in the center of the first row on the first balcony just after the doors opened for the night's performance. They had purposely arrived early, giving themselves ample time to acclimate to the heady heat and racket of hundreds of heartbeats in one place. Without a purposeful effort to hear the performance above the pounding rhythms of swarming life that was soon to surround them, the fine opera would sound little different than a songstress' voice against the overwhelming clamor of a thundering waterfall. By arriving earlier than most, they had the opportunity to filter out the background noise of the hundreds of beating hearts slowly,

109

over time as they arrived to fill the floor level and balconies to capacity. It would make the night much more enjoyable, for Lamond especially. It also gave him time to take in the magnificent décor of the theater, which was an ornate jewelry box of a structure, the stage its most prized jewel. Every square inch of the building was adorned in old world opulence, intricately carved embellishments gilded in gold dripped from every edge. The seats were upholstered in plush fabrics, the walls covered in richly colored and printed wallpapers. Lamond's eyes buzzed around the expansive theater, touching each beautiful detail like a visiting bee pollinating a garden, all without looking like a sightseer.

Valeria looked her handsome companion over from head to toe, admiring how far he had come, how much he had accomplished in such a short span of time. He wore a nicely tailored suit, the pants, vest and jacket with tails in black, with crisply starched white shirt and matching white bowtie. His hair was parted on the side, carefully combed and dressed, freshly shaven, nails impeccably clean. His top hat rested carefully on his knee, at least one finger on its brim at all time from fear of it falling. He had gone to great effort to ready himself, yet he was still uncomfortable, cramped, pressured. She could feel it emanating from him, hear his heart, but to mortal eyes he was the personification of easy calm, picture perfect down the cufflinks. No human among them would imagine it was such a momentous, stressful night for him.

He looked at Valeria and lightly tugged at his collar, pulling it away from his Adam's apple. She knew it was more than simple constriction that bothered him. It was the thirst, undeniable in such a high concentration of humanity. She felt it too, the scratchy, dry, burn on the back of her throat, amplified by the scent and sound of fresh, free flowing blood. It was like being a castaway at sea, dying of thirst while surrounded by an ocean of water, but unable to drink. She carefully bowed her head, acknowledging his concern, yet minding her carefully curled and pinned hair. Her flaxen locks had been rolled and the majority of it swept up into waves and curls atop her head, except for a small portion at the nape of her neck that had been curled and pulled forward to drape over her collarbone. Small crystal beads were scattered in between the curls, glittering in the warm light of the opera house, and tall feather dyed to match her dress added the height required by the style of the day.

* * *

As uncomfortable as he was, Lamond could not help but imagine Valeria was even more so, but she seemed to be perfectly comfortable within the layers, lacing, ruffles, and plumes of her wardrobe. To say she looked exquisite was an understatement. Her dress color was a bold choice, light chartreuse satin with a small floral print, embellished with ivory tulle across the low, square neckline and hanging from the bottom of the elbow length sleeves. Several of the crystals that accentuated her hairstyle also adorned the bodice, arranged in a floral pattern similar to the print on the satin. Ivory velvet ribbon added detail to the full of the skirt in an elongated, triple chevron pattern and tied in the back at the waist, which was also mirrored on the upper sleeves. The toe of one ivory satin slipper peeked from beneath the avalanche of fabric, tapping in anxious anticipation. She looked as if she belonged there, because she *did* belong there, dressed in finery, mingling with the highest echelon of Paris society. She was whatever she claimed to be, whatever status she desired, even a princess from a faraway foreign land if she desired to be so. None among them would doubt her claim for a moment. But he was a laborer, a commoner borrowing her husband's clothes for the evening, his hands still rough from countless days of backbreaking work. He shifted uncomfortably again, keeping a careful eye on his hat as he wiggled his cramped toes in his narrow, highly polished shoes. This charade was going to take some getting used to.

Much to his relief, the show started promptly on time. A brief prologue welcomed the audience and then the heavy red curtains parted and revealed the first scene, a large room with a hearth at its center, filled with servants busily preparing for some grand occasion, a ball. One unfortunate girl, wearing ragged clothes and soot, laments that she is not permitted to attend the fabulous ball with her wicked step-sisters.

"I know this story…" Lamond leaned over and whispered in her ear, just as Lucette was awakened by her fairy godmother.

Valeria smiled and nodded, pleased that he seemed to be enjoying himself, at least to a small degree. She clapped daintily as the first act ended and the curtains closed. It was good practice for him to be amongst humans in public. He deserved to experience the finer things that Paris had to offer.

Lamond could hardly take his eyes from the stage as the actors sang and danced to the perfectly, choreographed to the music from the orchestra below the stage. Only occasionally, when a soprano hit an amazingly high note, or the music ended with magnificent crescendo did he look to her, eyes full of wonder, as if to verify what he was experiencing was reality. Never had he imagined the simple childhood tale of Cinderella could take on such grandeur, could become so much more than its modest beginning. Vicariously, he shared the thrill of the opulent ball with Lucette, a commoner who now was anything but common.

The similarities between Lamond and Lucette were not lost on Valeria, despite having not thought of it before. She hoped Lamond would live happily ever after, just like Lucette.

After the fourth act, the final curtain dropped and the performers took their bows to splendid applause. Soon after, the crowd began to file out of the theater. As Lamond rose from his seat, Valeria took his hand and held him back. He sat back down and looked at her curiously.

"How are you feeling?" she whispered, leaning in close to his ear. "How is your thirst?"

"Parched," he answered, pulling his stiff collar away from his neck again.

"I think tonight is the night, Lamond." She smiled, patting the back of his hand reassuringly. "You're ready."

112

"Here?" He shifted around in his chair. "There are so many people here."

Valeria nodded confidently. "Exactly, that means more to choose from. I will be close by, if you get into trouble."

"Trouble?" Lamond's eyes grew wide, his mind racing through a thousand negative outcomes to his first attempt at procuring a meal on his own.

"If you should need help…" she quickly rephrased. "But you won't, because you are ready."

Unsure of how to proceed, Lamond walked slowly toward the entrance of the theater. He briefly looked around for Valeria, wishing he could spot her, but she was completely out of sight. He drew in a deep, unnecessary breath, and exhaled with a huff. As soon as he did, the mouth watering aroma of every human blood type danced across his sense of smell. Thirst clawed at him, and he cleared his throat in response. There were too many people, too much stimulation, too many eyes and ears to witness his actions. He wished Valeria had not been so insistent about the matter. Why did it have to be that night? He already felt like he stuck out like a sore thumb.

Lamond exited the theater on the swell of the human sea, shoulder to shoulder with hundreds of potential meals only an arm's reach away, sometimes less. He felt a small portion of his tension subside after he finally made it out to the street, the fresh air clearing his mind. Uncertain as to how to continue, now that he had given up the cover of the theater, he walked in the direction that most people were choosing. He felt like everyone around him must be able to sense he was a predator, the way a gazelle could sense a lion's hungry stare. He assumed Valeria was still close, but she remained frustratingly out of sight.

The longer he walked, the crowd thinned and with it his chances of procuring a meal on his own. The last thing he wanted to do was concede defeat, have to call out for Valeria to bring him something to eat like a helpless child. He was tired of being cared for, ready to be self-sufficient again, has he had always taken care of himself.

He could remember nothing of his mother, a sickly waif who had died of dysentery when he was just two years old. After her passing, he had bounced from family to family, one sympathetic heart to the next of the people who struggled to survive in the crowded swallow of the slums, slaved away with her in the garment factory, or just a kindhearted stranger that was simply unable to watch a child wither away on the street. His father's identity unknown, he was simply Lamond, Josette Delaflote's boy, one of the many unclaimed orphans of Paris.

He knew the poor of the slums offered the simplest solution to his problem, but for the very same reasons that caused him to resist them as an easy meal. These forgotten souls, the grimy bottom of the satin slipper that was Paris, already had enough grief and misery without his addition. He would have made the perfect morsel for a thirsty, heartless vampire when he was a child, huddled in the doorway to escape the rain, hungry, sick, and defenseless. Fate, it would seem, had other plans for him, but regardless, he found the notion of asking Valeria for help a better option that exploiting any of them.

He turned the corner on the next street, lost in thought with his head down, and headed toward home and defeat. He could see the glow of the streetlights reflected on his shoes. Without warning, he and another pedestrian bumped into each other, hard enough to knock him off balance, jarring him from his thoughts.

"My apologizes..." he said as he bowed to the young man he had collided with. "I was not minding my steps."

"Lamond..." a familiar voice spoke, his voice obviously sullied by overindulgence in drink. "Where the hell have you been? I haven't seen you since... since Thayer died."

Lamond's feet were frozen to the ground, slack jawed. So much had changed since the last time he had spoken with Andre. He was a different man, a different creature entirely.

"I… I have been staying with a friend… since the fire," he stuttered, swallowing hard before pulling at his collar again.

"Is that were you got those clothes?" Andre teased, looking his former friend up and down. His inspection and the abundance of alcohol in his blood were making Lamond uncomfortable. He could sense his building ill intentions almost as clearly as the booze on his breath. "What else did your friend give you?"

"Nothing…" Lamond tired to laugh it off, backing away from him. "I am a kept man, Andre. These clothes are just for show. She doesn't trust me with her money just yet."

Andre inspected Lamond with a skeptical glare, closing the gap between them again. "There's something different about you, more than just clothes." He pulled a small, yet dangerously sharp knife and gave Lamond plenty time to see it. He stepped close and tapped him on the chest with the flat of the blade, just under his chin. "See the thing is…that whole thing with Thayer don't sit right with me, the way you just disappeared and all. And now I find you, dressed to nines, all by your lonesome. I think you should start telling your old friend the truth."

"Back off, Andre!" Lamond growled, the burn in his throat shortening his fuse. He shoved his drunken acquaintance back with force. Andre stumbled and fell, quickly scrambled to his feet, and charged with his knife drawn back. Lamond sidestepped and the blade skidded across his chest, the tip slicing through his shirt and scratching across his chest. The scent of blood, his own blood drawn by a former friend, exploded on his senses, igniting the burning rage within him. He grabbed Andre's wrist and twisted it, forcing him to release his weapon. Impulsively, he lunged into his throat, sinking his teeth deep into Andre's flesh and quickly retracted. The bitter taste of a traitor's blood filled Lamond's mouth, gushing every time he screamed. After a few good drinks, the fire in his throat diminished, and he released his neck. "Not what you were expecting was it, friend?"

115

Lamond pushed him away and wiped the blood from his mouth on his handkerchief, throwing it to the ground when he finished with it, ruined. Andre scrambled backwards, holding his throat, blood seeping between his fingers. His eyes wide with horror, shock, unable to believe what had just occurred.

"Stay away from me!" Andre shouted, disappearing into the darkness and out of Lamond's life. He knew it would be for good, that he would not approach him again. He doubted he would tell anyone of their encounter, and doubted further that anyone would believe him if he did. With the last threads attaching him to his mortal life severed, Lamond buttoned his coat to hide his bloodied shirt, and continued toward home, feeling his wound heal with the aid of his attacker's blood.

Finally home, he slammed the door so hard as he entered that a painting was jarred from its hook on the wall. The frame busted and splintered from the impact. Valeria looked up from her reading and studied him, the scent of blood all over him. Lamond walked around the debris and headed toward his room.

"It's for the best, you know. It would be impossible to maintain old associations."

Lamond shot her an ice cold glare, knowing she had witnessed everything, but had done nothing to assist him. He yanked his bowtie from his neck and threw it on the ground in her direction before stomping upstairs, without a word.

***

7 June 1899- Now that Lamond has become more comfortable hunting, I believe it is time for him to learn a new trick. I want him to be self- sufficient as soon as possible. I do not intend to be his mother, nor his wife, and I do not wish for him the same measure of devotion that Vlad expected from us. I want to give him the means to make his own life, without my assistance so that I may go on to live my own. I

know I will share in the responsibilities for any lives he takes, since his existence is my fault, but it is his decision how he will adapt to immortality. I refuse to spend my life waiting to see if he will make a mistake, just so I can clean up the mess afterwards. He will live or die by his own actions, no matter how wise or foolish they may turn out to be, just as will I.

***

"Shouting at me will not make this any easier!" Lamond growled. Valeria rubbed her eyes vigorously before crossing her arms over her chest.

"I did not shout at you!" When Valeria heard just how loudly she was indeed shouting, she lowered her voice to a muted grumble. "I simply said if you would only concentrate instead of complaining, perhaps it would be easier!" A stiff wind blew a large section of hair down from her neatly styled bun and into her eyes and she hastily swatted it away from her face. She paced around the Eiffel Tower's top balcony, looking out at the lights from street lamps and windows that dotted the sea of darkness.

"Complaining?" he shouted back, forehead creased deeply above his brow. His blonde hair was frazzled into a spiny mess from the wind and from nervously running his hands through it, just before wringing them, repeating the process each time he looked over the rail. "Did you even hear what you said, what you told me to do? Are you out of your mind?"

She stood at a distance and watched Lamond, gripping the guardrail around the balcony with both hands, knees slightly bent. Perhaps jumping from such a height was too much to expect on his first attempt at transformation. She remembered the first time her body took on its other form, how she had effortlessly exhaled into mist to gain reentry to her castle. It had happened with ease, subconsciously, without thinking or trying. Lamond was over thinking, like a human, not willing it to happen as she had inadvertently done.

Lamond tugged uncomfortably at his collar, swallowing hard before shifting his shoulders in his tailored shirt and jacket. His restrictive clothes were not making matters any simpler. He took his jacket off and hung it over the railing, rustling his hair and rubbing his hands together again before peeking over the side. Valeria watched him from the corner of her eye, now standing by his side, and chuckled under her breath at his discomfort. He rolled his eyes at her and frowned, annoyed at her bemusement.

"I still do not understand how you did it."

"You will get used to it, I promise," she said, smiling wider than usual. She quickly stepped behind him and with both hands, pushed him over the guardrail. Lamond's screams of sheer terror sliced through the night like a knife as he plummeted toward the ground.

"Now, Lamond!" Valeria's voice shouted from the billow of shimmering mist that surrounded him, louder than the wind in his ears. "Just let go! I won't let you hit!"

He could hear his heart pounding in his ears for the first time since he had been reborn. The ground was advancing faster than he could process thought, racing toward him, yet the rest of the world seemed slower than normal. "Fog, Lamond! Think of fog!"

A barrage of images flashed into his mind as Valeria lent him a measure of her concentration. Encapsulated within his creator's haze, he saw the peaks of the Carpathian Mountains jutting through their cloudy blanket on an autumn morning. He saw fog rising from the Arges River as it snaked its way beneath Castle Dracula. He recalled his own memory of walking down the street on a foggy Paris morning when he was a child, his cheek kissed by dampness.

In an instant just as his fingertips touched the sidewalk, Lamond's body expanded beyond his understanding into a thick, rolling blanket of fog. He could feel Valeria with him, around him, inside him, as the fog spread out across the ground, like he was a stone dropped into a pond with its corresponding ripples. Smoky tendrils curled up at his edges, reaching skyward again, his consciousness within every droplet yet dispersed.

"Fly with me, Lamond."

Although she barely whispered, he could hear her clearly, yet unable to pinpoint the source of her voice. He was surrounded by her, saturated within her.

"Back up to the top."

He could feel the shimmer that was Valeria pull him upward, through the beams and girders of the Iron Lady. Intermingled, they poured over the first balcony, quickly overtaking the second. As they snaked up the tower's slender neck, she separated from him, flying into the opposite direction. They playfully chased and passed through one another, crisscrossing the tower like the lacings of a corset, before meeting again on the balcony.

Valeria stepped from Lamond's enveloping fog, moisture stretching across her disrobed body like a marble statue covered in dew. Her hair draped over her shoulders and down her back in stretched waves, heavy and damp like she had just bathed. The wire mesh of the balcony floor was cold beneath her feet, but just barely. A second later, Lamond materialized into his true self just behind her, pulling her back tight against his chest with one arm while he brushed her hair away from her neck with the other. She relaxed her head against his shoulder as he followed the gentle slope of her neck from shoulder to ear with his lips and tongue. A devilish smile parted his lips when she lightly giggled, certain she enjoyed the teasing tickle from his mouth, but was quickly surprised when she morphed into a veil of mists and disappeared from his arms. He looked for her in all directions, but was astonished to feel her vaporous form creeping up his legs from beneath the floor. She encircled his waist and curled up his chest with countless searching fingers. He held his arms out again, faintly able to feel her form in the moment before she became solid again, latching her legs around his waist and wrapping her arms around his neck, fingers lost in his messy hair. She pulled his face close to hers and looked into his eyes with silent intensity for a moment before kissing him, lightly tugging at his bottom lip before moving on to his neck and beneath the cut of his jaw.

He held her close, tight, afraid she might disappear again. Yet again, she had surprised him, becoming an offer she knew he would be powerless to refuse. He found her even more alluring, even more captivating, as he looked upon her now with his immortal eyes than he had while a human. Only now did he understand her unusual strength, the subtle coolness of her perfect flesh, the glimmer of blood red beneath the ice of her eyes. He understood in part, but he knew there was so much left hidden, so many secrets that she had not, and may never, share with him. He could feel energy building within her body, like a spring was coiling inside her, a hair trigger ready to release. His heart was pounding in his ears again, as loud as when he was falling. She was pure adrenaline, lightning in a bottle, life and death. He ran his hands up and down her sides, exploring the shape of her body from beneath her arms, sloping into an hourglass waist, and curving into shapely hips and derrière. She seemed so fragile, but he knew better. She was stronger than any marble pillar of Rome, where surely she would have been worshipped as a goddess in ancient times.

The cold edge of the steel guardrail surprised her when Lamond leaned her against it, providing her a seat. His body was nearly as cold as the steel, the same as hers, chilled by the constant breeze from the river. He had changed so much, not for the better or for the worse, but different. His blazing human heat was now the cool strength of a vampire's body, more than twice as strong as before. The light scrape of keen teeth now scratched across the tender skin of her breasts as he carefully pulled a nipple between his teeth, visiting both. Blazing heat no longer broiled from his loins, stretching to touch her, but coolness to match her own. The furnace of a human body had transformed into a cool, efficient machine, capable of creating hours of pleasure without tiring.

* * *

She shifted her hips downward, grabbed two handfuls of his firm buttocks, and guided him into her. The familiar sensation of sharing her body with a vampire lover returned, cool but immensely satisfying. No longer did she have to control herself, or fear harming him inadvertently. She could let herself go, finally able to abandon years of abstinence, as they rocked back and forth against the railing. She knew he could support her with no fear of tipping backwards as she leaned back to put her breasts back within reach of his lips. Electricity surged through her body, still unaccustomed to be being touched again, when he allowed his teeth heavier contact her flesh as his tongue flicked across her nipples once more.

Excitement fueled their movements with increasing urgency as the awareness of time eluded them, their passion unspoiled by fatigue or climate. Entwined as few others had ever been, it was possible to change into their incorporeal forms, singularly and both at once, to experience a multitude of pleasures impossible for human lovers. Lamond held Valeria aloft within his billowy fog, stimulating her entire body with rhythmic perfection beyond the confines of gravity.

"Come... back..." she urged with a whispery voice, trailing off the end of enraptured moan. He lowered her back onto the floor and rematerialized over her, without leaving her body. She playfully licked the point of one fang as she smiled at him, causing him to shiver with expectation. He could not imagine what she had in mind, what they had not experienced in their time spent high above the streets of Paris, but he knew it would be amazing. She pulled his neck down to her lips, kissing it fully from ear to shoulder, before bringing his ear to her lips. "Are you ready for this?" she whispered.

"Oh yes!" As soon as the words escaped his lips, she sank her fangs into his neck with lightning speed, puncturing his artery and suctioning the blood from the points of entry. The quick flash of pain only heightened his senses, nearly overwhelming him, as her tongue rolled against his neck with ease, charming his blood into her mouth. After a few sips, her head fell back, his taste filling her mouth and intoxicating her senses, the rush of another's life coursing through her body. She rolled her head to the side and waited anxiously, but only for a moment. As soon as his lips touched her neck, his fangs slid beneath her skin and the same sensation of pain laced pleasure blurred her senses. The world of humans became a backdrop, existing only of the peripherals of their consciousness. The quickening that burned like flames finally found its fever pitch and both came into blood- drunk, orgasmic, climax.

Lamond fell by Valeria's side, breathless although he had no physical reason to desire breath, only the residual instinct left from his human life compelled his lungs now. She smiled with her eyes closed as she listened to his racing heart, enjoying the afterglow of their performance.

"Is it always like that?" he asked, propping onto one elbow, looking down at her.

"This life is not without its advantages," she said as she slowly opened her eyes. From behind Lamond, a glimmer of light caught her attention. She quickly sat up, eyes wide in astonishment, and gasped. "Dawn!"

Lamond dropped flatly against the floor and Valeria collapsed across his chest, both trapped within the confines of their deathly sleep.

***

Valeria laid in perfect silence upon Lamond's chest, listening to the slow pulse of his heart. He was so soundly asleep, his heart rate so slowed beyond that of his waking beat that it seemed to have no rhythm at all, only pump on an occasional spasm. She could hear Paris coming to life below them, the dull rumble of a machine powered by human cogs. For now, the tower was quiet, only visited by the occasional bird looking for a place to rest. But she knew very soon, that would not be the case. The first visitors to the tower today were certainly going to have a view to remember!

A couple hours after dawn, Valeria could hear a cluster of heartbeats gathered together below. Muffled voices and movements were just outside the realm of her consciousness, on the fringe of her senses, as she lay cocooned within herself. Her immortal curse demanded payment in time, every day, without fail, the hours from dawn to noon were not her own. Only after centuries of unlife had she evolved the ability to whisper so quietly that no human ear was even capable of hearing her. With even greater effort, she could open her eyes or slightly turn her head. She knew the newborn Lamond was still trapped within the black, as though he did not exist during the first hours of daylight, and her best efforts would not be enough to reach him.

Faint tremors radiated up the Iron Lady's legs and spine as her elevators came to life, busily carrying the first groups of sightseers to the lowest observation deck. Valeria felt the anguish of growing dread as she helplessly waited for the visitors to arrive on the third observation deck and make their discovery. A man and his lover, found in naked embrace upon the third deck of the Eiffel Tower! Such a scandal! What a commotion! It would take an eternity to live it down. She groaned, although no one heard it.

Finally, the gasps and whispers came. She could feel the floor of the deck tremble as a horde of voyeurs with prying eyes jockeyed for a look at her and Lamond. Whispered insults, various sordid remarks, occasional complaints of being crowded or pushed, and the constant shuffle of feet overwhelmed her ears. A few poked them, a couple nudged them with the toe of their shoes, but their actions garnered no response. They had been pronounced dead at least five times already. Although undetectable to those looking down at her, she could feel the heat of shame blush her cheeks and chase down her neck. She knew the crowd would not disperse until someone carried them away, like two carcasses salvaged from a flock of vultures.

After what had felt like another lifetime spent as the center of attention high above Paris, Valeria heard a handful of male voices with heavy footfall disperse the onlookers. After the crowd had been chased from the scene, they returned. She felt the hands of these strangers roll her from Lamond's chest, grab her by the arms and legs, and lay her on a stretcher, covering her from head to toe with a sheet.

"Looks like he went out with a bang..." One man jeered as Lamond was laid out on his own stretcher beside her. She heard the sheet snap as it was shook from its folds before covering Lamond.

"What a way to go." Another answered as the stretcher was lifted, her body supported by the taunt canvas between its poles.

Valeria groaned again.

***

8 June 1899- I am mortified! I woke today from my sleep, naked upon the coroner's table. Lamond lay on the table beside me. Thankfully, the coroner had yet to start an autopsy. In addition to being a dreadfully disgusting and painful experience, it would have been nearly impossible to explain or erase from the coroner's memory. As it is, he is astonished. He claims it is a miracle, that Lamond and I are lucky to be alive. We survived a near death experience with hypothermia in the middle of summer no less, due to the height and wind at the top of the tower. However, we may be charged with trespassing and indecent exposure.

Chapter Twelve

Lamond and Valeria, hands clasped, spun quickly around the crowded dance floor, passing shoulder to shoulder with numerous other human dancers. Laughing riotously, they paid no mind to their sharp teeth, their pale skin, or their lack of fatigue. That was one of the many beautiful things of the Moulin Rouge. Everyone was enjoying themselves too much to worry about their differences. The upper class aristocrat was welcome to dance with a lower class laborer. It was liberating, bohemian, sensual. The dance floor was always full and the drinks never ran out.

Even though Lamond had enjoyed the proper and reserved presentation at the Opéra-Comique, he had found true entertainment in the extravagant cabarets of the Red Windmill. He was not alone. It was quickly becoming one of the most popular attractions in all of Paris, drawing visitors from across the globe. With so many people, so much activity, so much excitement, it enabled he and Valeria to hide in plain sight, to live as the humans lived, to love life. The brightly colored costumes, boisterous music, abundance of electric lighting, which was strung liberally across the ceiling and gracing chandeliers, and the smell of champagne, absinthe and sweat, created the environment that was often imitated but never duplicated. The Moulin Rouge was nothing short of a phenomenon, loved by the living and the unliving.

Remembering that they should rest, Lamond and Valeria sat at one of the small tables that surrounded the dance floor, warmly lit by a small lamp with a red shade. They had chosen a table against the wall, toward the back of the room, allowing themselves as much privacy as there was to find. They huddled close to each other and Lamond wrapped his arm around her back, pulling her close. Valeria leaned in against him, resting her head under his jaw, her arm stretched over his chest. He felt warm, almost heated to human temperature by the abundance of body heat around them. She lightly played with his hair, twisting it around the tip of her finger.

Lamond purposely remained silent, knowing that approaching her with conversation might burst her bubble, allow her to realize she was enjoying herself, enjoying his company. He chose instead to feel her, the energy of her body, her quickened breath, and her eyes, full of life, as she enjoyed all that the cabaret had to offer. She very seldom allowed herself to relax, to cut loose and simply enjoy living eternally, less and less since the events at the Eifel Tower.

Much to his surprise, he felt her lips touch his neck just above his collar. He instantly felt his chest fill with excitement, the hair on the back of his neck standing on end, his skin becoming doubly sensitive. Since their near vivisection, she had begun to pull away from him whenever she noticed she was getting closer to him, denying herself of any affection, especially physical. He did not know if she was aware of her new behavior, if her fears were motivating her on a subconscious level to keep her distance, or if she was purposely punishing herself for their close call. She lightly tugged on his earlobe, teasing him with her sharp teeth. He quickly turned his head and caressed her face, kissing her fully, tasting her, taking her in before she realized she had faltered and run away again.

Before them, the dancers began to pour out from backstage, rushing out from both sides of the curtain like rivers of brightly colored, ruffled dresses and black stockings as the *Infernal Gallop* was being played. The ladies swung their dresses back and forth wildly, displaying their fancy undergarments to the cheers and excitement of the audience. They coyly covered their mouths, a faux sense of shock, after they flipped their dresses over the heads, yelping and shouting to those watching. As the performance approached a fevered pitch, Valeria leapt over Lamond's legs and straddled his lap, facing him. She lifted his face with her hands, returning his long, deep kiss, her tongue chasing his. Her sudden outbursts of desire, although welcomed, always took him off guard, never able to anticipate when she might lose herself. It seemed tonight that the intoxicating atmosphere of the Rouge had been too much for her to resist. She lightly traced the side of his neck with the tip of her tongue, from collar to ear, before whispering a request.

"Find us something to drink…" she said suggestively, leaning to the side so he could take in the sight of the dancing ladies. "I'm thirsty."

Ten minutes later, Lamond's chair was pushed into a darkened corner, a blonde woman on each leg but only one of them had a pulse. He did not know if Valeria was setting him up for some elaborate test that she intended for him to fail, or if she was simply living in the moment, for a moment. She looked at him, winked, and pulled the dancer away from her business of kissing Lamond's neck and unbuttoning his shirt, and kissed her passionately and intentionally long before releasing her. Lamond felt as though he was going to explode, certain if he had not already died, his heart would not be able to endure it. A glimmer of her sharp teeth caught the light as she tugged the dancer's taste from her bottom lip briefly before melting against him, kissing him longer and with even more intenseness than the last. He could taste the hot, lingering flavor of human on her tongue, transferred to his as it darted in and out from between his lips.

Valeria gently nudged the dancer toward him, inviting her to partake as though she was offering her a scrumptious dessert or glass of the finest wine. Lamond looked at Valeria, still half expecting her to change her tune and instantly become enraged that he had one along with any of it, but he saw she was intently focused on the side of her neck, her eyes wide with anticipation of what was to come. The next thing he knew, the woman's warm and voluminous breasts were pushing against his chest as she kissed him. He could feel the heat emanating from her red hot tongue warming the inside of his mouth. He heard her softly whimper through the kiss; a sound of pain laced pleasure, endorphins flooding her taste. He rolled his eyes and could see Valeria had made her bite, washing her neck with kisses and soft licks between drinks.

The woman was blissfully unaware as the entry wounds numbed and blood thinning agents were introduced into her circulatory system by Valeria's venomous kiss. She released her neck, exhaling in near orgasmic satisfaction, licking the residual stains from her lips. She beckoned for Lamond to partake, and he quickly latched onto the dancer's neck over the incisions that Valeria had just made and took in a few quick drinks. Valeria twisted his hair around her fingertip again as he drank, just behind his ear, but shifted quickly in time to catch their dancer friend when she began to swoon.

"Lend me your hanky, please," Valeria said, quickly applying it while still folded to her neck as she lounged across her arm. She shifted her weight toward Lamond, handing over the duty of supporting their victim. She removed Lamond's tie, pulling it from his collar and tying it around the dancer's neck in a wide, billowy bow, using it to disguise the makeshift bandage as well as keep it in place. Carefully they propped the dozing woman in the corner to sleep off her encounter, little worse for the wear. They slipped out of the dance hall, past the unsuspecting and inebriated patrons, and out into the humid night air.

Just outside the doors, basking in the red glow of the windmill, Valeria fell into Lamond's arms, drunk on the dancer's blood and pheromones. They swapped her flavors between them, their mouths still warm from their drink. He could feel the shape of her body hidden beneath the layers of their clothing as she pressed against him, searching, feeling, squeezing with their hands. In a heartbeat, she took his hand and pulled him away from the Rouge and down the dimly lit street in search of a more private area.

Finding a narrow street or alleyway in which to indulge a quick indiscretion was nothing new in Pigalle. In that regard, Lamond and

Valeria were no different than any human couple. Once they had found a reasonably private area, Valeria quickly began to unbutton his shirt, his lean and muscular frame dimly lit by moonlight. Simultaneously, he pulled her tucked blouse loose from the waist of her skirt and lifted it over her bosom, instead of trying to navigate the tiny buttons that lined her spine, and untied the ribbon on the front of her camisole. He quickly cupped one of her breast in his hand, feeling its soft firmness, before opening his mouth wide to draw her nipple and its surrounding halo between his lips, allowing his fangs to lightly graze her skin, leaving two thin red lines across her perfect white flesh. The unique taste of her skin, perfume, and blood welcomed him, invited him to return.

From their hideaway, they could still hear the raucous music and foot- stomping dance of the Rouge, could hear the shouts and squeals of joy amongst the veritable crashing sea of heartbeats. They could feel the energy of the can-can dancer's blood coursing through their veins, invigorating them, fueling the fire, her spark of life was now a part of them. Another kiss shared the last hints of her taste between them.

Frantically, Lamond unfastened his trousers and she quickly slipped her hand through and grabbed his proud and anxious member in her hand, passing his full length through her hand, up and down, several times. His groan of yearning pleasure caused her to smile widely, devilishly, as she enjoyed his expressions. A couple chest expanding breaths and he started to gather and lift the layers of her skirt and petticoats. After a determined and almost frustrating search, he found her shapely and strong thighs and buttocks, feeling her statuesque body with his whole hands, kneading and embracing the contours of her shape. Hidden beneath her slips and skirt, her legs were adorned by silk stockings, held in place by ribbons at the thighs and undergarments were loose legged with ruffles at the edge. She held her layers up with one hand, the other firmly locked behind his neck, as he lifted her from the dirty street, pushing the leg of her underwear out of their way. Her legs locked around his waist, her weight supported effortlessly.

If they had chosen to do so, they could have faded into mist and fog, left the hassle of their clothing on the ground, and enjoyed a rooftop view of Paris as they made love. But they were intoxicated by the red hot, flesh and blood of humanity, their smell, their taste, their touch, and craved to experience sex like the impassioned humans they had pretended to be, messy, awkward, and at risk of being caught. They wanted to feel the fabric of her clothing bunched around them as he lifted her up and down on him, the warmth radiating from the brick wall behind them, the creak of shoe leather as her clasped ankles shifted with their rhythm.

If they had chosen to do so, they could have made their love for hours, until dawn. But they needed the adrenaline rush of a secret, risky encounter. One hand grasped the back of Lamond's neck, the other warmed by the brick building as she pushed against it, Valeria looked intently into his uniquely green eyes, which were now brown around the circumference of his iris, backlit by the lightest shade of crimson. Their heavy breathing maintained speed with the rising momentum of their movements, his arms close to her sides as he supported and lifted her, one side of her sculpted derrière in each hand, her breasts rising and falling just out of his reach of his lips. He could feel climax building inside her, a quiet tremble of anticipation enveloped her as he held her closer, lightning in a bottle. She leaned her forehead against his, their noses touching, as she was overwhelmed by unfurling ripples of pleasure. He could feel her cool breath on his face in short whispery puffs, following the staccato-like rhythm of her quick, abbreviated sighs.

Her breathless voice was the last nudge he needed, the spark to his fuse, quickly burning, sending him to his own intense finish. Wisps of her hair, which had fallen loose from its pins in their excitement, brushed across his face like golden strands of spider webs. He pulled her as close as he could possibly get, one arm crossing her back so he could hide his hand within her tumbling curls, and rested his back against the bricks. She responded by wrapping both her arms behind his neck, and for a moment they were silent, breathing in and existing only in the envelope of energy they had created together. Their hearts communicated through their chests in their own coded language of beats.

He was the answer to her heart's lonesome call and she was the light that had chased away the darkness of his menial existence. Lamond was taken by her, possessed by her, a love that bordered worship. Valeria could feel herself giving in to him, falling in love with him, quicker and with greater intensity than she ever imagined she would ever experience again. It terrified her.

***

10 July 1899- I know this feeling, and my heart welcomes it, but I am afraid. To say I am afraid is not sufficient, I am scared to death. I have lost everyone I have ever loved and everything I have ever cared for has turned to dust. My budding feelings for Lamond are tempered by fear for him. It is dangerous to love me. In the end, it seems nothing good ever comes from it.

***

24 July 1899- Lamond has asked me to join him every night for two weeks, bribing me with every activity, location, or flavor he could think of, but I have refused. He makes me reckless, clouds my judgment. There is no good reason why we did not get in trouble for our little indiscretion with the can-can dancer at the Rouge. His initials were embroidered on the corner of the handkerchief for goodness sake! When we are together, we push each other, encourage each other to behave in ways we might not if we were not, in ways that draw too much attention. It is not that I do not enjoy his company, because I do; it is just not prudent to behave as though there are no consequences. There are always consequences, karma, whatever one prefers to call it. I

saw it happen to Fleur. I saw it happen to Vlad. His recklessness nearly killed me. For the best interest of all involved, I have to keep a level head and not let my feelings influence my behavior.

All my frolicking about has distracted me. There are still things I have promised myself, promised Ilona, and I assume to an extent promised Vlad, that I would see done. Emil is raised, for better or worse, he is a man now. But Van Helsing is still alive, and that just cannot be. What a shame it would be to allow myself to continue this game, this fairytale, and allow that old bastard to die a peaceful death from old age. I have become increasingly aware that I need to reorder my priorities.

***

2 August 1899- I assume it was only a matter of time. It is a scent I remember all too well, the scent of another woman. I have pushed him to it, nearly forced him to it, but I cannot deny that it pangs my heart. If I would allow myself, I would care deeply for Lamond, but it was too much, too quick, and at the wrong time. Distance will be best for the both of us.

***

The scent of Lamond's cologne lingered in his wake as he passed Valeria on his way out for another night on the town. He was dressed well, nice pants and shirt, unbuttoned just enough to hint but not to scream.

"You should go out with me tonight, Valeria." He chimed with a smile, quickly taking her hand and waist for a moment to steal a quick, spinning dance. She pulled away from him, as quickly as she could reasonably do without being overly impolite.

"Thank you, but I don't think I will be going out tonight," she said, faking a smile.

"What is wrong with you?" He sighed, backing away from her. "You used to be fun. We would go out, dance, drink, make love under the stars. But now you just sit here, like an old maid."

"It is called being cautious, Lamond, something it would not hurt you to practice from time to time," she growled, annoyed by his reference.

"That's all you ever say, cautious, cautious, need to be cautious. To hell with cautious! When have we ever gotten into any trouble? Never, not even when we almost got ourselves cut open by the coroner. How much worse trouble can we get into than that?"

"It's just not wise to keep risking it, to keep pushing until something horrible does happen. Slayers..." She started down her usual rant, but he cut her off.

"Oh god, here we go with the slayers again! Where are they, Valeria?" He held his hands out, looked all around the room. "I don't see them, never do see them, and I see plenty."

"I'm sure you do see *plenty*," she gouged. A hint of jealousy showed through her carefully manicured exterior.

"Don't you do it! Don't you try to make me feel guilty because I enjoy my life!" Lamond fired back, his cheeks beginning to turn a healthy shade of pink. "Night after night I ask you, beg you, to do something other than collect dust. You might be fine spending the rest of eternity in this house, but I am not!"

Valeria huffed, crossed her arms and refused to look at him. She hated him when he was right.

"Get mad, get good and mad. Then maybe you might do something, make a move, prove me wrong. You know, there may come a time when I am done with fighting with you, tired of begging you," he continued, knowing she would not relent, but he at least wanted to make her think, force her to realize she was making herself a prisoner in her own home, by her own choice.

"I never asked you to stay, Lamond," she said, a flinch in her expression revealed what she was far too proud to say. It had hurt her to say those words to him, and she had hoped to hurt him with them. It worked.

Lamond dropped his head, her words stinging him. He looked up and searched her expression for a reason for her cold, spiteful words. Her face was frozen, except for a light quiver of her bottom lip that escaped her control. She refused to blink, as a tear would have certainly fallen from her lashes if she had.

"Have it your way, Valeria," he whispered before quietly leaving her to her bitterness.

***

Lamond stomped down the sidewalk, hands rammed into his pockets. The sun would not set for another hour, but he did not care. Anywhere in Paris was better than being trapped in the house with Valeria when she was in such a mood. He gritted his teeth, his fangs scratching the inside of his bottom lip. It was beyond his understanding how anyone could be as stubborn as she, why anyone would be content to wallow in their past pain as much as she did. What sins did she feel she needed to atone for before she deserved to live again? He could not imagine and she was certainly not forthcoming with any details. She had refused to tell him anything about her past, why she was in Paris, who she was before she arrived.

Despite her rejections, she was still the most intriguing woman in the city. She was a stone cold beauty from another land, from a place and time of fables and old wives tales. She was ancient yet eternally youthful, fragile yet stronger than a bear, a thousand stories to tell yet she chose silence. She was the most seductive, most exciting woman that had ever shared his bed, but she could also be the coldest, most unapproachable ice queen in the world. Her duality was exhausting.

But now she had gone a bit further, as though she wanted him to leave, but lacked the courage to tell him outright. He groaned inwardly, quietly complaining to himself. Their squabble had dampened his mood and was a wet blanket on his libido. Now he just wanted a quiet place to think for a while. Women were the same, alive or unliving, unpredictable, moody, and damn confusing.

Day or night, finding a quiet place for an individual with such sensitive senses was quite a daunting task. He felt he was drowning in an ocean of sounds and smells. The sounds of life surrounded him, coughing, laughing, talking, the sounds of work, the sounds of entertainment, and every assorted smell that accompanied all those actions stressed his nerves. His mind heavy with thought, he understood for the first time why Valeria so valued her privacy, the quiet sanctuary of their home. He walked in the direction that would put the most distance between him and the clamor of city life, honing in on a calmer place but unsure of the destination.

He descended a flight of stairs, spiraling downward from street level to the underground as the last rays of sunlight illuminated the rooftops. Only the very brave or the very foolish delved too deeply into the honeycomb of chambers, quarries, sewers, and miles of tunnels beneath Paris. A century earlier, one unfortunate explorer entered the catacombs and was swallowed by the darkness, lost. His body was found eleven years later near an exit, just beyond his reach. Lamond was neither brave, nor foolish, but simply confident the catacombs no longer offered any dangers for him. The coolness and darkened silence was soothing, amplified by the knowledge that unlike human explorers, it was impossible for him to be lost. No matter how far he sank beneath the surface, it would never be so deep that the distant call of beating hearts above could not call him back to the land of the living.

Four hours past sunset, Lamond wound through the tunnels beneath the city like a rat in a maze, curiosity driving him further and further into places he would have never dared to tread as a mortal. The choking darkness, passages reduced to nothing more that slivers between fallen sections of tunnel, and flooded rooms were just a few of the traps that lay in wait for the unlucky wanderer. But now he was considering staying underground for a couple nights, maybe closer to a week, until he could wait no longer to feed, just so his curiosity could be sated. He stopped at a doorway and read the foreboding signage above it.

"Arrête! C'est ici l'empire de la Mort," he read aloud, standing before the door of iron bars that blocked the section of the catacombs that had been repurposed as an ossuary from any uninvited guests who had failed to pay admission. He could smell decay and soil, floating out of the darkness like foul breath from a gaping mouth. He crossed his arms over his chest, his lips drawn into a frown as he thought of Valeria and her gloom. "Stop! Here lies the empire of the dead. Thanks, but I just left there."

Bored and musty, Lamond finally emerged from the underground through a manhole, chilled and looking for warmth, forgoing his previous thoughts of an extended stay. His explorations under the petticoat of Paris had worked to calm his nerves, but had left him lacking. If he had wanted to sulk about darkened hallways like a phantom, he would have stayed at home. He had been given a second chance at life, had died for it, and he intended to live. He dusted off his pants and shoes, straightened his sleeves, and looked around to see if anyone had noticed. While a passerby might be surprised to see a man as well dressed as Lamond pulling himself out of a manhole, seeing a boiling fog seethe out of the opening and reform into a stylish man in the middle of the street would have drawn even more attention.

He smiled as he walked toward the garish lights of the Pigalle dance halls, still going strong despite the late hour. The music seemed to inject life back into his veins, the life that he had felt being sapped from him while in the catacombs. Stepping inside his favorite haunt, the Moulin Rouge, he was immediately overwhelmed by a gust of body heat, the smell of sweat and booze, music and heartbeats, laughter and singing. He could feel energy building within him, like a machine had been switched on inside him, its magnetic pull instantly detectable to the humans that surrounded him. Company would not be in short supply.

***

11 August 1899- For the first time, Lamond did not return home. I am sure he was not alone, but I only hope he was cautious. I would hate to learn of his exploits by reading of them in the morning paper. He enjoys living the carefree life of a young man and he deserves to be happy. I am too old for such frivolous things, as he will one day be. But for now he enjoys pretending to be human, at least appearing to be a human with a certain measure of specialness, which is certain to bring him all manner of attention. He lived his entire life with nothing, being nothing, so I am happy that at least now he is enjoying himself. I was fortunate to have been born into a wealthy family, a loving family, and given a comfortable upbringing, which I have been able to maintain for the majority of my existence. He should have no less.

***

13 August 1899- Lamond finally returned home, smelling like a prostitute that has not bathed in days. Having the good manners to wash before returning to my home should not be too much to expect.

Chapter Thirteen

A balmy night settled over Paris, the humidity high and the air charged. She could feel the barometric pressure dropping, clouds unfurled like thick layers of dark wool batting. The wind, which had been a light, whispery breeze an hour prior, now rustled the foliage loose from the numerous trees that lined the city streets and stirred them in the air, giving the illusion that the city was inside the dome of an enormous snow globe. As she sat atop the Arc de Triomphe and watched the weather churn into frenzy, she knew if it was possible to look inside herself, the same chaotic scene would be unfolding.

Unlike the swift summer thunderstorm, her personal storm had been slow brewing. It was a conglomerate of complacency, loneliness, depression, rejection, sexual repression, and malnourishment, all brought to a thunderhead by Lamond entering her life instead of exiting his own. Even though he seemed to relish his new life and all the sins and pleasures it entailed, she still felt guilt for his existence, responsible for his actions.

Lamond's confidence had grown and his lust to bed or drink every young woman in Paris had become insatiable, for which she knew she was very much to blame. In the beginning, he was afraid to even step outside their apartment without her by his side, content to spend his nights with her alone, but slowly and gradually, she had pushed him away, retreated back into her shell. Whenever he managed to break down her defenses, it would only be a temporary lapse, a singular heated encounter. Later she would build a new wall, make another excuse, and tell herself another lie, afraid to let him linger too close for very long.

It seemed he had finally given up on her, and now he was ready to start his night at the last ray of daylight and raced the dawn home every morning, except for a handful of occasions when he had stayed out for days on end. He had not yet killed, which spoke volumes of his control and quick acclimation to his new life, yet she could not help but remind him time and time again just how thin the thread that tied humans to their lives truly was. Several times she had warned him and he had listened to her words without objection, yet the look in his eyes was unmistakable. He judged her to be a hypocrite and he was justified in it. She vigorously rubbed her eyes, hoping to wipe the mental image of his condescending glance from her memory. Not only had she pushed him away, rejected his affections, she had become little more than an annoying governess, and now a part of her wished she had not been so quick to shun him.

A clap of thunder rolled across the city, a crackling and hollow timbre, and the first fat drops of rain splattered around her. The weather was forcing her indoors, yet she was not ready to return home and did not want to be in the presence of strange company. With a huff, she left her physical confinements and allowed herself to be tossed about in the wind in her shimmering, ethereal form. She felt like a tiny raft afloat in the ocean, a single grain of sand waiting to slip down the bottleneck of an hourglass, no different than any leaf on the wind. She knew what she needed to do to ease her conscience, and she meant to do it, but the first step was going to be difficult to take. She had grown comfortable in Paris, had allowed her liaisons with Lamond to push her broken memories and wounded heart to the side. Her close call with the coroner after their exciting night in the arms of the Iron Lady had sobered her, reminded her of the work left to be done. She could run no farther or wait any longer.

She had ridden on the current of the storm unconsciously, only to arrive back at her own door. As beautiful as Paris was, and even though she had grown to love the city far more than she had ever imagined she would, she knew what the churning in her heart meant. She had ignored her mission long enough. She had enjoyed her Parisian distraction, but it was time to move on. She would speak to Lamond the next day. As she slid through the open window, she wondered how he would respond when he learned he was being left behind. Would he even care she was leaving or would it break his heart, just as hers had been broken by her creator, her husband, time after time?

She chose to develop just outside her soggy clothing, quickly wrapping herself in a thick robe. She piled her dripping garments into a wash basin and retreated to bed, covering herself from head to toe under the luxurious linens. No matter where she was in the world, as soon as she allowed herself to feel settled, to have a sense of home, she was forced to pull up roots and start over. Begin again. Emil's words pierced her heart for the thousandth time.

***

15 September 1899- I lie in bed tonight as I have so many nights, waiting on dawn, preparing for war once more. I feel torn between the comfortable life I have found here in Paris and the mission that brought me to this city in the first place. I almost allowed myself to forget that I am not a casual tourist or even a new resident. I am only passing through France on my journey to Amsterdam. The thoughts of travel do not inspire me as they once did. I long for home, any home, anywhere that is mine. I doubt I will ever truly have a home again, not as humans do. I could live a lifetime's worth of years and never age a day and all the while my neighbors would be dropping like flies of disease and old age. I worry I will never be home again, not as I was in my castle with Vlad. I long for the simplicity of life I enjoyed in the early days of our marriage, before everything changed, before we changed.

I cannot help but wonder how Lamond will react when he learns I am leaving. I do not expect or want him to moan and cry for me. He has found great happiness in his new life, entertaining every barmaid, seamstress, grisette, or female member of aristocracy he can lay fang to. Of course all I have acquired in Paris, aside from a few personal effects, will be his. What he chooses to do with it will be up to him. I may return to Paris to find my lovely apartment on the pleasant side of town has been transformed into a sheik's harem, Lamond lying on a stack of pillows atop a mountain of lovely concubines. It is good for him and the rest of Paris that such unions to do not produce children or Lamond's prodigy would most likely overrun the city by the end of next year.

***

"Amsterdam? I don't understand…" Lamond said, rustling his hand through his hair, pulling his shaggy bangs back from his face as if to see her point more clearly. "Why do you have to leave Paris? Life is good here, Valeria. Even you could be happy here, if you would let yourself."

"I *have* been happy here. Happier than I have been in a long time, but there are things I must do." Valeria's eyes briefly became distant as she searched through the litany of heartaches pushing her toward Amsterdam.

"See! That is how it is with you, always looking back, never looking forward to the future!" he spat, hands flung into the air. "You know, I have lived with you since April and I don't even know his name. Actually, I know nothing about you, but you know everything about me. If you are leaving, I think I deserve to know something beyond your name."

"Deserve?" Valeria bristled, offended he had drug Vlad into the conversation. She knew he did deserve to know more of her than she had given him, but to have it demanded of her infuriated her.

"Yes. Deserve," Lamond stated firmly, not backing down. "You killed me; it's your fault I'm like this. I think I deserve an explanation."

142

She huffed, crossed her arms over her chest, and looked away, refusing to watch him gloat. She hated being wrong, especially if it mean he was right. She took a deep breath to compose herself before speaking. "What do you want to know?"

"Everything. Where you…"

"You are not getting everything," she interrupted, face set like stone. "What *must* you know?"

"Who are you?" His voice rattled with a hint of laughter, not with humor but disbelief. "How did you become a vampire? And what the hell is in Amsterdam that's so important?"

Valeria walked to the sofa by the window and plopped down, propping herself into one corner and offering the other side to Lamond with an outstretched hand. She pondered how much she would have to tell him to satisfy his questions and how much she could leave out. "Well my name is Valeria Kara…"

"I know that already," he interrupted, watching her shrewdly. He knew what she was plotting. She shot him a glare that insured she would not continue if interrupted again. "Continue, please."

"Valeria Karajan of Romania. I married Count Vlad Dracula of Transylvania on the nineteenth of May in the year 1460, a patriot of his homeland. Most of the first two years of our marriage was spent apart as he waged war against the invading Ottoman Empire. One night he returned home changed, no longer the man I knew, yet strangely still himself. A part of me knew what he was but refused to believe, even when he began to drink my blood. In the end when the Turks finally arrived at my castle, he abandoned me, just left me there. Instead of being captured by our enemy, I took my own life. I leapt from the top of the castle battlement into the river below, but I did not stay dead." She held her hand out as if to display herself. "When he finally did come home, he killed my lover and moved his second wife into my castle, still human and very pregnant. Her name was Ilona, cousin to the King of Hungary. In an attempt to save his heir, he turned her as she died in childbirth. She became a vampire, the child was lost, and he left again.

143

Ilona and I learned to exist together, Vlad hopped in and out of our lives, still fighting his war. He faked his death in 1476 and we left Transylvania for a very, very long time."

Lamond sat motionless, silent, soaking her story up like a sponge. He wanted to remember every word because he knew she may never tell it again.

"Eventually we ended up here, in Paris, around 1780. Two wives proved to be insufficient for Vlad, and Fleur made us a family of four. She was a courtesan, an intolerable woman of lower class. Ilona and I were both of noble birth and we refused to accept her into our lives. The further we pushed Vlad away, the closer we became. I loved her with a passion that I did not know I could possess for a woman. We became wives to one another, effectively divorcing Vlad from our lives. He spent years alone with Fleur, much to her happiness. Finally we returned to Transylvania, where Vlad, Ilona and I did reconcile somewhat. Ilona even took in a human boy, adored him as a son. Emil. Eventually Vlad left the three of us for England, which took much of the wind from Fleur's sails and made her a measure easier to live with. When Vlad did return home, it was in a rush with the smell of another man's woman on him. This man and his merry band of crusaders followed him, one of which was old and very wise to the weaknesses of our kind. They followed Vlad to our castle. First he killed Fleur, and then Ilona."

Lamond sat in silence, riveted, allowing Valeria a moment to her thoughts. The pain the recollections caused her was evident on her face, by the creases in her forehead, the bottom lip she lightly nibbled, despite her effort to disconnect and rush through her history. She was mere inches from Lamond, at arm's length, but she was thousands of miles away. Her eyes were blank, lost, drowning in the ocean of her past, guilt, loss. He wanted to pull her close, hold her in his arms, kiss her, anything to pull her back to the present but he knew better. He dared not touch her. She was not a woman who would accept rescue from another. She would have to save herself, swim for the shore of her own strength. Any attempt on his part to pull her back and she would only jump back into the depths of her despair once more.

"He hammered a wooden stake through their hearts as they lay helpless, just before sunset. You cannot imagine the sound that made, wood shattering bone, bursting their hearts. If that was not enough, he cut their heads from their necks, disgraced them. Twice I heard the knife tip scrape against stone bottom of the sarcophagus when it parted their flesh. It sounded like the scream of train's brake in my ears. The others killed Vlad shortly thereafter. I was not with him when he died. He was alone." Valeria's face bent with disgust, pity, grief, and guilt.

"How did you survive?" Lamond ventured to ask, entranced and terrified she would end her story.

When she continued right where she had paused, and he doubted she had even heard his question. Her eyes were downcast, voice less a whisper. "Ilona did not pray or beg to be spared. With her last breath, she begged me to care for her son. I promised her I would do it, that I would protect him with my life. When the slayer stood over me, I begged that old bastard with my eyes to let me live, not for myself, but for the sake of an innocent soul. Maybe he felt that, maybe he fell under my charms, I cannot say for certain." Finally her eyes met his and she addressed his presence once more. Her was face glistened with tears, reddish streaks on marble skin. "Not a day has passed since that I have not wished, prayed, that she had lived instead of me. It should have been her, not me."

He risked touching her by taking her hand in his and whispered. "Is Ilona's son in Amsterdam now?"

She looked at him strangely, processing his misguided question. "Emil? No, he is in Brasov, where I lived before coming here. He works in a print shop, learned the trade quickly. He is a man now, no longer wants or needs me in his life." A quick sniff and she wiped the tears from her face with her fingertips, drying them on the side of her dress, as if she hoped to erase any proof that she has shed tears. Lamond knew he had picked the scab from another wound. "Van

145

Helsing, Ilona and Fleur's murderer, is in Amsterdam. He will die for what he has done."

"Who killed Vlad? Do you plan to kill him as well?" Lamond dared to ask once more.

"No. Vlad asked for his trouble. He tried to take another man's wife and he died because of it, brought death to Ilona and Fleur and nearly killed me," she said before suddenly jumping to her feet and disappearing into her bedroom, but returned quickly. She handed Lamond a book. "Here, read this. If you have any more questions, I will try to answer them tomorrow before I leave. I am tired and wish to retire for the evening. Goodnight, Lamond."

Lamond sat in silent wonder, holding her copy of *Dracula* by Bram Stoker in his hands. He heard her bedroom door close, the lock turn.

***

16 September 1899- It is on nights like this that I wish I could find comfort in a bottle as humans do. A well aged bottle of good Parisian wine would be good medicine for my frayed nerves, if I could only hold it down. Instead I would have to search down a human who had already enjoyed the wine and drink from them, once removed. Finding a slobbering drunk is easy, finding someone with actual taste is much more difficult and I haven't the patience for it tonight.

Instead of leaving tonight as planned, I bared my soul and past to Lamond. I am sure it served as great entertainment for him, as he has undoubtedly had questions of me since the night we met. I revealed more than I had intended, more than I ever told Emil, more than anyone else living knows of me. Perhaps tomorrow my spirit will feel lighter, having confessed my sins so to speak. But tonight, it is simply compounded, pushing me deeper, making me smaller. As I lay on my bed and write, I do not feel as though I have the strength to lift my head. Ilona, sweet and beautiful, gentle and kind, will haunt my dreams. She does this without her knowledge or consent, as it is my own memories of her that will torment me. She is in a place beyond my reach, a place of beauty and peace. I refuse to believe in a Heaven that she could not be a part of. She is in paradise, listening to the voices of angels. She so closely mirrored one herself during her time on Earth. She was my angel, my source of peace.

Perhaps I will try the wine once more tonight.

***

Safe in the sanctuary of her bedroom, Valeria poured herself a glass of the rich, potent wine she had recently acquired. No matter how hard she tried, she had not been able to get the thought out of her mind. The possibility of reprieve, no matter how slight, from the crushing emotions her confession had brought to the surface had proven too much to ignore. Willing to try anything to loosen the noose, she remembered a beautiful vineyard not far from the city. Years ago when she had visited Paris with Vlad and Ilona, the vineyard was thriving and it had survived despite the revolutions and hardships France had faced. She liked their mettle.

It had taken more than a little convincing to gain entry at such a late hour, but finally the owner conceded to her charms. She had made it worth his while, purchasing three bottles of his most expensive vintage at double price, a small fortune made in one night. After the transaction was complete, she waited patiently for him to return to bed and fall back asleep. She drank from him before returning home with her purchase, slipping out through an open window, a shimmer on the balmy summer air.

Now back at home without alerting Lamond and her belly already half full, she held the glass to her nose and sniffed the beautiful bouquet grapes, sun, and time, and then cautiously took the first sip. It was an explosion of flavor and heat, the tartness puckered her mouth. Finally gathering the courage to swallow, she felt the foreign substance scald

147

her throat and clash with the blood in her stomach, like oil and water. At first she thought she would immediately reject it but after a few minutes, her stomach calmed and she felt the first hint of warmness in her cheeks by the bottom of the first glass. Another glass and the tension began to relax from her shoulders and neck. Her system seemed to accept the wine more with each sip. Forgoing the glass, she turned the bottle up and downed about a quarter of it before sitting it back down. She felt her face become more flushed, her eyes become heavy, her mind quieted. She allowed her eyes to close and she savored the thick, comfortable blanket that was being wrapped around her senses. She lifted the bottle again and took several more gulps. It burned less and tasted better with each drink. Her stomach stopped protesting altogether.

The warmth spread from her mouth, down her neck, across her chest and all the way down to her belly. Not even basking in front of Serghei's forge had she felt such warmth, not even while lying in the blacksmith's strong, protective arms. Not since her human days could she recall such warmth, not since her wedding night celebrations when she and Vlad had danced, ate and drank the night away, surrounded by her family and guest in her Father's house.

Grasping the bottle by the neck, Valeria rose to her feet, stumbled, and then regained her balance. She held her left arm in front of her, as if she were caressing a phantom partner, and held her right hand and the bottle high, as if she was holding his unseen hand. She recalled the steps, from her mind to her feet, and began to dance. Lost in memory, she could see her husband's face, smiling and full of human life. She recalled the beautiful embellishments of her dress, embroidered flowers and silk ribbon trim, small carved buttons. She could smell fresh flowers and candle smoke. She could feel his hand on the small of her back. She could hear the chatter of the guest and the beautiful music of the flute and lyre. She and Vlad spun around the chapel floor of her father's estate, smiling, happy, and drunk with wine and love. Her feet came to a stop, but her head continued to spin. Another dance around the floor for old time's sake, one more dance with her husband before sobriety and the dawn took him back to Sheol.

***

Valeria woke, groggy and sluggish, at the strike of noon. Even though she had delivered her from helpless slumber, she found it difficult to open her eyes, even more difficult to move. Her head felt like it was inside a stockpot and a brat child was banging the side with a large, metal spoon. The sun was too bright and even the birds chirping outside her window were too loud. Another noise, a low rumble, a snarling wheeze, roared in her right ear. She rolled her head slowly to investigate. It felt like fluid was sloshing in her head, just like the wine had churned in her belly the night before. She gave firm instructions to her eyes to open their lids and find the source of the racket. Her vision was blurry, clearing only after several squinting blinks. Beside her, Lamond snored like a hibernating bear. He lay on his stomach, his head on her pillow, mouth half open. One sharp tooth peeked at her from behind his lip. He had one leg flopped over hers, her arm halfway under his chest, naked. Just then, the light flickered through the gently swaying trees, reflected off his marble-like buttocks and glared straight into her eyes.

"Oh god…" She grumbled, squinting and rubbing her eyes with her free hand, instantly aware of her own nudity, like Eve in the garden. She racked her brain, desperately trying to recall anything from the night before. She remembered talking to Lamond, giving him the book, and then slipping away to the vineyard. She dropped her arm lifelessly off the side of the bed and her fingertips immediately found the cold glass of the empty wine bottle. She had spent the last weeks separating herself from him, encouraging his womanizing and independence while she plotted her departure from Paris, severing his dependence on her and her reliance on him. Now he lay naked in her bed again, and she could not remember a single thing they had done. For all she knew, they

149

had fornicated right in the middle of downtown Paris, right on the street in front of anyone who cared to watch. Had he drank from anyone, had she? She could have killed someone, even drained and slaughtered half the city, and she would not have remembered it. She was clueless, having no idea how greatly the alcohol had affected her. Lamond was the only hope she had of regaining any insight of her lost night.

She shook Lamond, pulling her other arm out from underneath him and sat up beside him. He frowned, but did not wake up. "Lamond, wake up!" she said, giving him a good shake. Finally he began to stir.

"Good morning, beautiful." His eyes only half open. Valeria sighed.

"What happened last night?" she asked impatiently, offering no salutation in return.

"Isn't it obvious?" Lamond smiled slyly.

"I gather that much. What I mean is how? How did this happen?" she asked with less patience than before.

"Well… it happened here on the bed, over there in the floor, and on top of that dresser for a time." He smiled broadly. "You were quite acrobatic."

"Damn it, Lamond! You know what I mean to ask!" she growled.

"You really don't remember." He chuckled. "I knew you were drunk! You drank that whole bottle of wine and managed to keep it down? How?"

"No, I do not remember. If I could remember, would I be asking you?"

"Alright, don't get bent out of shape," Lamond huffed, seeing she would be no fun. He rolled over and propped himself up on his elbow. "After our talk, you gave me that book, and then stomped off, all moody and dark like you always do. You locked yourself in your room. A few hours later, right when I was getting ready to go out myself, you met me in the sitting room. You had a half empty bottle of wine in your hand. You looked at me, smiled and said, want to have another go? You looked like you were drunk off your ass, but I thought that was impossible. Of course, I was happy to oblige."

150

"Did we leave the house?"

"No, the dawn arrived much too quickly." Lamond smiled, stretching over to tuck her hair behind her ear. "I wish we had gotten an earlier start."

She quickly pulled away and stood, leaving him on the bed. "Thank you for seeing to me, Lamond. I appreciate that you were here. I will not be so careless in the future."

"What are you running from, Valeria?" he spat and unexpectedly rushed to her. In an instant he was by her side took her by the hand.

"I do not run from anything!" she growled, insulted by his confrontation. She yanked her hand from his.

"Really? You have been running for years. Hell, you have been running from me since the night I died."

She shook her head. "You cannot understand..."

"No! I *do* understand, much more than you think. I understand that you had a horrible marriage to man that did not love you, who left you, got himself killed. I understand that you lost Ilona, and that you loved her very much. I know you had a stepson that turned his back on you, turned you out of your home." He dared to pull her close to him, her shoulders in his hands. She could not raise her eyes to look at him, yet she did not pull away. "I know you are alone, your family, everyone you have ever known is long dead. I know you are afraid to let me in, because you think I will disappear just like everyone else you have ever cared about. I know you care for me, and that it scares the hell out of you." He could feel her tremble in his hands, silently fighting, desperate to keep her composure. She bit her bottom lip, doing her best to hide the tear that ran down her cheek from him. Gently, nervously, he placed his hands on either side of her face and lifted her head to see her face. He wiped the tear away with his thumb. "Now, do you want to know what scares me?"

She finally opened her eyes and whispered as he brushed her hair from her dampened face with his fingertips, combing through the strands of gold. "What?"

"That you will let it all swallow you. That you will hang on to all that pain so tight it will kill you. That's what scares me, Valeria. That one day it will take you." He pulled her into his arms, holding on as if he was trying to save her life. "Sooner or later, you are going to have to let it go. You are going to have to move on or there will be nothing left of you."

Wrapped in his arms, her head on his chest, she finally spoke. "That is why I have to go to Amsterdam, and then England. I have to end it. It is a thorn in my brain. It won't let me be." She could hear the slow rhythm of his heart, fluttering with passion and compassion. "When it is done, I will come back to you a whole person."

"Let me come with you..." he said, hoping to persuade her but knowing better.

"No. I have to do this alone. If I fail, I will no doubt die. I killed you once already and I am not about to risk it. But if I succeed, I will need to learn how to live again and then I will gladly accept your help."

Part Five:
The Dish best served Cold

Chapter Fourteen

22 September 1899- I arrived in Brussels last night and stole away the morning hours safely atop a house, basking in the warm sun like a lizard. I am but a few days away from Van Helsing's throat, but I cannot be reckless. He is nothing if not resourceful. I will not underestimate him, the lengths he is willing to go or how far he will push others to achieve his own agenda. If not for Van Helsing, Vlad would have no doubt added Mina Harker to his harem. Of course we had planned to kill her as soon as she entered the castle, but none of that is important now. I am all that is left of that life, a relic of a tragic past. I no longer intend to be tethered to the past. I will live, even if it kills me. I am going to live beyond this, with or without Lamond, with or without Emil, with or without anyone. I intend to live, but first, Abraham Van Helsing is going to die.

The forest on the outskirts of the city is beautiful. I believe I will spend some time there, a place to rest my mind and prepare for what is next. I have been in the city so long that I am accustomed to the noise, the constant drum of hearts. I have allowed my sense to become dull, gotten a bit lazy. Lamond has shown me an easier life, a calmer pace. I had the illusion that much of the time I spent with him had been wasted, that it was keeping me from my mission, but now I realize it was important. Time well spent. Aside from letting my hunting skills wane, it has helped my heart to heal. I believe there is much I can learn from this modern man on the ways of the world. We may spend days, years, or centuries together, or not another hour, only time and the outcome of this trip will tell. I have been harsh with him when unnecessary, selfish with my affections toward him. But I have finally realized that I will be eternally thankful to my accidental friend and everything he has brought to my life.

***

Valeria crouched low to the ground, her clothes shed to the minimum. Barefoot and wearing only her white, lace trimmed bloomers and camisole, she crawled across the forest floor like a stalking lioness, over and through the underbrush as silent as the prey she sought. Her senses were so alive that her entire body seemed to crackle with electric energy. The scent of the earth and decaying leaves filled her nostrils, the cool air of the forest on her skin, ears alive with every chirp, chatter, and wing flap of warm life. Her eyes could see deep within the shady areas of the wood, detecting even the best camouflage efforts. She felt like a tightly coiled spring, a snake prepared to strike, a hair- trigger trap ready to snap.

Slowly she crawled, low and tight to the ground. Just ahead of her, a young red deer nibbled the tender grass growing beneath a cluster of beech trees. The evening sun filtered dim through the trees, casting a warm glow across the landscape. Valeria could hear the incessant buzzing of insect wings, abruptly stopping when a fly landed on the deer's ear. It snorted and wiggled its ears to scare away the uninvited guest, continuing to eat. As the buzzing fly left to annoy those with less sensitive faculties, Valeria crept closer to her target. Leaf debris, dead grass and spindly twigs littered the ground. One step closer and a rotten twig snapped beneath her foot and she instantly froze. The deer's head jerked up and searched for the source of the noise, quietly chewing a mouthful of grass. She dug her fingernails into the soft soil and looked toward the sky. The sun was taking its sweet time.

The deer felt Valeria's penetrating stare and looked straight at her, ready to flee at the slightest provocation. She closed her eyes, lowered her gaze, and held her breath. The tension between hunter and prey was palpable, almost visible. The birds around them chirped oblivious and merry, the insects called to the night hiding just beyond the horizon. If she moved so much as a fingertip, leaned to the left or right, or even lifted her head too quickly, the deer would disappear.

Finally a rush like warm water washed over her, starting at her head and cascading all the way down to the tips of her toes. The sun had finally given over the reins to her powers, stoking her already heightened senses like a bellow to a fire. She inhaled deeply, taking in the symphony of life around her. She dared to lift her head and look at the deer, which had not taken its eyes from her. She curled her toes into the dirt for traction, and steadied herself like a sprinter on the block of a one hundred meter race. She inhaled again, tasting the scent of her prey, smiled, and shot toward the deer. The startled creature bolted, charging headlong into the forest along well traveled paths that Valeria was not familiar with.

She trailed the deer at a close pace, only a few feet away at times, through the ever darkening forest. It would eventually tire, but she would not. It would be blinded by darkness when she could still see. It was only a matter of time. She could hear its hooves thundering against the ground, pausing to leap over a fallen tree or tangle of brush, only to return at the same frantic pace. She could hear the breath rushing in and out of its lungs, its heart beating with the rhythm of a runaway locomotive. Blood. She could hear its blood churning in its body, speeding down the highways of its circulatory system, funneling in and out of its heart. It was only a matter of seconds before the lactic acid built in its muscles, slowing it against its will.

The deer began to decrease its speed and the duration of its jumps lessened. Valeria maintained her grueling speed and closed the gap. She grabbed at its hind quarters, but the deer deviated and she missed. The deer ran slower still, but Valeria held her cruising speed, closing the gap once more. She was so close she could see the individual hairs of its ruddy coat. One more push and Valeria charged forward, running alongside instead of behind it. The deer attempted to change course once again, but she leapt and wrapped her arms around its neck and yanked it toward the ground with all her weight. They stumbled as the terrified creature drug Valeria through the thick underbrush and scrub. Finally succumbing to exhaustion, the deer collapsed. She dug her heels into the dirt and maneuvered it to the ground, leaping onto its side like a lioness securing a gazelle.

"Shh…You're safe," she whispered as it struggled, whining pitifully. Its heart was pounding like thunder, a film of terror across it dark eye. She encased the deer in a shimmer of mists, like it was covered by a comet's tail, and held it firmly still. "Good job, little one. See you again tomorrow."

She quickly lifted into the air, giving the deer a wide berth to gather itself. In the blink of an eye, it was back on its feet and had disappeared into the dark of the forest. Her own feet back on the ground, Valeria was greeted by a dry, scratchy throat. All the energy she had expired during her exercise would have to be replaced, but not at the expense of the deer. She had only drank from an animal once in her unlife, a wolf, after a failed attempt to end her own life by starvation. It was something she had no intentions of doing again, unless under the similar distressed conditions.

As she walked back to retrieve her dress and shoes, she listened to the complex melody of the night. The wind whispered secrets in her ear and the owls questioned her intrusion as the rising moon illuminated her path. It had been quite some time since she had spent any time in nature, not since arriving in Paris. It was soothing, even in her most difficult, lowest times, to be in the midst of life, free of judgment and scorn.

Finally she caught a glimpse of her dress hanging from a branch, billowing in the light breeze like a misplaced ghost. She could have drifted there much faster as mist on the wind, but deliberately chose to walk, to take her time. So much of her life had been spent traveling to one destination or another, to another challenge to overcome, another danger to escape. She had never truly been given the chance to enjoy her travels, another aspect of her life she intended to change. She gathered her clothes, but stopped short of putting them back on. She was covered, front and back, head to toe, in dirt and deer hair. Dinner would have to wait.

***

October 1899- My time in the forest has been good medicine for my soul, so much that I have lost track of time. I only go into the city when I need to feed, and return as quickly as possible. I laugh out loud at myself, lying high in the trees like a jungle cat without care. I have even slept there on a few occasions, but I prefer to not risk falling to the forest floor in my sound sleep. I prefer to sleep under the open sky beneath the underbrush in places inhospitable for humans to tread, so deep within the forest I have no fear of being discovered. I feel alive with energy in this place. My woodland friends have been wonderful exercise, much to their reluctance. I know that I will not be facing a foe as quick as a deer in Van Helsing. He is but a husk of a man, old and withered by time, but I am certain he will have some sort of defenses that will need dealing with. He knows what it is that he has wronged, the creature that I am. I cannot help but believe that he knows I am coming. I do not understand how he knows, but I am almost certain of it.

I know the time has come for me to continue my journey, to do what I must to so that I may continue with my life. I have to set things right, avenge Ilona and Fleur, and I supposed Vlad as well, and at least some measure for Emil. I will remember my time here in the Sonian forest, when the world beyond the trees becomes too much to bear.

***

159

29 October 1899- I finally arrived in Amsterdam last night. I learned the date by the paper I picked up off the street upon waking. It is difficult for me to believe I was in the forest for so long. It is no wonder I received such a peculiar look from the clerk when I paid for my room, a month in advance, looking as I did. Yet another reason I prefer to stay in the quaint establishments of a city. The staff is not so easily alarmed and asks no questions as long as the money is good. I plan to be as quiet as a church mouse, listen and speak only when I must. I will resist the urge to be hasty, to bear my fangs and stalk the city until I find him. Someone will reveal the location to that shriveled up old bastard in due time.

***

The cool whisper of ocean air hinted of winter's approach, a salty kiss upon Valeria's cheek, but waning autumn had yet to release her grasp on lovely Amsterdam. Clusters of brightly colored leaves still adorned the trees, the sun still brave and warm. Valeria, well dressed and manicured once more, strode through the heart of downtown, with a parasol and her hat brim pulled low. The city was inviting, beautiful, and of pleasant temperature. She quickly understood why her nemesis had called this distinguished city his home. If he had not done so already, she would have considered it a home for herself.

Amsterdam was two hundred years older than she, a trait she always admired in a city. The architecture had remained beautiful while changing and evolving with industry. Canals encircled the heart of the city like hedgerows. The train station hummed with life and the zoo displayed exotics from across the globe, not to mention the various museums, theaters, cafes, boutiques, schools and universities. The de Wallen, the oldest part of the city, displayed its living wares behind red lit windows. Ladies of easy virtue lured customers with the siren's song, offering every pleasure imaginable, so long as it was paid for in advance. Boredom would certainly be hard pressed to reside in Amsterdam.

For almost three weeks, Valeria had been a silent tourist, nodding when spoken to, returning to her room in the de Wallen in plenty of time to greet the dawn in safety, feeding as mist from the destitute in the alleys throughout the city. They were an unpalatable, but a safe source of nourishment that required no invitation. She had enjoyed walking through the various squares, down canal lined streets, browsing the markets and mixing in the frantic energy of the festivals that seems to pop up for one reason or another every other day in one neighborhood or another. The air carried music and laughter, the rich scents of foods and drinks from a multitude of cultures, the smoke of cigarettes and industry smokestacks. But her fraternizing had not been without purpose. While she intertwined, she listened, scanning conversations for the name she needed to hear, Van Helsing. She found it to be an unusual name, even in his homeland where she had assumed she would have to fish him out from hundreds bearing the same surname. But almost a month had passed and she had not heard a single mention of the name, until by chance she heard it mentioned while passing a café near the university.

"...Hoogleraar Van Helsing..." She had caught only a whisper, but she was certain of what she had heard. The young woman and her companion were discussing a Professor Van Helsing, no doubt they were students at the Municipal University of Amsterdam where he was a professor. She knew from reading Bram Stoker's Dracula that in his professional capacity, he was a professor, a vampire slayer in his free time, a murderous hobby. She wanted to jump in the middle of the conversation, ask twenty questions before introducing herself, demand to be taken to him, threaten them with life and limb if they denied her, but instead she sat on the closest bench to the couple and tuned in on their conversation.

As she eavesdropped, she wished she had taken time to refresh her Dutch while in Paris instead of relying on the crash course she had

161

received after arriving in Amsterdam, a byproduct of another hasty decision. However it was unnecessary to understand everything they said. If Van Helsing was a professor at the university behind them, it would be simple enough to find him, possibly follow him home. She felt her stomach drop, her nerves instantly frayed, and the warmth of the day seemed to dissipate. It was not foolish to believe that he would have individuals close to him, bound together by similar views or perhaps in his employment, that would kill her if given the opportunity, take pride in the act.

She cautiously stood and looked around, as though her gaining the knowledge of his location had somehow triggered an alarm, alerting him to her presence. She walked past the couple, who were still chattering on the bench, as humanly as she could, overly careful to not draw attention to herself. Her mind raced with possibilities, anxiety beginning to take hold. What if the young man and woman on the bench were not students, but aligned with him somehow, spies that knew how to spot the subtle differences in human and vampire kind and would alert him to her presence? Perhaps it was not a coincidence that they were right there where she needed them to be but placed there, sentinels on guard. She was finding it difficult to resist the whispers of paranoia.

The walkway to the University entrance seemed to grow longer, the shadow of the trees darker, the structure taller, more foreboding. She stopped outside the door, unable to continue without invitation. She realized if she had been given an engraved invitation to the university, she would be lacking the courage to take even one more step.

"Damn him!" she muttered under her breath, cursing him and her fearfulness, pacing in front of the door. She had traveled the breadth of Europe to be where she stood, a veritable arm's length from her target, only to find herself incapable of continuing. Why had fear waited so long to dig its claws into her heart? After all, he was just a man. But somehow this mere human had been the undoing of everything, the taker of her life though she lived, had grown larger and intimidating in

162

her mind. That was why she could feel herself tremble instead of rushing inside to meet him with fearless courage. Despite all odds, Abraham Van Helsing thwarted her and her sister wives attack that night in the swirling snowstorm, protecting not only himself, but Mina Harker as well. Their failure, *her* failure, had resulted in the deaths of Ilona and Fleur. Now she was taking the fight to his door, on his territory. For the first time since meeting Lamond, Valeria felt grievously alone and wished she had accepted his offer to accompany her. Her pride had displaced her better judgment yet again.

As she pondered and paced, a polite and well groomed young man exited the university, dutifully holding the door for her to enter. Instinct overrode her fear and she quickly passed inside, accepting the offered invitation, but with no idea of how to proceed. The door closed heavy behind her, echoing in the expansive room that felt as quiet and lifeless as a tomb. She began to walk without direction, listening to the sound of her shoes on the marble floor as she searched for some sort of guidance.

"Hallo, kan ik u helpen?" A light touch on her arm and a quiet voice, fractured by old age, startled her. An old woman with hunched shoulders shuffled out of the doorway just as she had passed it, intersecting their paths. She waited patiently for Valeria to respond, her kind face deeply creased with wrinkles, white hair pulled tightly into a neat bun. Her eyes looked watery, a shade of grey-blue that only age could give.

"Ummm…" Her Dutch eluded her momentarily. "Ik ben… Ik ben op zoek naar Hoogleraar Van Helsing." She hoped she had gotten close enough to asking if she knew where she might find Proessor Van Helsing for her to understand. The woman nodded knowingly, shuffling to her desk. She unfolded her glasses, which hung from her neck by a piece of twine tied to the end of each arm, and placed them low on her nose.

"Bent u Roemeens?" she asked with a pleasant smile, her eyes nearly disappearing within her wrinkles. She had detected Valeria's resilient Romanian accent.

"Ja," she agreed, hoping to play down any shock or hesitation in her voice or behavior. The last thing she needed was gossip within the university concerning a young, nervous blonde woman from Romania was searching for Professor Van Helsing. She smiled with tightly sealed lips and waited patiently.

"Ah!" the elderly woman said triumphantly, finger pushed firmly against the page to mark her discovery, offering Valeria to read for herself as she read it to her, "Afdeling Wijsbegeerte."

Philosophy department, she was almost certain that was the proper translation. She committed the words, their spellings, to memory.

She pointed her bony, arthritic finger behind her, motioning as if she was leaping over buildings as she counted them. "Een, twee, drie."

Valeria bowed her head low in gratitude. "Dank u wel."

The woman took her glasses from her nose, smiled and nodded before shuffling back toward the room she had appeared from.

As Valeria returned outside, she could hear a clock somewhere on the campus chime five times. She knew the autumn sun would quickly fade into night and restore her powers, but she chose instead to walk away, to return to the security of her room. This time, she would not allow her emotions to propel her. She would be cautious, observe the building, learn the daily routine, and look for a weakness to exploit. She had already been invited in, so she could move when the time was right. If she was very lucky, she would be able to spot her prey as he left for the day, follow him home. Perhaps karma would allow her to kill him as he slept, just as he had killed Ilona and Fleur.

***

26 November 1899- For three days I have known where to find Van Helsing, but instead I have hid in this room, gutless. If Vlad were here,

he would have already taken care of this business. He would have devised a cunning plan to draw him away from his routine and safety, ambushed him, and the matter would be done. If Fleur were here, she would have already walked straight up to him, looked him in the face and gave him a piece of her mind before ripping out his throat in front of all of Amsterdam. If Ilona were here, I would have had the courage to protect her, protect Emil, and I would have confronted him the night I learned his location. If Lamond were here, I would surely have already thought of a way to dazzle him, to look special in his eyes. He would have no doubt helped me with the task and we would have made ourselves merry drunk on the old bastard's blood, perhaps even had a nice romp in his bed. But I am alone and alone I have sat, for three days. For someone who has lived for four and a half centuries, three days should be a fleeting moment, a breath, but it has felt more like three years. It is the weight of shame.

I will return to the university today to watch for him. I believe I will be able to sense his closeness when he steps outdoors. The salty air will enhance his scent, his stink, and I will be one step closer. This will end soon, for I will be unable to tolerate myself or these four walls much longer.

Chapter Fifteen

Valeria sat downwind of the Philosophy department, a bloodhound wearing a nice dress with a parasol. To the outside world, she was another beautiful woman in Amsterdam, relishing a fair weather day before winter took hold again, watching the blossoming sunset. In reality, her senses were on fire. While she would have to wait for sunset for many of her abilities to activate, her exquisite senses were passive. In such close proximity to the university, the drumming of heartbeats was nearly overbearing, combined with breathing, laughing, talking, and eating, her keen sense of hearing was almost useless. Picking Van Helsing's voice out of the crowd, even though it echoed clearly in her ears and dreams, would be impossible.

She assumed he would be late to leave his studies, but she wanted to be close in the slim chance that he might leave before dark. She casually watched the sun set behind the city, waiting to be fulfilled. The peaceful orange and pink hues were vibrant, more like a summer sunset than late autumn. With the last brushstrokes of daylight still clinging to the edge of darkness, the sun bowed his head and Valeria felt night breathe life into her once again. She closed her eyes and felt the wash of energy embrace her. She stood tall and stretched, not because she needed to but for the pleasure, like a housecat stretching her back after warming in the sunlight.

She strolled to the main entrance of the building the elderly woman had directed her toward days earlier with greater confidence. The wind blew lightly on her face, chilling the air temperature while saturating her in the scents of hundreds of humans. Just as before, a well mannered student held the door for her and she comfortably accepted his invitation. As soon as she stepped over the threshold, she felt a shiver of trepidation chill her heart. The building was an expansive structure of marble, cold and silent. She felt like she was walking into the gaping entrance of a cave, only to realize too late it was the mouth of a vengeful dragon.

Soon the moment she had waited fourteen years to realize would be reality. She would kill Abraham Van Helsing and avenge the deaths of her family and the ruin of her life. She felt a flutter of nervous energy replace the hesitation and she quickened her pace through the winding hallways, following the signs to the Philosophy department offices. Even though she had rehearsed the moment she would confront the slayer a million times in her mind, now that the time was at hand, a perfectly laid out plan eluded her. She would have to wait and see the monster's lair and then rely on her instincts to guide her. Escaping did not concern her. She would simply fade into mists, slip out beneath a door, through a keyhole or cracked window, or hide in any container of large enough volume to hold the entirety of her substance until she could make her escape. She would kill if it meant saving herself, but only as a last resort. She had no quarrel with anyone else in Amsterdam, even if they were in the good doctor's service. They would only be doing what they had been led to believe was right and spilling their blood would only justify false doctrine. Save Jonathan Harker and Bram Stoker, she was finally at peace with the world, even at peace with Emil. One day, she hoped to find peace with herself.

The faculty offices of the Philosophy department were abandoned, with the exception of a single heartbeat in the office at the end of the hall. For Valeria, it was the end of a very long, winding, and hateful road. She longed for the relief that would come when it was finally finished. For Van Helsing, it would be the end of his life's journey, an existence built on a foundation of hate and genocide in the name of God and science.

She allowed a portion of her body to become mist, her feet and most of her legs, so she would not produce footfall. She could feel her heartbeat quicken pace, the blood accelerating through her veins. She stood with her back against the wall, the open door only inches from her hand. Although she required no invitation, she wanted him to ask her in. She wanted him to know his arrogance had been his own undoing. She knocked on the frame, careful to stay out of view.

"Come in." His voice rang in her ears like an alarm bell on a fire truck. It was only two words, but they stuck straight in her chest, the fight or flight reflex activated. She squeezed her eyes closed, so tightly it hurt. For a split second, she had the impulse to run from the man that had become the monster of her nightmares, the murderer of her family.

"Valeria! Valeria I am afraid!" Ilona's last words sliced through her mind. She could see Ilona's dress lying in her tomb, filled with ashes so reminiscent of her form it was as though her features had been sculpted in sand. "Valeria, please!"

Her eyes opened, cold and distant. Her body became fully flesh and she set her jaw. She turned into the doorway and bravely walked into the room. Abraham Van Helsing sat behind his desk, piled high with books and papers, his head low and writing with such conviction that he neglected to look up to see who entered his office. She stood before him, waiting for him to look, close enough she could pull him across the table and tear out his throat before he knew to fear her. Instead she waited patiently for him to acknowledge her, a last lesson in humility.

"What is it?" he spat, annoyed by her disregard of his importance. As soon as he looked up, as soon as his eyes connected with hers, the color faded from his face, his mouth agape. "Mein Gott!" he gasped and pushed away from the desk, nearly flipping himself backward.

"Hello, doctor," she said quietly, hiding the inferno of rage and hatred that was boiling steadily toward eruption. "It has been a while…fourteen years. Did you think I had forgotten about you?"

Van Helsing stood slowly, cautiously, and paced backward away from her. His eyes were wide with fear and disbelief.

"Did you think I had forgotten about that night in Transylvania?" She quickly leapt over the desk and closed the space between them, sending a flurry of papers into the air. She stood face to face with him, gritting her teeth so hard that her fangs raked at her gums. She could smell the stink of fear on him, exuding from every pore. "Did you think I was too afraid to find you?"

She pushed him back, causing him to stumble, but not quite enough to knock him to the floor, like a cat playfully tossing a mouse before killing it. "Did you think you would not have to pay for your sins?"

The old man bristled with bruised self- righteousness. "Sins! Dracula was a monster! I carried out God's work!" he boasted, chest full of pride.

Valeria refused to back down. "You are right, Vlad was a monster and he died for the choices he made. But Ilona and Fleur had done nothing to you and you slaughtered them like lambs," Valeria growled, her cheeks warming and ears burning, her nose nearly touching his. Van Helsing cowered slightly, refusing to look at her terrifying, yet beautiful countenance. "You are nothing but a murderer. For all your righteousness, you are no different than me."

Van Helsing fell back and leaned against the fireplace mantle, clutching his chest. Sweat was no longer confined to the fine dew on his brow, but streaked down his cheeks like tears. Valeria studied him closely, listening to his hearbeat, guarding herself for a deceptively played trap. His aged heart tripped occasionally at its accelerated speed, struggling against the added stress, but she knew better than to underestimate him. He panted heavily, leaning so deeply that it seemed he would collapse if he had not been able to support himself on the mantle.

Suddenly, with no outward indication, Van Helsing lunged at her. With adrenaline coursing through his veins, he slashed at her with a silver knife collected from mantle. She jumped back, her body quickly becoming a cloud of mist. The knife passed though with no effort or injury, but she could feel the scalding burn of the poisonous silver as it interacted with her body on a molecular level. She quickly lifted away from him and hovered over head, well out of reach of his desperate slashes.

"Is this the best you can do, slayer, after fourteen years?" she chided, listening to his heartbeat, reading it like a gage of his frustration.

"Face me, like a man not a coward!" Van Helsing blustered, his face red hot.

"Like a man? Now, why would I do that?" Her whisper filled the room, echoed like a shout. Valeria shot down from overhead like a streaking comet, wrapping herself around him like a straight jacket. She restricted his wrist and hand tightly, aiming his hand toward the fireplace. She manipulated his arm, demanding it to move. She clenched down on his wrist at the precise moment and forced him to throw his weapon into the fire. "How does it feel to be helpless, old man, helpless like Ilona and Fleur?" she said, her lips only a breath from his ear. Her voice was purposely alluring, feminine, emphasizing that he was being broken by a woman, above all else. "How much money did you make selling my soul to Stoker?"

"I did no such thing!" he spat, as strongly as his constricted chest would allow him to speak.

"Liar!" She tightened her grip. "I suppose you just gave it to him for nothing?"

"I had nothing to do with that book!" he said, a little more desperate than before.

She bore down tighter, like turning a corkscrew. She could feel his brittle ribs begin to warp under her pressure. "Do not lie to me!"

"I swear!" he wheezed, his face changing from red to purple. "I did not give him the journals!"

His words clicked in her mind. "Maybe you did, maybe you didn't, and maybe it was Harker."

"I beg you! For God's sake, do not involve Jonathan." Van Helsing spoke with desperation. He tried to turn his head, hoping to find her face so he could look her in the eyes as he pleaded.

171

"Oh! For God's sake, it would be a pity if young Quincey should get caught up in the middle of this!" Valeria teased, mocking him with what she knew what would hurt him most.

"He is just a boy!" he shouted, writhing with fury against her confinement.

"What of Ilona's son? Emil was just a boy when you murdered his mother, destroyed his family!" Valeria's eyes flashed red, washing all she could see in crimson, seething rage. She felt every translucent particle, every glimmer of herself, compact around his ancient bones. A loud crack, followed instantly by a wail of pain, announced a rib had been broken. "It was I that told Emil his mother was dead, dried his tears, felt him tremble in my arms. He did not understand hate until then, until you! Damn you, Abraham Van Helsing! If ever a man deserves to burn in Hell, it is you! I would deliver your soul to the Devil myself if I had the power!"

"Mercy…please…mercy…" he begged, his voice raspy and faint, breathless.

"No," she whispered. Her face was scarcely visible, an outline of herself. "We can have none of that."

Valeria smiled fiendishly as cruelness twisted her thoughts. She tightened her grip on her victim further. Again it was followed by another loud crack, his left humerus shattered. He gasped, and as he opened his mouth desperately for breath, the mists of Valeria rushed down his throat. Van Helsing gagged, drowning on his attacker. Within the blackness, she felt her way into his lungs, clogging them. Having released his arms, the professor swung wildly with his unbroken arm at the cloud of iridescence that circled his head like smoke from a chimney until asphyxiation felled him to his knees. Within his chest, Valeria followed the sound of his thundering heart, down the alleyways of his arteries until she arrived inside his heart. As she filled the chambers, she thought of Ilona and Fleur, of the last moments of their lives. She could still hear the hammer strike the stakes, shattering their sternums before gouging into their softly beating hearts. She congealed, as concentrated as she could make herself in her incorporeal state. The hammer of her memory struck again like thunder and Valeria willed her substance to expand into a thousand small daggers, her particles like shards of glass. The beating instantly stopped and the dark cavern that was once his heart began to collapse. She funneled out of his gaping mouth as he lay on the carpet like a fish on a dock, eyes glassy, his face blue. She rematerialized before him, covered in a sticky sheen of his blood, her hair stuck to her face. Blood readily flowed from his mouth and nose, pooling around his head. Valeria felt bile rise in throat at its scent, the odor equal to rotten eggs or spoiled meat to a human nose. Finally, Abraham Van Helsing, the slayer of legend, the murderer of all she loved and valued, was dead. She spit on his corpse and chose to walk out the door instead of floating in the mists. It was finished.

Valeria walked down the dark corridors of the university, passing no one. Outside again, the wind was blowing in rain that was on the brink of freezing. Like the university, the streets of Amsterdam were deserted. The stinging, pelting rain soaked into her dress, diluting the residue of Van Helsing. As she walked, the gravity of what she had just done began to settle on her shoulders. Wide ranging emotions swayed her heart, back and forth from hateful fury, to cold sorrow, to victorious revenge. She had expected to feel overwhelming satisfaction after killing Van Helsing, but was instead shaken to her core. She tried to laugh, a faux celebration, but she shivered and had to struggle not to cry. She had faced her monster, stared her nightmare in the eye once more and lived, but she was not unscathed. She had done more than confront him, more than dealt his death. She had been inside the body of living man. She had heard his heartbeat from the inside, ventured into the dark chambers and had brought it crashing down. Chilled, exhausted, and blood starved, she could feel herself begin to shake. She wiped her face, swiping the hair and tears from her face with trembling hands. She had allowed herself to become soaked through, hoping the rain would wash away her pain with his stink. She hoped it would

173

cleanse her, heal her heart and bring her peace. She hoped she would no longer feel compelled to go to England to seek more war and pick more scabs, but all the rain in the sky above her would not be enough.

She shuddered against the cold and wrapped her arms around herself. As she walked down the puddle strewn street, a single muffled sob escaped her quivering lips despite her best effort. She forgot where she left her parasol. Her dress was ruined and would have to be thrown away, dirty water filled her shoes. Suddenly, she was overwhelmed with loneliness and wished Lamond was by her side. She needed to be held, to be embraced against his strong chest and listen to the whisper of his heartbeat. But she was alone in a city of strangers, far from any place she had ever called home. She was shocked by her own admission of weakness, that yet again she had become dependent on another. The dam of her emotions finally burst and Valeria fell to her hands and knees and cried right in the middle Amsterdam. Her sorrows carried above the howl of the wind, harmonizing with it. It was a broken rhythm of sobs and gasps for breath, pinkish tears falling to the ground, mixing with the rain. Her life had been nothing more than a parade of misfortune. She had been born noble, married a Count and lived in a grand castle, and for a time, her life had been perfect. Now misuse, tragedy, the selfish actions of others, and her own hasty decisions had left her with nothing, without even a fresh dress to change into.

With a long, whimpering sigh, she released herself from the shackles of her physical form again, relishing the freedom and obscurity of her vaporous incarnation. It was the only way to feel clean again after invading such a dark and hateful space, the only way to escape the crushing weight in her chest. She cast herself thin, wispy and faint on the wind, rolling with the current of the storm until she could no longer stand the cold. Finally relenting, she slipped into her room through the open window. She collected herself, but left her clothes in a soggy pile on the floor. A nearly spent candle shone dimly on the small table, the only light in the room. She had purposely left it burning, although she did not need the light to see in the dark. The room did not seem quite so empty then, even if it was just the meager glow of a small candle. She crawled into bed, completely wrapping herself in the linens, drying her hair. It was still hours before daylight but she welcomed sleep early. From her cocoon, she yearned for metamorphosis, to live as a new creature, free from the heartache of the past. Begin again.

***

28 November 1899- I have done that which brought me to Amsterdam. The old man is dead, by my hand but not by my bite. I would not taste a single drop of his foul blood. I thought I would be relieved, that a great burden would be lifted from me by his death but my heart is still heavy. So much has been done but there is still so much to do. I will travel to England, since I am certain now that Harker was Stoker's informant. It is only logical. Mrs. Harker is credited in his book with collecting the journal entries and such into a chronological work. I imagine there is some grain of truth to this, since so much of the book is based on actualities.

If I recall correctly, Vlad bought property in London. By rights, this should be mine. I think I will call on the good solicitor soon, see if he remembers me. Perhaps I will also pay Mr. Stoker a visit, to congratulate his achievement. Harker is first and then Stoker, if time and worry permit. Harker is the whole purpose of my visit to England and I cannot endanger that by making a pest of myself in London and risk Stoker informing Harker of my approach. As tempting as it is, I will pass this first opportunity by and stay my course.

Chapter Sixteen

Jonathan Harker rubbed his eyes, stretching them wide against fatigue, determined to finish reviewing the handful of documents that were stretched across his desk. The weary December sun had long given up on him, having set hours earlier. Mina sat across the spare bedroom that had been converted into Jonathan's home office in a comfortable armchair studying a passage from Psalms, enjoying the modern electric lamplight and the last hours of the evening. Young Quincey was early to bed and early to rise, a good student and obedient son, older than his ten years.

A soft knock at the door alarmed them both, nearly causing Mina to leap from her seat. She placed her hand against her chest to calm her racing heart as Jonathan passed her on his way to the door.

"This just arrived for you Mr. Harker, urgent delivery." Mary the housekeeper informed, handing him a package.

"Thank you, Mary," he replied. She nodded and slipped away. Jonathan closed the door and returned to his desk.

After neatly stacking the papers to the side, he inspected the package. Having no return address, he carefully opened one side and peered inside. It contained several small books, old, weathered, some nearly falling apart, and a sealed envelope. Intrigued and hoping to discover the identity of the sender, Jonathan opened the letter and pushed his reading glasses up on his nose before reading.

March 15, 1897

Friend Jonathan,

If you are reading this, then it would be that I have passed into the sweet hereafter. I apologize for the shock I am sure this must cause you, and to poor Madam Mina. Forgive me, friend Jonathan and dearest Mina, but there is something that I must confess, lest I be denied entry by Saint Peter. I reveal this with great shame, the burden of which I have felt heavy in my heart every day and I must confess it, not to a priest but no less a man of God.

Friend Jonathan, I implore you to forgive the weakness of this old man but that night in Transylvania I faltered...

The letter continued, but Jonathan was unable to grasp its full meaning, unable to see through the haze of shock that blurred his vision. He could feel his heartbeat throbbing on the side of his neck, his breathing quick and tight. Mina watched him cautiously, recognizing the symptoms of raw and unsympathetic panic washing over him.

I beg you forgive me friend Jonathan and dearest Madam Mina. I was indeed a fool, but my failure has haunted my days and nights since that night and I do not wish to carry the burden into death. I pray now that you will forgive me then, when it is time that you should receive this letter. Pray pity upon the soul of a weak old man, as I have prayed for a blessed life for you both and young Quincey every day of my Earthly life and will, if it does please our good Lord, look upon you protectively from Heaven until it is that we should be reunited there.

"Your friend"
Van Helsing

Jonathan took off his glasses, closed them with trembling hands, and placed them in his shirt pocket. He took a handkerchief and wiped his eyes, trying in vain to hide the depth of his emotions from his attentive wife.

"Jonathan, what is it?" she whispered, having left her chair to stand by him at his desk, her hand on his shoulder.

He looked up to her and swallowed hard, and then cleared his throat. "Mina dear, I do not know how to tell you this." He took her hands in his and kissed the top of each. He looked older, due to the worry on his face and his silvery hair, having long lost its color early to stress and burden. "Abraham Van Helsing has passed away. It would appear that two years ago he arranged this to be delivered upon his death."

"Oh, Jonathan!" she gasped and pulled her husband close, nearly falling upon his shoulders as she wept. He urged her to stand and walk to the sofa on the opposite side of the room and sat with her there. Her face buried in his shoulder, he held her close, knowing she felt such gratitude to the doctor.

They both knew that without Dr. Van Helsing's intervention, she would have succumbed to the dark whispers of the Count and been added to his dark coven of brides. Jonathan shuddered inwardly and pulled her closer, stroking her arm with his thumb as he held it.

"Considering his age and a life of hard work, I knew it would be soon, but the last time we spoke he seemed so strong, so full of life. I do not think my mind ever fully accepted that one day he would die, that he was just a man that could die. He gave us so much."

"He was a great man, a champion for good," he agreed, resting his cheek atop her head. "We were fortunate to have known such a man."

"Quincey..." Mina whispered, covering her mouth in realized shock. "How will we ever explain to Quincey? He will be heartbroken."

Jonathan thought for a moment of his son's namesake, the friend they had lost. So much effort and loss had been given Mina's behalf. "He will understand just as we must understand. A man so great as

179

Abraham Van Helsing, so loved by God, must finally be given opportunity to have his reward. If ever a man should be blessed, it would be him."

"Well said, Jonathan. We will speak to Quincey tomorrow after breakfast. I do not think I could bear to tell him tonight, even if he was still awake," Mina whispered through her tears.

"It is good he is asleep. It gives us a little time to nurse our own hearts. We will explain as best we can tomorrow and when we can explain no more with logic, we will hold him and tell him the rest with love," Jonathan said, gently kissing the top of her head. He closed his eyes and bit his lip, knowing that neither Quincey nor Mina would know the whole truth enclosed in that letter. He would keep his mentor's secret and pray for the rest of his life that Van Helsing's weakness would not become the tragic ending of his fairytale life. He would pray that the Dracula's widow stayed in the shadows and everyone could continue to believe that their hero was victorious.

***

Jonathan Harker's Journal

4 December- The great man, Abraham Van Helsing is dead. The light of the world is dimmer for its loss and the Harker household will most certainly mourn his death. Mina retired early, tired with grief and sick with emotion. Little Quincey was already asleep, thankfully. It will give me time to think of how to best tell him. His little heart will be broken, its first such injury, for Van Helsing was like family to us all, but to Quincey, he was a like a grandfather or dearest uncle. However broken my heart may be, my grief is somewhat overshadowed with the dread knowledge held in my late mentor's letter. For the love of all that is holy, does this foul woman still live? I had rested well over the years with the knowledge that the Count and his ilk had been blotted from the

face of God's good Earth. I have slept well and rarely would the memories of those horrible days come back to haunt me or Mina. If this damned creature does yet live, she has been quiet in her hunting. My trained senses have not detected any sign of her in print, wire, or by word of mouth. So for now at least, I believe I will bear this burden of knowledge in silence and spare poor Mina the worry and my departed friend further shame. I will hide these journals, just as the great man did himself. Rest thee well dear doctor, to you I owe all that I hold dear.

***

Diary of Countess Valeria Karajan- Dracula

15 December 1899- I have booked passage to England from Amsterdam aboard a comfortable ship, which should be departing shortly with the tide and arrive tomorrow afternoon, exactly as I need it to. I could have made the sail shorter, as well as my overland travel, if I had instead departed from Calais to Dover, but I dare not traveling back into France without informing Lamond, and I am not about to do that. I am certain he would accompany me if I asked him, but I am still unsure how much of his motivations toward me are his own or out of some loyalty he feels to me as his creator. I have felt the control of another on my life for centuries and I will not exploit him. If I should somehow fail, after what I already done, then I was not worthy to carry out this task. Then he would certainly be free of my influence, if he is not already.

As pleasant a city as Amsterdam, even in the depth of winter, I am happy to be away from it. Van Helsing was quite the local celebrity, a starring role in Stoker's novel, so being found dead in his office under the most unusual circumstances has stirred up the entire city. Speculation to his cause of death has been wide and varied, including

181

everything from poisoning, to an aneurism, to witchcraft. Surprisingly, death by vampire has not even been offered as a possibility.

***

The winter sun set early over Paris, filling Lamond with the power of the night just as the electric lights began to reinvigorate the city. Valeria had been gone from Paris for nearly three months, effectively putting his afterlife on hold. He had only imagined what life outside her proximity would be like, how he would be changed. Months ago her absence would have been a license to behave in any manner he pleased with whomever he wanted, but now it seemed more like holding his breath than anything else, waiting for her return. After months together, moments of intense closeness and honesty, he yearned desperately to be back in the glow of his softly burning star.

The light of the first stars began to punch pinpricks out of the night's dark canopy. It was the lightly glowing stars that reminded him of Valeria, not the garish or bold. The gentle flicker of a blue hot star, quivering in the distant background, its deceivingly cool exterior disguising its molten hot heart, was Valeria. He looked toward the North, the direction of her destination, counted the stars and rubbed the space between his brows with his fingertips to alleviate the pressure. Something important had happened, in Amsterdam he supposed, something that had affected Valeria so strongly he had felt it through their bond, resonating like the strings of a guitar across the miles. He could only imagine that she had succeeded in killing Van Helsing, as he could not comprehend any other outcome. His mind could not process the thought that he could have slain her instead, that her light no longer shone. He wished she had allowed him to follow her, and had considered using the vibration of their connection to track her down, but he knew how crafty she could be. If she chose to avoid him, she would be able to do so despite his best efforts or intentions, assuming he could even cross the French border. As much as he wanted to help her, as intensely as he desired to save her, to love her, he knew she had to first save herself.

The return of dry thirst in his throat reminded Lamond it had been several days since he had fed. He had kept his encounters with others to a businesslike relationship, withdraws as needed. The scent of human women, which had first lured him like nectar to a pollinating bee, was no longer so desirable. He knew then for an undeniable fact, no other woman on the face of the earth could ever compare to Valeria. No other star in a thousand years of night skies would ever shine so bravely, so beautifully, or captivate him like she had. He could no longer see the light of any other star. More than just a star, she had become his sun, the object which his world now revolved.

***

18 December 1899- Arrived in Exeter this morning just before dawn, and after my nap I decided to explore the city a bit. It is simply lovely, even in the dead of winter. A fresh snow had encapsulated the world in white, slowed the pace of life. It looked as though each building had been accented with white cosmetics, lying on every possible edge. The cathedral, mentioned in Stoker's book, is quite simply stunning. It is the gem of the city, but not the only beauty. The clock tower is quite impressive, but it reminds me of Brasov, which reminds me of Emil, which sours its beauty in my eyes, but ever so slightly. It is like seeing a flower and remembering the funeral of a loved one which it graced. One can still appreciate the beauty, but no longer can gaze upon it the same way.

I do not know what to expect from Harker, aside from shock. I wonder how the solicitor in him will react when he sees that I have sought him out to do business, to lay claim to property. As Vlad's, or should I say Count de Ville's widow, the four properties he purchased in London should be mine, assuming this information is accurate. I do not know how foolish he will allow his bravery to make him. Supposedly he is the man who actually took Vlad's life, again as stated by Stoker. After all this time, after he has made a life with his wife and son, I would hate for my hand to be forced. He was only protecting that which he loved, that which was his. I do not fault him for this, but I am not so prideful that I will not admit, to these pages at least, that looking upon the face of my husband's killer will break my heart, just as seeing Ilona's killer did. Vlad loved me, I know this. He loved Ilona and Fleur as well, in his way. He just loved everything else more, especially himself.

I am tempted again by the sweet whisper of intoxication, not just of blood, but of wine as well. Now that I know it is possible to do so, I am surprised how many times since I have considered giving in to the warm, forgetful comfort that can come from the combination of blood and wine. I could all but taste it that night in Amsterdam and I would have surely sought out both if I could have mustered the strength to pull myself from the bed. I cannot allow myself to be weak, especially not now, but I am weary of being strong. It is as if the meaning of my name is a curse. It is though it mocks me and I will never find anything but heartache, nothing but reasons to endure, to be strong.

Lamond's words echo in my mind, his fear that I will allow this pain to swallow me. I feel as though I am in the midst of a dark, churning ocean and my neck is scarcely above the surface. Wave after wave threatens to hold me down, to make me sink. I sometimes wonder how terrible it would be, to just give in and rest. I cannot entertain these thoughts for very long before my face breaks the surface and I gasp again for breath, for life. I hope, nay, I pray that I do not give in. I know there is much rough water ahead of me, jagged rocks, howling winds, but I may have finally found an island of refuge in my handsome Parisian.

***

Wearing the most stylish dress she could acquire before leaving Amsterdam, Valeria gazed at the residence of Jonathan and Wilhelmina Harker from the dry and warmth of the horse drawn coach. Reluctantly, she stepped onto the frozen street and the coach quickly left, clopping into the snow covered distance to find the next fare. Finding him had been easy enough. Stoker stated that Harker had been made partner before his employer, Peter Hawkins, died and had been made quite wealthy. After a short visit to the offices of Hawkins and Harker, posing as the widow of a former client, Count de Ville, and the careful deployment of charm and batted lashes, she had walked away with an address to the Harker residence. It stood in an upscale, beautiful neighborhood, just as she had suspected it would.

Valeria had gathered from her conversation at the office of Hawkins and Harker that Jonathan often chose to work from his home. His failing health was blamed, having taken a turn for the worse in recent years. He was prone to bouts of weakness which left him bound to his bed for weeks at a time. They offered no mention of Stoker's book or how much, if any, compensation he might have received from its success. Regardless, it seemed he had paid a hefty price for his wealthy life. His new found celebrity status had not agreed with him as well as it had Dr. Van Helsing. Instead his nervous condition had suffered greatly from the stressful ordeal in Transylvania and with the unwelcome attention brought upon his family by Stoker's book. Where Van Helsing had thrived in the spotlight, Harker had withered and withdrawn.

The street in front of the Harker home was covered with at least four inches of snow, deeper in some areas. Valeria frowned, thinking of the dirt and slush that was soaking into the hem of her skirt, coat and boots, but she could lay them out to dry later after concluding her business. She smiled when she noticed the bank of snow that had been piled against the gate surrounding the property, pushing it open a few inches. She eased the gate open a little further and tiptoed atop the crusted slush

185

and up the sidewalk, which had been freshly scraped and salted, toward the inviting home. At the door, she tapped the brass doorknocker and waited for response. After waiting a reasonable amount of time with no response, she tapped the knocker against the strike plate again, but with a little more force.

Finally the door opened. "Harker residence, ma'am, can I help you?" a young boy around the age of ten asked. She immediately recognized his likeness to Jonathan, dark hair and the contours of his face. Quincey.

"Yes. I am here to speak with Mr. Jonathan Harker regarding matters of business," she responded, giving no indication that she knew his name or the identity of his father. She could see he was making a great effort to be a proper adult and responded as though she had not noticed he was a child, exactly as he was hoping she would. He nodded his head in agreement and opened the door for her.

"Yes ma'am." He led her toward a drawing room and offered her a seat. "Your coat please." Valeria obliged him and he accepted it carefully, noting the wet hem.

"Thank you, sir," she responded, wondering if she would ever see it again. Her exits were often hasty and had cost her many coats, hats, and parasols over the years.

"I will inform Mr. Harker you have arrived." The young gentleman walked away, seeming quite pleased with his performance and reception.

Valeria smiled, entertained by young Harker's heartfelt attempt at adulthood. She remembered Emil, how he had behaved so similarly on the rare occasioned when they would venture from their cabin and associate with other humans. He wanted to handle the business, wanted to be the man of the house, long before he had the understanding of how to strike a deal or recognize a sham. He would become so frustrated when she had to speak over him, override his authority in front of others that he would fume for hours afterwards. Valeria smiled again, and then promptly pushed Emil from her mind. She took the morning paper from the table and began to read, hoping to keep her nostalgia at bay until she could occupy her mind with the business at hand.

She had not finished reading the first page when Harker suddenly appeared in the doorway, obviously having just readied himself for proper business. Although he was perfectly dressed, freshly shaven and every hair in place, he was slightly winded, his face and neck still bearing the slightest sheen of moisture and she could smell the scent of his shaving soap and freshly applied cologne.

"I apologize for the delay ma'am, I was not expecting..." He stopped, frozen in his tracks and thoughts. His hand was mostly outstretched to shake hers, but would move no further, his words stuck in his throat. He had recognized her. She could see the Adam's apple in his throat struggling to release his voice, his eyes wide and unblinking. She stood appropriately and nodded her head, a muted bow, and took his unresponsive hand and shook it. She sat back down and waited for shock to release him. He looked to the chair across the table from hers and leaned to grab it by the arm, almost pulling himself toward it, unable to take his eyes from her for more than an instant.

"It is I who should apologize, Mr. Harker, for calling unannounced." She smiled pleasantly, playing the same game with the father as she had with his son, pretending not to realize his condition.

He looked at her, squinting for a moment before taking his glasses from his breast pocket of his vest. He put them on with visibly shaking hands. The color had mostly drained from his face, leaving his complexion to nearly match his prematurely white hair. "Wh... why are you here? Why now?" He finally sputtered out, staring desperately to convince himself that his eyes were not deceiving him.

"Well it is not for the same reason you last visited my home, I can tell you that," she replied with searing sarcasm.

"Quincey!" he gasped and looked around the room wildly for his son, without leaving the chair.

"Your son is fine, Mr. Harker. He does you proud. You and your wife have brought him up well. How is your wife? Better than your friend, Dr. Van Helsing I hope."

Harker swallowed hard and loosened his tie slightly. "M...M...Mina, Mina is well. Thank you. Van Helsing is... Dr Van Helsing is dead."

"Yes. I am aware of his passing. His death was unfortunately necessary, as was much the situation with my husband. Your wife need not know of our business or my visit today, unless you prefer otherwise."

"Mina is not here. She went into town this morning. I am out of my medication." Harker blinked, his head twitched slightly, as if he was a robot that was unable to understand its last command. "You...you killed Van Helsing."

"Yes. He was a murdering bastard, killed my lovely Ilona and Fleur in cold blood. He got what was coming to him, Mr. Harker, just like my Vlad got what was coming to him that day in Transylvania. You were protecting your wife, nothing more." Valeria's mind conjured a vision of what Vlad must had looked like the moment before Quincey Morris plunged the knife into his heart and Harker severed his head from his neck. She rubbed her eyes and then nervously checked her upswept hair, something to do with her hands to calm herself. "But that is in the past. As I said, I come today on business."

"Business?"

"Yes Mr. Harker, business. You are still a solicitor, are you not?"

"Yes of course but..."

"And while under the employment of my late husband, you purchased several properties for him in London, correct?"

"Yes..."

"Correct me if I am wrong, but as his widow, I am entitled to these properties. By law, they are mine, yes?"

"Well... yes. Under normal circumstances the deceased man's property would be passed along to his next of kin, firstly his wife or children, but…" Harker squirmed uncomfortably in his chair, loosening his tie further. "Those properties have already been sold."

"Sold?" Valeria questioned, leaning in toward him.

"When no next of kin of Count de Ville came forward to claim the properties, the estate passed to the Crown by Bona Vacantia and the proceeds went into the Treasury," he explained nervously, sweat beading across his forehead. "Van Helsing said you were dead, that he had…that he had killed you with the others. I had no idea you were alive until earlier this month, when I received his letter and package."

"A package? What kind of package did he send you, Jonathan?" she inquired, her interest instantly shifting away from the properties.

"Please… let me get it for you. It should be yours." He cautiously stood and walked out of the room backwards slowly before turning and running further into the house when out of sight. He quickly returned with his forehead and collar further dampened with sweat. He handed her a parcel, still partially covered in the wrapping it had been mailed in. She looked inside and could see an opened envelope inside and several books. She took one from the parcel, a small volume bound in dyed blue leather. She opened it and found that it was Ilona's neat, elegant script adorned the yellowed pages.

"It is Ilona's journal," she whispered breathlessly, carefully closing the book before holding it close to her chest. She could faintly detect her touch on the pages, the weedy floral scent of the lavender sprig she often used as a page marker still lingered. For a moment she closed her eyes and forgot the purpose of her visit, surrounded by Ilona's faint, gentle presence.

"That is everything. I have kept nothing. I apologize for the confusion with the properties, but it is quite out of my hands." Valeria could tell that he was hoping to rush her out and knew at any moment he could revoke his son's invitation and force her onto the street.

"Does anyone else have a copy of these journals, Bram Stoker perhaps?" Valeria asked quickly before he remembered his ability to evict her from his home. "I would be willing to bet you a earning a nice

189

little sum from selling my family's secrets. Was he your first buyer or just the highest bidder?"

"I… I do not know…" Jonathan babbled.

"Do *not* lie to me Harker; you are terrible at it," Valeria said, agitation highlighting her words.

"It was not Mr. Harker, ma'am. It was me," a quiet, elderly female voice with a strong Cockney accent broke into their conversation, shattering in the room like a wine glass breaking upon the floor. An older woman wearing the traditional black and white dress of a housekeeper stood in the doorway, tall and slender, her hands clasped in front of her. Her head hung low on her chest, as though she did not wish to see who was in the room. "I'm sorry to be listening in on your business, but when I walked past this room, I felt a chill off this one and I knew I had to confess. If I had not got my dress tail wet outside with the snow and had to change, I would have never have let this one in. Poor Quincey answered the door, trying to be helpful."

"Why, Mary?" Harker gasped.

Valeria could see that he had not suspected such treason from their trusted employee, that he was wounded by the betrayal.

"I know you always suspected Mrs. Harker, and I wish I had the courage to tell you before now, but you must believe me when I say it was nothing personal, sir. I saw that file Mrs. Harker had typed up and with all the talk I had overheard, it all sounded so interesting. I thought someone, a playwright type or an author might pay nice for such a thing so I wrote out a copy of most of it, little bit at a time."

"Have we not always looked after you, Mary, paid you a fair wage?" Harker questioned, hoping to understand her motives.

"Yes, of course, Mr. Harker. You and Mrs. Harker have always been kind and fair with me, and tending to Quincey has been nothing but joy. But times are changing, Mr. Harker. Not much work left for housekeepers, especially not old ones like myself." Mary's shame would not allow her to lift her head. She quickly swiped tears away from her face and sniffed. "I just thought it would be nice not to be a burden on my children when I get too old to be of service, that I might be able to leave a little bit behind to them and my grandchildren, make life a little easier for them."

Valeria sat silent, baffled by the housekeeper's revelation. A woman she had not even considered, a name mentioned only once in Stoker's entire novel, had been the downfall of her relationship with Emil, not Harker. All the energy she had spent hating him for exposing her most painful secrets to the world had been misguided.

"Oh Mary, do you realize what you have done? What she has done because that book was published?" Harker spoke out, pointing at Valeria. His condemnation took her off guard, almost insulted her, but she said nothing, let the scene play out uninterrupted to see what else she could learn from it. "She is here because of you! She could have killed Quincey, all of us, just like she did Van Helsing because of that damn book!"

"I thought he would change the names and places, Mr. Harker! I could not believe my eyes when I saw yours and Mrs. Harker's names on the pages, and little Quincey too." Mary broke into sobs, her frail body wracked pitifully. Valeria felt a wave of pity swell up inside her heart for her. "I never meant to put anyone in danger, please believe me!"

"I would have found you anyway, Harker. I didn't need that book to track you down," Valeria broke in, surprised she was coming to the rescue of the one who had unintentionally brought her so much grief. "You came to my home first, remember?"

Harker turned to Valeria and straightened his tie, wiped sweat from his brow. She knew he had finally remembered his wild card and was preparing to play it. "Mrs. Dracula... or Mrs. de Ville, whichever it is you prefer to be called, I am afraid I can be of no further assistance to you and..."

Valeria carefully cut him short, rising to her feet with her hand held before her to stop his words before he spoke them. "I understand, Mr. Harker. I thank you for the package and your time." She quickly walked toward the door to let herself out, her invitation still intact. She passed a woman in a thick coat and hat at the entry way, brushing against her in a rush to leave before Harker could say anything else. "Excuse me, ma'am," she said politely to the lady of the house, purposely avoiding eye contact.

"Jonathan, who was that woman?" Mina Harker asked as she dusted the snow from her hat, watching Valeria disappear into the swirling white of the returning foul weather. She rubbed her arms to warm herself, as though she had caught a greater chill from touching Valeria than she had from the frigid weather, an inner chill.

"Oh...just a woman seeking advice after the death of her husband is all," he answered vaguely after an extended pause. He could not pull his eyes away from the direction Valeria had disappeared into, as though he was stuck in a daze.

Mina looked at him curiously. She took her husband by the arm and pulled him back from the doorway, which was being swept with snow from the blustering wind, and closed the door. "Will she be back?"

Finally Jonathan was able to focus and he looked at her earnestly and wrung his hands to warm them, suddenly aware of the cold. "I do not believe so."

***

19 December 1899- I visited with Harker earlier today, only to find it a total waste of my time and that I soiled my nice dress and shoes in the slushy, dirty snow for nothing. The houses Vlad bought have already been claimed by the Crown and with it any money that could have been mine. I didn't necessarily need the money. I have always been able to get what I need. More than anything, I wanted them because they were his. Even though we were married for centuries, I do not have a single possession of his, not one memento of our life together. I have been forced to uproot and resettle so many times that it is difficult to hold on to anything for very long. Most precious to me,

and most certainly worth the trip, was getting our diaries and journals back after all this time. Van Helsing had certainly spent a great deal of time studying and traveling, as I do not even know where he found them all or if there are more still unaccounted for. I cannot wait to read them, even though I cannot help but feel that I am betraying Ilona and Fleur by doing so. To have something of Ilona's, something that was dear to her in my hands again is such a joy. I hear her tender voice in my mind as if she is sitting beside me, though I have only read a few pages of one journal. It will be interesting to see what was going on in Fleur's mind as well, to read what she never revealed. I am sure she will have a few choice words about me! I hope they do not hold my prying against me, especially Ilona. It will be bittersweet to be so close to her again, to read her most private thoughts, and yet be so very far from her. It will wound me, I am certain of it, but it is something I cannot resist, despite the pain, like a moth to a flame. I can almost feel her energy on the pages with my fingertips. I can certainly detect her scent. I do not think there will be a day, no matter how long my life may be, that I do not think of her, miss her, and love her. Gentle Ilona, you certainly bewitched me.

It was interesting, and perhaps also worth the trip and my forgotten coat, to discover it was not Harker or his wife that sacrificed my story to Stoker, but their housekeeper. It played out like a bad detective novel, a weak plot unraveling to reveal the surprise villain. But perhaps I left Exeter with something more precious than money, an open invitation to the Harker residence should I ever need to return, thanks to young Quincey. However, I do not foresee needing to return to Exeter or have any further dealings with Harker. It is too risky. Making myself a nuisance would only result in being hunted by slayers or some other zealot who would kill me to save me, since he is now a celebrity if he likes it or not. Now I am off to London. I go to find Stoker and make certain there will be no sequels to this damn book that has caused me so much grief, salted my wounds. He will have to find a new muse. From there, I do not know. Perhaps I will return to Paris and see how Lamond has fared in my absence, see if he meant the sweet words he promised before I left.

***

The office door of the late Dr. Abraham Van Helsing opened slowly, creaking as it moved across the floor like an old man's bones. It had been nearly a month since the professor's death and despite the thorough cleaning, the room still smelled of blood. Arminus and his two associates walked cautiously, their long white coats nearly brushing the overlapping Persian rugs. They fanned out across the room as silent as sailing ships, careful not to disturb anything. He had brought his gifted and capable protégés, Tobias and Vincent, to assist in the investigation. Each was fully aware of the importance of their visit and would dare not touch a single object. He would have preferred to inspect the scene of his former colleague's death sooner, ideally while the corpse was still on the floor, but that would have been impossible. Travel from Budapest to Amsterdam in the dead of winter could still be challenging, even with the conveniences of modern transportation.

Arminus departed with his cohorts as soon as he received news of Van Helsing's death, a letter sent posthumously to his own office at the University of Budapest. Quite some time had passed, but to his well trained, scholarly eye, he was certain to find at least a shred of evidence that the investigators had overlooked. His hands hidden beneath the bleached wool coat, Arminus froze in the center of the room and silently searched with his eyes, crawling over every surface to find that which did not belong to his fastidious colleague. Tobias and Vincent followed suit, using each of their senses to the height of their training, hoping to catch a whiff of the faint vapor of past events.

For five minutes the men stood motionless, silent, waiting, listening, and desperately hoping to channel the memory of room. Secrets had soaked into the oak flooring and paneling, into the woolen rugs, and silk upholstery, recorded upon objects conceived of nature like a phonograph. He walked to Van Helsing's desk and sat down in the well worn chair, placing his hands on the marble desktop. There was something in the room that did not belong, something out of place, a splinter under the surface. He searched the room with his eyes from the perspective of the desk once more for the clue he needed, Tobias and Vincent stood silent and motionless as statues. The wind blew through the branches of the tree just beyond the window, flickering and diffusing the morning sunlight before it passed through the panes of glass. A glimmer of highlighted brass caught Arminus' eye from just beneath the sofa, on the fringe of the light's reach. He walked toward the sofa, bent and plucked his prize from beneath the furniture, a powder pink parasol with a ruffled trim and a shiny brass ferrule.

"She was here." Arminus spoke with authority, presenting his find to his associates. He lifted the parasol to his nose and inhaled deeply. "Abraham's fears were realized and my suspicions were true. The fair one killed Abraham. I am certain of it and since she was so polite as to leave behind something belonging to her, finding her will be a simple matter."

***

20 December 1899- London, the world's largest city. I have only been here a few hours and I already want to leave. The air is filled with so much smoke from the multitude of industrial smokestacks that it has created a grey blanket that nearly blocks the clear sky entirely and literally chokes it inhabitants to death, as if the outbreaks of cholera and other diseases were not enough to concern them. Noisy automobiles fill the streets, electric wires crisscross overhead, and there are so many pedestrians milling about at any one time that it is nary impossible to avoid being bumped into, or being pushed into someone by another. Horse drawn carriage work busily alongside the commotion, adding their girth and smell to the cacophony of the city. A part of me wonders

195

why Vlad was attracted to this city, what drew him here. It is so different that his beloved Transylvania, but I assume it is safe to say that Vlad enjoyed variety in his life. The over-populous of the city would allow someone like Vlad, or myself, to hide in plain sight. There are plenty of people from which to feed and plenty of places to safely hide away, especially when considering he had owned at least four residences around the city. I can understand the reasons behind living in a metropolis like London, but as to why he chose this city and not another is a question I will most likely never be able to answer.

The harbor is crowded, the boroughs are crowded, the streets are crowded, but the pubs are crowded above all, but at least I have found a comfortable place to rest. I have forgone my habit of lodging in the poor neighborhoods of a city and have chosen instead a bit of luxury. The newly opened Savoy Hotel is as comfortable and beautiful as anyone could expect. My room is wired for electricity, as is the entire expanse of the building. It even has the accommodation of a private washroom, with running hot and cold water. I soaked in a hot bath for over an hour upon arriving, reheating the water as soon as it started to cool. My God, it was fantastic! I forgot about feeding, about Van Helsing, Harker, Stoker, everything, and was content to wrap myself up in the comfortable bed linens, as warm as a boiled fish! I wish Lamond was here to experience this. If he is able to leave Paris, as I hope he is able, I will bring him here to experience the luxury for himself. I catch myself thinking of him, wishing he was here more than I ever imagined I would. I do not know what to make of it.

Soon I will meet Stoker, if for no other reason than to scare him senseless. But until then I will be comfortable, read from one of Ilona's diaries, and live the good life for a while. Tomorrow I will have another hot bath.

***

22 December 1899- I have been fortunate to locate the Lyceum Theater and identify the man himself, Bram Stoker. I have searched for three men and have found each of them without much difficulty since none of them have had any reason to hide. None of them had the notion of repercussions for their actions, responsibilities to taken. I am curious to see how Stoker responds to an adoring fan, unknown to him to be his greatest critic. His book has not been the greatest success with this tight laced, repressed society. Fortunately for him, he has had better success as the theater manager and assistant to its brightest star, Henry Irving. It will be interesting to see how he reacts on both accounts, to the admirer of his work and to a character in his story which has come to life.

***

Holding a bouquet of roses and her copy of *Dracula*, Valeria stepped from the carriage and stood before the towering columns of the Lyceum Theater. With the main entrances closed to the public, Valeria resorted to the service entrance. The stage doors to the theater were busy with people coming and going, busily preparing for the next performance. A young stagehand graciously held the door open for her, seeing her hands full. He nodded and smiled, looking over his shoulder to lengthen his glance of her. She smiled with tight lips, but playfully winked, a lighthearted moment to brighten her mood.

Only minutes after arriving at the Lyceum, Valeria nearly collided with the author himself.

"Excuse me, Mr. Stoker?" she asked quietly. He immediately halted and raised his head from the handful of papers he was studiously reading.

"Yes, of course," he responded quickly and courteously, accepting the bouquet of roses almost automatically, as if it was a familiar task.

"Mr. Irving will be most appreciative of these. I will place them in his dressing room. Is there a card?"

"Mr. Stoker, those are for you," she whispered, diminishing with faux shyness. She sheepishly presented him with a copy of his book, a first edition. "May I have your autograph, please?"

He was astonished and for a moment unsure of how to respond. She could see that he was not accustomed to such attention for his work, overshadowed by the owner and star of the Lyceum, Henry Irving. "Certainly." He took the book and his polished exterior cracked ever so slightly with a hint of pride, like a fine china teacup with hairline, feathery cracks in its glaze that did not compromise its integrity. "May I ask your name, ma'am?"

"Valeria Karajan- Dracula," she answered, allowing her full, dangerously beautiful smile to grace her lips. She could feel the edges of her fangs lightly scratch her bottom lip. "I have traveled very far to meet you, Mr. Stoker, from Transylvania. I have already met Mr. Harker and Dr. Van Helsing. Your book was like a map, showing me where to find them, and you."

She watched the color fade from the author's face and he took a single step back. Like a gazelle afraid to run for risk of inciting a chase, he stared his predator in the eyes, frozen in place. He looked about the entrance of the theater for anyone else who might bear witness, but found himself to be suddenly, and strangely, alone. "I thought it was fiction, all of it, nothing more than a story except for the names of a few individuals to give it some authenticity."

"Mr. Stoker, I find that with most fiction, there is a kernel of truth. However you have done such a superb job crafting this story that I doubt any readers will ever suspect it was based on the deaths of an actual family, of my family." Valeria's eyes turned steely, the illusion of timidity long gone. She could hear his heartbeat racing, smell adrenaline mixing in his blood. "But you had no way of knowing that did you? Who could ever believe this fantastic story could be based on true events?" His respiration quickened, chest visibly rising and falling as she took a step closer to him.

The entrance became flooded with workers once again, a brief reprieve from their tense conversation. She watched the people pass around them uncomfortably, Stoker's bouquet of roses trembling in his hand like a white flag of surrender. The room emptied and left them alone again. He nervously moistened his lips, pursing them tight. She could see that he wanted their meeting to end, but was too afraid to flee. She held her hand out to take back her book.

"Thank you speaking with me, Mr. Stoker. I appreciate your time. I felt you would want to know there was another side to this story. I do not anticipate reading a sequel." She led him to the response she wanted to hear, placing her book under her arm.

"No, ma'am."

"Thank you." She shook his hand with an ungloved hand, just so he could feel the unnatural chill of her touch. "I am looking forward to reading more of your work, just not about me." She smiled again and winked, taking her leave through the main entrance doors and disappearing into the numerous pedestrians filling the streets despite the numbing cold.

The author stood in disbelief, rubbing the coldness lingering on his hand from her touch. He had just experienced a dreamlike opportunity, an impossible moment for a creator of fiction, but meeting this character in the flesh was an experience he hoped to never repeat. He looked at the bouquet, an obviously expensive purchase, and retrieved the card nestled amongst the stems, scratching a drop of blood from the side of his finger on a thorn in the process. The message was simple.

"Best Wishes"
> \- Mrs. Dracula

***

22 December 1899- Later- I have met with Stoker, although now I am uncertain as to why I felt it so very necessary to meet him. I had no intention of harming him. I assume I wanted the satisfaction of knowing that he understood the words he had written were not without their weight, that much had been risked and lost as a result. I have lost my nephew, nay I have lost my son, and he has lost yet another mother. Van Helsing is dead because his book told me his name and where to look for him, finally sending him to answer to his beloved creator for murdering in His name. Harker had to face his demons once more and look upon me as more than a simple monster or insatiable fiend, but as a woman, a widow. His housekeeper had to confess to her sneaking and sticky fingers. I wanted to see Stoker, but more than anything I wanted him to see me. I wanted him to know Valeria, not simply "the fair one" as I was reduced to in his novel, but as a woman who had been hurt, broken, and nearly died during the course of events he fictionalized. I wanted to ensure that he would write no sequels at the expense of my unfortunate family. I wanted him to know I was watching him and that he, like the others, was all too easy to find.

***

24 December 1899- Inclement weather and the Christmas holiday have delayed my leaving England. I had anticipated being home by now, home being Paris with Lamond. I believe I will send a telegraph to our address. Even if it is delivered late, Lamond will know that he was in my thoughts and that I plan to return to Paris soon. No doubt he is concerned for my safety. Perhaps I will send one to Emil as well, assuming he still lives at our former address. While I have not formally observed the holiday for many, many years, I feel this Christmas would be a proper time to look beyond the shortcomings of my past and look

forward to the future, not only for myself, but also for those who are dear to me.

Christmas was always a dark, cold day when Vlad was away. I would hate to think that I might be causing Lamond the same feelings, although I do not imagine he cares for me the same way I desperately loved Vlad. I do not know if it is love that motivates him, infatuation, or some dark bond between master and creation that neither of us fully understands, but if it is the latter, I hope to one day undo that bond and give him back his free thinking mind. I hope he will care for me still, since I cannot help but believe a least a measure of my feelings for him are genuine, that I can begin to love again. Even though Emil may wish not to think of me, he will know that I am thinking of him, that he is loved more than he can understand, especially now. My nephew, who became my son that is now absent from me, the child I fearfully loved that has become a man. He became a part of my heart, the part that is now broken by my exile from his life. I hope Ilona has been looking down protectively upon him these months, looking after him since I am no longer allowed to do so. I hope she is not angry with me. Although I failed Emil as a mother, I hope she understands that I did my very best, that I tried to raise him in a manner she would approve of. I hope she knows she is remembered this Christmas. I hope the angels of Heaven will whisper in her ear and tell her she still is loved, that her absence has not diminished her place in my heart. I do not believe Vlad to be in the same Heaven as Ilona, yet I cannot bear the thought of him suffering for all eternity in Hell, though many, even I on occasion, have said he deserved it. For all the pain he caused me, for all the heartbreak, I hope Vlad knows he is still loved as well. I do not think I will ever be able to stop loving him, not completely, if nothing else in a fond memory. And I hope, if nothing else, Fleur knows that I no longer wish to kill her.

I have made great effort to move beyond my past, beyond the ties to my last name, but now I know that regardless of how hard I try to make the past right, it never will be. There is nothing left now, nothing more I can do for anyone or myself other than move on and try to live again. Try to begin again.

Part Six:
Lost

Chapter Seventeen

27 December 1899- I have fed cautiously, discreetly, and I know I have done nothing to raise suspicion or draw attention to my presence in London, but I cannot help but feel the weight of eyes upon me. Just like I could feel Lamond lurking about in the shadows, I know without doubt I am being watched, but I do not know why or by whom. Perhaps I should have taken Lamond's advice and left well enough alone, left Van Helsing, Harker, and Stoker alone, or at least allowed him to come with me. My mind tells me that this is impossible, that I am only imagining this warning in my heart. But I have grown to trust my heart and I know with all too much certainty that many things that should be impossible are very possible indeed. I wish to warn Lamond, to tell him to flee Paris, but I still have no way of knowing if he can leave the city, or what would happen to him if he attempted to and was unable. What if the eyes that are bearing down on me have no knowledge of Lamond and my warning inadvertently revealed him? What if I lead them back to Paris? What about Emil? Would those who hunt vampires also seek a human, just because of their associations?

I remember that night in Transylvania when Ilona, Fleur, and I looked out across the frozen countryside and knew that we would be facing men who wanted to kill us. We knew that we may not survive the night. We knew no one was coming to save us. I feel that fear returning, spreading from my heart, tightening my chest, and up my neck to strangle me. But this time I am alone, wishing I was not, like I have so many times on this journey through my past. My mind tells me

205

I am tired, sick with emotion from all that I have done and remembered, but my heart knows the truth. It is not my imagination! Someone is watching me and for all my otherworldly powers and abilities, I cannot see them but my heart whispers to me, warns me, and tells me to be ready.

***

29 December 1899- I have waited as long as I can. I am thirsty and I will not risk the journals I received from Harker or this one in which I am writing to fall into the hands of another. My thoughts will be my own. Ilona's and Fleur's thoughts will be safe, private. I can feel the circle around me closing. I am a fly on a web and I can feel the vibrations of the spider as he approaches. I will face this enemy as I always have, as best and as brave as I can. I do not wish to die, yet I know I may not survive, certainly not unscathed. I feel darkness, a negative energy about me, emanating from my stalker, but different than the very ordinary human slayers that took Fleur in Palermo. I will fight as I always do. I will be strong. If these unseen hunters think they have found in me an easy prize, then they will be very disappointed. I am sick of hiding. I am going to find them.

-Valeria

***

Valeria closed the cover to her journal and placed the pen back in the inkwell. She felt the variations of the cover with her fingertips, the microscopic flaws and blemishes. She tried to stay focused on the task at hand, which was protecting the journals, and not dwell on why she had chosen to sign the last entry, but she understood her motivation. It was her farewell in the event she did not survive her encounter, her

206

farewell to Lamond. He was the only one she could entrust the journals to, her only friend left in the world. She took her journal and slid it in with the others, carefully reclosing the package and pasting her Paris address over Harker's before retying the string.

She quietly closed the door to her hotel room and walked down the hall, her head held high. None of her other belonging mattered, only the journals. She held onto the package tightly, listening with the depth of her ability and scanning every corner and alcove as she descended the stairs toward the lobby, wishing it was sunset instead of mid-day. She walked up to the front desk, hoping she did not appear as unsettled as she felt.

"Could you please add this to your mail?" she asked politely, placing enough money on the top of it to cover the postage and trouble.

"Of course, ma'am, and will you be staying another night?" the polished attendant asked, placing the parcel under the counter.

"Unfortunately not, I am leaving London today," she replied, wrapping her scarf around her neck and tucking it down inside her new coat.

"We hope you will return to the Savoy Hotel, ma'am. Your stay has been   a   pleasure."

"I certainly will and thank you." She carefully smiled. She pulled her hat low on her head and tied it securely below her ear. The sun could not set quickly enough.

Feeling a measure of relief, knowing the parcel would soon be on its way to Lamond, Valeria took to the street. She needed to find a meal, needed to have a provider in mind and a plan to facilitate her drink at the break of sunset. but for the time being, she needed the security of a crowded, public space. She hoped whoever haunted her footsteps would be too cautious to attempt anything in public, in front of mortals. She could only speculate as to why she could not sense the ominous darkness that had threatened to consume her for the last three nights during daylight hours. It was as though whoever sought her needed to

207

wait until the night invigorated her with the fullness of her powers to hone in on her, or until the night gave them their own abilities. Regardless, it was the only advantage she had.

Every person she passed was scanned with a skeptical eye. She had to be careful not to look too closely, to not stare too long. Just as a deer knows when it is being watched by a carefully hidden wolf in the woods, humans could sense when they were being eyed by a predator. If she allowed her gaze to settle on a human for too long, they could detect something was off with her. It could make humans uncomfortable, cause them to want to distance themselves and bring unwanted attention upon her. She mulled the events of the nights immediately following her meeting with Stoker over and over in her mind, hoping to remember a misstep, something she had done to draw her predator out. Had they followed her from Exeter, or perhaps even Amsterdam? She sighed and refocused her eyes, realizing she had been absent from the present, lost in thought. Nothing stood out in her memory, nothing to hint to why she had suddenly become so interesting. She hoped it was not connected to Paris. She had allowed herself to become carefree, intoxicated, and even taken into the custody of the morgue while she and Lamond slumbered away in their deathlike sleep. Of all the places to draw the attention of such an enemy, it would be logical to think it had occurred in Paris as she frolicked about with her lover, but she was certain she had only been followed for a few days. What was she missing? Where was the line connecting her to those who she knew, without doubt, meant her ill will?

She stepped inside the first tavern she could find with an open door and took a seat at the table closest to the fireplace, listening to the grit and peanut shells crushing under her shoes. The patrons were so inactive she was unable to tell if they had started drinking early or if they simply had not made it home from the previous night. Regardless, she was not alone and she knew many more patrons would be arriving soon. She rubbed her eyes, irritated by the dry heat of the fireplace, and waited. At least daylight hours were shorter during winter, but that meant she had less time to prepare. The circle was closing, her hunter was getting closer.

***

Valeria looked behind her and flashed an alluring smile at the tipsy man struggling to follow her down the dimly lit hallway. He lost his balance and briefly leaned against the wall to steady himself. She laughed playfully, beckoning him to continue before backtracking and taking his hand to lead him quicker. The night was approaching, only a few minutes of daylight remained, and with it would come the prying eyes of her stalkers. Rounding a corner, Valeria pressed her unwitting accomplice's back against the wall. Seconds ticked by, the anxious quickening of the night began to crawl beneath her skin like static. As her chosen patron fumbled with the button on his pants, she kissed the side of his neck and detected a hint of sawdust residue on his skin. Tick, tick, tick, the night teased her with its approach, taking its time. The man struggled to make sense of the multiple layers of her coat, dress, and petticoat. Finally the sun released its hold on the day and the night overwhelmed her in a wash of sensation, enlivening her body from the crown of her head to the soles of her feet with a rush of energy that was almost as good as sex. For a moment she could not feel the man's hands on her body or smell the sawdust on his skin and clothes, fully absorbed within the embrace of the night. A quiet sigh escaped her lips, close enough to his ear to make him shiver. She grabbed a handful of his peppery black hair, yanked his head sideways and, sank her teeth into the side of his neck. She struck with practiced precision, quick as a snake's bite.

Invigorating blood hastily sped from her punctures, fright accelerating his heartbeat and giving haste to the flow. He began to struggle, attempting to escape his diminutive attacker, but was unable to break free of her grasp, unable to push away from the wall. He attempted to scream out, but she quickly released his hair and covered his mouth instead, bracing his head against the wall securely. In the fading light, her pursuers were gravitating closer to her with each drink. The chemical cocktail in her saliva mixed in her victim's bloodstream, working in tandem with the alcohol to reduce his strength and coordination, preventing his wounds from clotting, and tranquilizing him into submission. He collapsed to the floor and she followed him down, sitting across his legs to support the weight of his upper body as she finished her meal. The tavern girl who passed them thought little of the scene, accustomed to witnessing inebriated patrons hiding away in darkened corners in to engage in clumsy, brazen sexual acts.

Valeria released her victim when he was sufficiently sedated and her blood reserves were replenished, propping him against the wall to sleep off his encounter. He would wake in a few hours with a headache, exhausted, and a bruised neck, but otherwise unharmed. She stood, wiped her mouth with her hand, and straightened her clothes and hat. In his drunken stupor, her unlucky friend and never managed to navigate the button on his own pants, much less the complicated trapping of her attire. With only a moment's grooming, her appearance was perfected. She quietly walked toward the main hall of the tavern, resisting the temptation to fade into mist and slip through a crack outside. The weight of those searching for her now pressed down upon her like she was deep underwater and she could not afford to use her abilities for anything less than an emergency, knowing each time signaled to them like a lighthouse.

Outside the tavern, the streetlights were beginning to flicker into life. Only a handful of London's sturdiest or most destitute citizens dared to face the cold, their dark silhouettes backlit against the fading light, hunched and slow moving like ghosts looking for a place to haunt. Valeria could hear their heartbeats, smell their blood from a block away, but she still could not discern the locations of her stalkers. She could feel them but could not see them, sense them but unable to pin them down. They were everywhere and nowhere. Somehow they were hidden from her senses and she began to understand with sickening dread that her pursuers had some sort of supernatural abilities at their disposal as well, cloaking them. She quickly intermingled with the heartbeats and scents of the street denizens, standing behind a handful of people with ragged clothes and dirty, malnourished faces who were burning pallets and scraps of broken furniture in the back of an alley. She hoped the shield of humanity would be enough to confuse them until she could get a better understanding of what faced her and equally hoped that her nice clothes and appearance of stature did not start a commotion amongst those she was counting on to hide her. She needed a moment to think, to settle her thoughts and nerves long enough to devise a plan. At least in the alley she had a means of escape, unlike confines of a tavern or other building.

Valeria felt like she was in a straight jacket, her choices limited. The wind blew strong, funneling down upon them by the narrow alley. The humans shuffled nearer to the fire, huddling closer to each other to brace themselves against the cold. The adults pushed the children closest to the warmth and used their own frail bodies to block the wind as best they could. A little girl with tangled hair caught Valeria's eye, her face reddened and chapped by the cold. Her mother struggled to keep her shaggy shawl wrapped around her shoulders. Behind her, the freezing homeless pressed in tighter, urging her closer to the meager fire. The little girl watched her quietly, silently. She was no older than Emil had been the night Vlad brought him to the castle, breathless and cold. Tempting his wives to feed from a helpless child was calloused and heartless, one of his lowest acts. It would have stripped them of their last shreds of their humanity, tightened the grip on the chains held tightly by their husband-master, reduced them to dependant animals.

Valeria shuddered at the thought, sick at her stomach. She looked away from the little girl and searched with all her senses for those who sought her. The sourness in her stomach lingered and she felt as though she was going to vomit. She closed her eyes and hoped it would soothe her belly if she let them rest. The people around the fire shuffled, bumping against her on all sides, their odors and filth rubbing off on her. The scents saturating her nose were quickly becoming unbearable and she knew she would not be able to linger there for much longer. She rubbed her face and held her handkerchief to her nose. Suddenly she felt a strong, viselike hand on her arm and the strength rushed out of her body, pouring out of her like a broken hourglass. Her eyes popped open and she realized that she could not hear the heartbeat of the man at the end of that hand, his fingers interlaced with a rosary. He stared at her with steely eyes, grey like dirty ice, cold and emotionless. Her stomach dropped and she feverishly struggled against his grip but was unable to pull away.

"Let me go!" she shouted, eyes wide with fear. She looked to the freezing huddle, desperately hoping that someone would help her. They pretended not to notice, looked away, and hung their heads low, unwilling to add to their own suffering by interfering in the problems of others. The mother turned her young daughter's face away, covered her eyes with her hand. Again, Valeria implored them for help. "Help me! Please!"

Beneath the ragged robes of a homeless beggar, the man took a silver crucifix on a chain from the pocket of his white wool coat. Another man, wearing a similar disguise, appeared from behind her, grabbed her other arm and together the first wrapped the chain, deceivingly thin, around both her wrists. Together they pushed and pulled her away from the crowd and into the engulfing darkness just beyond the reach of the fire. The first attacker locked his arms around her, reducing her strength to less than that of a healthy human woman of similar size. The second, a broad shouldered man with a bushy red beard and shaved head, slid silver knuckles engraved with a cross onto his right hand and cracked the joints of his fingers.

"Hello, Countess," he said smugly. Valeria spit in his face. His face twisted in disgusted rage. He drew back and swung. The impact against the side of her head was concussive, her eyes rolled back and her world went black before she hit the ground.

***

Valeria awoke to the distinct rocking pattern and the rhythmic clack of a train as its wheels crossed the ties of the track. The light stung her eyes and she tasted blood in her mouth, her own blood. She turned her head and felt searing pain, like a red-hot poker had been stabbed into her skull. She instinctively lifted her hand to caress her injury, but found her wrists to still be bound with the silver crucifix chain, the skin beneath burned and peeling. She gently touched the source of the throbbing pain and found a large knot protruding from her scalp, busted and scabbed, her hair matted with dried blood. Squinting against the glaring sunlight, her eyes felt filmy as she tried to see where she was. She was surrounded by steel bars, a jail cell. No. It was a cage, the bars fashioned in such a manner that a crucifix was patterned into all four sides. She was being transported like a circus animal, a caged oddity, a hunter's trophy.

She struggled to recall the events that had led to her situation. She remembered a little girl in her mother's arms, cold, eyes dark like spent embers. A strong man with the crucifix grabbed her arm, another man with a silver cross on his knuckles. Darkness. How long had she been unconscious? She knew she was traveling on a train, but she was certain, during fleeting moments of semi-lucidity, she had felt herself crossing water. Once she had even smelled the salt of seawater. Had she crossed back onto the mainland of Europe? When had she boarded a train and where was it going was? She had far too many questions for her aching head to process and not nearly enough answers to quiet it.

The numerous blessed objects surrounding her made it almost impossible to estimate how long she had been unconscious and had stripped her of her accelerated regenerative abilities. Judging by the

213

burn in her throat and the wound on her head that was still fresh and oozing, she assumed it had been two possibly three days since she fed from the man in the tavern but the holy items aggravated her perception. The blood she had taken in the night of her attack would do little for her in their presence. Her body would continue to crave nourishment but would gain nothing from it. It would flow through her like a sieve. Eventually, if she did not find a way to escape, little would remain of the woman she once was. She would become a ghoul, consumed by endless hunger, immobilized by the blasphemed symbols of a loving God. The cage would become her eternity, decorated by symbols of sacrifice and forgiveness but used by those consumed by hate as weapons, an immortal reduced to undying, loved to death.

***

Lamond shredded the brown paper wrapping on the package he had just received, addressed from London. It must be from Valeria. When the telegraph arrived at Chirstmas, he had been most pleasantly surprised. Not only was she healthy and well, she was thinking of him and had intentions of returning to Paris soon, returning to him. Now three weeks later, a weighty package arrived at their door. He felt almost childlike anticipation, beyond surprised that she had taken the time to get him a gift. He pulled the box open and removed the contents. Books, some of which were so old they threatened to fall apart in his hands. He gingerly opened one of the oldest books and read the handwritten pages. He discovered it was not an ordinary book, but the diary of Ilona Szilagyi, Vlad's second wife, Valeria's beloved. The next book was much newer, a journal written by Fleur Boucher, the third wife. If Valeria was planning to return to Paris, why would she mail these most precious possessions? He could not imagine a reason she would let them out of her sight, much less risk losing them in transit. He saw a letter sticking out of the pages of the newest book in the collection, one that he immediately recognized. It was the journal that

Valeria was currently keeping. Puzzled, he took the letter and left the book open to the page it had marked.

Lamond,

I hope that this letter and package finds you safe and well. For reasons that I still do not understand, I am being followed. Hunted. I could not risk these journals being taken from me, so I have entrusted them to you, my one and only friend. I beg you to keep them safe. Be on your guard. I have no way of knowing if those who hunt me will come for you next. I am sorry Lamond, if you are in danger. It seems all I have done is wrong you. I pray for your safety and ask you to do the same for me. Until we meet again...

Fondly,

Valeria

Lamond set the letter aside and picked up her latest journal, reading the page she had marked. It was her last entry. He puffed, sending his long shaggy bangs blowing around his eyes. He hopped to his feet, sending the chair sliding back and began to pace. Still holding the journal, he swung his arm as if he was going to throw it, or perhaps striking at the unseen foe that Valeria mentioned. He felt helpless, juvenile, only able to set on the side and wonder what was happening to her. He gently tossed the journal to the table and continue to pace like a caged lion.

"Damn it, Valeria!" he said aloud in frustration, rubbing the back of his neck as it began to tighten. "Why do you have to do everything alone?"

He wished she could hear him, that he could hear her response. She was too proud to ask for help, but he understood what she was thinking when she wrote her last entry, what was unseen between the lines. She was in over her head, swallowed up, just like he was afraid she would become. She was asking for help. She was apologizing. She was telling him goodbye.

Chapter Eighteen

Valeria faded in and out of consciousness, trapped within the confines of her holy cage. It had been nearly three weeks since the abduction. The benefits of the blood she had taken that night had long since passed, her thirst accelerated by the presence of the holy crucifix. She woke briefly, roused by the scraping squeal of the cage bottom sliding across a floor. A thick, black canvas tarp prevented her from seeing her location, as well as blocking anyone from viewing the sickly, captive woman held inside. She could sense it was daylight hours, even though the night shed little compassion upon her in her current condition.

The entire world seemed to move around her at an accelerated rate. She thought of Lamond and hoped with all her heart that her package had reached him safely. Mounting nausea boiled in her stomach from the overwhelming odor of garlic and vertigo induced by the crucifixes that surrounded her. She regretted refusing Lamond's offer to travel with her, but regretted dragging him into her life and problems even more.

She drifted out of consciousness and fell into a dream, a memory of the first night she saw Lamond. He was having a rollicking good time with his friends, eating and drinking, enjoying life. It was his energy, his fullness of life, the warmth of his sun kissed skin and golden hair that had drawn her to him. She had stolen a measure of that energy when she took his blood, stole his life. She had never intended to know him beyond a single night of lust and glorious gluttony, but against all

217

odds, he fought back from the shadow of death. He had become so much more to her, a friend, a lover, a tenuous tether to a happier future. She focused every ounce of her strength on Lamond, as if she was hoping to span the distance between them with a psychic bridge. Her eyes closed and though she wept, her parched eyes unable to produce tears.

"Find me, Lamond," she whispered so quietly no mortal ears would hear her speak her supplication. "Please."

The black shroud was yanked from her cage and blinding bright sunlight poured into her eyes. She huddled into the corner of the cage farthest from the door and tried to discern her situation through the glare. Powerless to defend herself, the bald man from the alley with the thick red beard opened the door and ducked into the cage. He forced a heavy rope between her teeth, like a bit for a horse, and tied it behind her head. He yanked her to her feet by her bound wrists, her shambling legs scarcely able to support her, and led her from the cage. Though her vision was distorted, she attempted to store an image of her surroundings. The cage she had been transported in stood in the small courtyard, which held a curious fountain. Comprised of three stacked, concentric basins, the water fell like rain from the smallest to the largest before collecting in the pool beneath, but atop the highest level burned a small flame, unhindered by the water. The building's exterior was nondescript, gray stone wall with the only opening was the door she was being led toward.

"Please Countess, come in," he teased, permitting her to cross the threshold. They passed several closed doors as she trudged down the dimly lit hallway, which eventually led to a downward spiraling staircase. Like she was descending into Sheol, she could feel the damp coolness of the underground level, smell the earthen floor. Finally arriving at their destination, she was lead toward one of three empty cells, each equipped with barred doors that were constructed to feature a crucifix. Opening the door, he pushed her inside and quickly slammed the bars closed. Again she pushed herself into the furthest corner like a frightened animal. Dust from the hay that lined the floor floated in the dim torchlight, like flecks of snow. "I hope you find the accommodations to your liking, Countess." He chuckled smugly before walking away.

Valeria snarled quietly, disgusted as she watched him walk away. She wondered how cocky he would be when she tore his throat out and licked his blood from her lips. Scalding hot emotions wrapped around her heart like razor sharp talons, rage, hate, malice. She thought her revenge had exorcised those demons with Van Helsing's death, but they had returned with searing intensity. For every ounce of despise she felt for her abductors, she knew they were but a symptom of the true disease. There was a greater foe that had yet to make an introduction, but she could sense their presence within the structure. Fire and water, surrounded by enemies, long suffering at a quiet smolder, she would not be snuffed out easily.

***

Valeria could feel death setting in on her as she ponderously picked her shedding hair from her coat, one strand at a time. She had to feed soon or she would become nothing more than a dust filled mummy. The faint, nearly undetectable shiver of day changing into night rippled through her body and just as she had expected, the man behind her confinement was unable to keep his distance.

She watched him approach through her eyelashes, pretending to be unaware of his presence. He wore a white coat like her two abductors, who followed closely behind him. Embroidered in silver thread, large crucifixes stretched across their shoulders and down the length of the garment, front and back. The pungent odor of garlic surrounded them and she could see long bowie knives secured to their belts, wooden stakes secured on the opposite side. The proximity of additional blessed objects, the garlic stench, and roiling testosterone made her nauseous.

She swallowed hard against the rising bile, raising her head to recognize them.

"Countess Valeria Dracula, it is an honor to finally meet you, face to face. I am Kristof Arminus. I am a scholar of antiquities, a collector of ancient knowledge, and a historian of the esoteric. You already met my associates, Tobias and Vincent," he said, motioning first to the bearded thug and then the other. "I have lost a great colleague and dear friend because of you. It was quite a mess you made in Amsterdam, but it made it quite simple for us to find you," he stated everything quite cordially and waited, as if he was expecting her to lift her hand so he could kiss the top of it.

Although he behaved as though they were being formally introduced, Valeria was not swayed by his charade. She turned her head away and feigned interest, but all the while her mind was on fire. She had heard the name before. Arminus. She studied his face in his mind. Middle aged, olive skin, long black hair liberally mixed with white and pulled back so tightly he would appear bald in silhouette, clean shaven, average height and weight. In street clothing, his appearance would be mostly unremarkable, aside from his nontraditional hairstyle. He referred to Van Helsing as a friend and spoke with an accent she recognized, Ilona's accent. Arminus was Hungarian. Finally the information clicked in her blood starved mind. Had she been in better health, the connection would have been instantaneous. Arminus of Budapest University, the scholar Van Helsing consults in Stoker's book.

"Van Helsing was a murdering bastard that deserved to die." She looked back to him again and stared into his eyes to better assess the threat. It was time to test his patience. "I spit on his body when I was done with him. I had a drop of his blood on my tongue. I would rather feed from a dog."

Arminus stiffened, twisting his head quickly to relieve the tension between his vertebrae with an audible series cracks and pops. Clearly she had gotten under his skin, but he kept his composure. "That is no way for a lady to speak, Countess."

"What do you want, Arminus? If you wanted me dead, you would have had your cronies behind you to do that while we were in London." She gouged, smirking at his henchmen. "You got me, fair and square, outwitted me with your fancy little coats. Why?"

"Because I needed a new volume in my library and you, my dear Countess, are a living memoir of the last four and a half centuries. We have many things to discuss about your peculiar nature." He informed with an arrogant smile, confirming her position as little more than an object to be studied.

"That is certainly unfortunate. My poor treatment by your goons has left me with a bit of a head injury, bruised my brain most likely," Valeria quipped, straightened her back. Her pride was still strong as she nursed the wound on the side of her head. "I can't remember a damn thing."

"That is unfortunate," Arminus responded, sticking his arm out to hold back the man he had called by the name Tobias. A stern glance was all that was necessary to reprimand and send him stomping off like a scolded child. Arminus remained calm, despite the web of sweat that covered his forehead and his reddened cheeks. "Luckily, I am also a man of science. If your memory fails to improve, I will simply have to dissect you to gain the answers I seek."

***

Trapped in the darkness of his sleeping mind, his body paralyzed by the morning sun, Lamond struggled against the suffocating black. He felt panicked, as if he could feel something approaching him so vast, so overpowering that he was helpless against it. It was there, darkness within the black, toying with him, biding its time. It would hold him hostage, just like the sun, until a moment before noon, and then it would engulf him. He wanted to move, run, crawl, float away like a wisp of fog, but he was powerless, less than mortal. Looking down at his body, he saw it was not his own, but that of a woman, someone he recognized. Valeria. Her body was bound from top to bottom with rough rope like a rick of kindling, arms pressed tightly against her sides. The darkness was heavier now, thicker, colder. He could feel it creeping up her legs, around her shoulders, over the crown of her head, like sinking in tar. Painfully slow, he sank deeper and deeper into the void, covering her hands, spilling over her thighs.

"Help me!" he screamed desperately with her voice. "Somebody please, help me!"

The thick as molasses darkness filled her ears, covered her throat and the rest of her body until only her face was visible. The black was filled by whispers, others that had been swallowed. They cried out in terror and pain, oblivious to anything but their own suffering.

"Oh God, no!" He heard her scream as the overwhelming void crept up to the corner of her eyes, just up to her nose. "Please! Lamond, help m…"

Her last cry was cut short by the blackness pouring into her mouth, down her throat. He could feel her gag, choke, and drown.

Lamond sat straight up in bed, coated in pink tinted sweat, screaming like he was being murdered. He hastily rubbed his face, swiping and scratching at the blackness from his dream. Finally he regained his composure and flopped back down upon the bed, sinking only in pillows. The sheets were damp and cold with sweat. He closed his eyes and rubbed them, still aware of his own accelerated heartbeat. He had begun the dream as himself, lost in the dark, but it ended with him inhabiting Valeria's body. He had experienced her emotions, felt her terror, and heard her calling out to him from a place he did not know. She was in trouble, without doubt. She was in desperate need of help, in more danger than he could even imagine simply because she was so readily asking for his assistance. She had no hope of helping herself or her pride would never allow her to ask anyone for help, not even him.

Lamond walked to the window and opened the drapes, leaning against the sash. Even the cool winter sun felt warm on his bare chest. He closed his eyes, filtering the pale light with his eyelids. His dream had addled him, chilled him to the core. He knew it was more than his misfiring brain trying to make sense of his longing to see Valeria again, his worry for her safety. It was a message, an insight to her situation. She was overwhelmed, overtaken, in danger.

"Hold on, Valeria," he said aloud, knowing it was impossible for her to hear him, but hoping against reason that she could somehow sense his words, sense his desire to find her. "I just need you to show me where you are."

***

The midday sun slowly loosened its grip on Valeria, although she did not wake as quickly as she normally would. Her blood starved brain functioned slower, saving resources whenever possible, drawing blood away from her extremities. Her legs and arms were drawn, her hair had mostly fallen away, and her lips had receded to expose her fangs. She could hear footsteps without heartbeats approaching.

"Hello, Countess, are you awake?" Arminius asked, walking without fear to the bars of the cage. His associates followed suit and stood on either side of him. Valeria held her calm, pretending not to hear his question or even acknowledge their presence, but she was more than aware of them. While their matching coats camouflaged their heartbeats from her, it did nothing to hide their scent. Their blood rushed just beneath the surface of their skin. A concentrated scent bloomed from one of them, the aroma of shaving soap with just a hint of blood drawn by a slip of the razor. Fiery thirst surged up her throat from her belly, urging her body to react. She fought back her impulse and remained motionless.

"Mr. Arminius asked you a question." One of the thugs, Vincent, walked around to the corner of the cage that she was huddled into. He reached his arm into the cage and smacked the back of her head. Valeria's eyes rolled dryly in their sockets, lips snarled.

"Vincent, no!" Arminius shouted. Vincent startled, and in the split second he looked up to address his warning, Valeria lunged.

Grabbing his wrist, she pulled his arm closer with every ounce of strength she had remaining. The bony fingers of a living corpse dug into his forearm and in the tender inside of his bicep. The thin chain that had bound her wrist fell from her. Her wrists had withered away from their bindings, enabling her to slip out. She bit into his wrist and tore away the flesh and sealed her mouth around the gory fountain that sprung forth. Her attack had been launched in the blink of an eye. Hot, life-giving blood poured down her throat like a funnel. Her emaciated body had forgone the reflex to swallow and simply allowed it gush down and absorb, soaking into her mouth, throat, stomach, lungs simultaneously.

Vincent screamed and struggled to free himself, bracing his foot against the bars and pulling. Arminius and Tobias raced toward him. The force of his struggle was dragging his flesh through her teeth, tearing and deepening as it went. She bit down harder, her fangs digging against the bone. Arminius dared to reach his hand in and push her head back but she buckled down and braced the entire weight of her body against his arm, glaring at him like a lioness protecting her prey. He quickly retracted before she had the opportunity to change targets.

"Help me, Arminius!" Vincent screamed. Tobias drew a knife from his belt, unmistakably silver, and drew back, aiming at Valeria's head.

"No!" Arminius shouted and yanked the knife from his hand. Instead he plunged the knife into Vincent's arm, inches away from her mouth. Vincent screamed in pain and shock, staring at the knife that had intersected his arm, its tip protruding from his flesh beneath.

Almost instantly, Valeria released him, sputtering and spitting out the last tainted mouthful. Vincent fell backwards, holding his arm and the knife above him, panic overwhelming him. Arminius took off his belt, calmly removed the sheaths and other equipment, and then cinched it around his associate's arm above the elbow.

Valeria walked to the other side of the cage and sat down to watch the show, feeling a sliver of life return to her. Like a sponge, she could feel her body filling back out, reconstituting itself from her meager meal, but she knew it was only temporary under the influence of the blessed décor. They would be even more cautious in the future and another opportunity would be difficult to come by.

Arminius left Vincent writhing on the floor distracted by his anguish. He returned shortly, carrying an axe at his side. He tapped Tobias on the shoulder and nodded. He dutifully agreed, taking a stake from his belt as they returned to Vincent.

"Don't fight, Vincent." Tobias said ruthlessly, jamming the stake between his teeth like a bit before he could respond. He stuck his knee into his associate's chest and secured his arm to the floor. Arminius stepped on his hand and drew the axe back over his shoulder like a lumberjack. Vincent's eyes grew large and he furiously shook his head in protest. Valeria could hear his teeth sinking into the wooden stake, his heart racing out of control.

Without hesitation, Arminius dropped the blade on his forearm, just below the elbow. The steel blade dug deep into the dirt floor of the subterranean lair. Vincent's body lifted off the ground as he howled in pain, the restricted blood still bubbling from his stump. He struggled violently for a moment, his entire body flopping as though he was being electrocuted. Finally he slumped, his head rolled to the side, the stake fell out of his mouth. He was unconscious.

"Tobias, a torch please," Arminius said, businesslike in his tone. Quickly he returned and handed it to his leader. He snuffed it out on the floor and then pushed the smoldering end against Vincent's wound several times until the bleeding stopped. "Please make him comfortable while I speak with our guest."

"Yes sir," Tobias answered. He locked his arms under Vincent's and pulled him away.

Valeria watched him drag his friend away, and looked back at the axe and the severed forearm briefly before looking to Arminius with a

225

lofty, unimpressed expression, challenging him with the twitch of her eyebrow.

"Well that was most unladylike, Countess," he responded. His calm tone scarcely able to hide his underlying rage, his hands still covered in blood.

"You abduct me, stick me in a cage and starve me like an animal, just to scold me about *my* manners?" Valeria responded, indignant and emboldened.

"An eye for an eye, a tooth for a tooth, is that how we should proceed?" he asked, his calm tainted by threat.

"Go to Hell," she spouted. "I'm not afraid of you."

"I could leave you in that cage, let you starve. I could throw fire in there with you, burn you alive, trapped. No way for you to escape." Arminius tried to make himself larger, threaten her.

"But you won't, will you? You spineless, son of whore, you won't do anything to me. Coward. You didn't even lift your hand to help them bring me in," Valeria responded smugly, saying anything she could think of to anger him. "You cut your man's arm off, but you didn't hurt me, because I am important to you. More important that your lackeys, obviously. He doesn't need both hands to keep you satisfied, does he?"

"You should hold your tongue, Countess, or you might just lose it." Arminius gritted his teeth, struggling to keep his composure.

Valeria licked the blood from her upper lip, suggestively slow, and defiantly flipped up her middle finger.

***

Valeria waited patiently throughout the night for her abductors, but as dawn began to whisper its approach, they had not returned. They were waiting for the coming of the dawn to suppress her, make her easier to deal with. The energy she had stolen from Vincent was slowly beginning to wear away, trickling away like a bucket with a slow leak, but she was still dangerous. She sighed loudly, shook her head. She had let her nerves get the better of her in London, gotten herself worked up, and they had gotten the upper hand on her because of it. But now she would see them coming, their only way to approach through the door of her cage. If either of them were foolish enough to approach her now, they would leave without their throat. But they were not foolish and she was running out of time.

Seconds ticked and Valeria could feel herself slowing down, like a windup toy at the end of its turn. She leaned back against the bars, her eyes closing despite her effort to keep them open. Like she was being blanketed by heavy snowfall, the weight of the dawn heaped thick upon her, soaked into her like dampness. If she had been well fed and not under the influence of the numerous blessed items around her, she would have been able to enlist her years of practice to keep her eyes open, retain some of her faculties. She would have still been frozen, nearly paralyzed by the death sleep, but able to see and hear. The dawn's curse was strong and she was diminished. She felt herself sink into the darkness, unable to keep it at bay any longer.

Like she was under the influence of a tranquilizer, Valeria could hear footsteps, muffled voices, sense motion around her. She felt hands being put on her, pulling her from the corner, removing her coat first, followed by her shoes, skirt, blouse, and corset, leaving only her undergarments. She felt her body being placed in a chair, cuffed at her ankles, wrists, and across her chest, like she was in an electric chair. Her consciousness slid back beneath the surface and she was engulfed by sleep.

***

Somewhere in the city, church bells chimed twelve o'clock. Arminius and Tobias stood looking down at Valeria, slumped in the chair, waiting. Less than a minute passed before Valeria woke with a start, instantly struggling against the confines of the chair.

"Welcome back to the land of the living, Countess," Arminius said, reminding her of her former title once again. It seemed to entertain him to remind her how far she had fallen, highlight her misery. "I want to apologize for your treatment. I detested putting you in that cage in the first place, as you said, like an animal. And while I cannot allow you to move freely about the premises, I hope you at least find this chair more pleasing."

"You could let me go, that would please me," Valeria chimed as Arminius pulled a stool in front of her and sat on it. Tobias stood beside him with his arms crossed behind his back, his long beard lying over his proud chest.

"Perhaps, but we have too much to discuss. As I mentioned before, this is why we brought you here. I do not wish to kill you, Valeria, only talk to you concerning your...condition."

"You could have talked to me in London. I would have even bought you a drink," she responded with clear distrust. "Why bring me to Budapest?"

"Clever girl." Arminius smiled, clearly impressed by her deduction. "Budapest is my home, and we had reason to believe you would be...less than cooperative. I seek knowledge, Valeria, knowledge that only you possess, since your husband is dead."

"What does Vlad have to do with this?" she snapped, unintentionally revealing he had struck a sensitive cord. Her patience with him was wearing thinner as the conversation stumbled along.

"He created you, did he not?"

"Why are you bothering to ask me a question you already know the answer to?" she spat, resenting his badgering.

Tobias shuffled uneasily from foot to foot, obviously unaccustomed to negotiation in place of action.

Arminius cleared his throat, adjusting his approach. "Of course, Count Dracula was not born a vampire. We know well from history he was first a man, a brave warrior for his people. But he was not simply

228

an arm for a sword. The power of his mind rivaled his accomplishments on the battlefield. But I assume you know this as well."

"Vlad loved his country more than anything, certainly more than me. There is nothing he would not have done to protect it."

"Is this how he gained entry into the Scholomance?" Arminius nearly leapt from his seat in anticipation. "Did he make some sort of deal for victory on the battlefield?"

"I don't know anything about a Scholomance," she answered honestly, yet flatly. She could tell he did not believe her. "I had never heard of it until I read that damn book of Stoker's. Why don't you go ask him?"

"Valeria, you do him no injustice in revealing this knowledge." He was almost begging her, leaning closer to her as if to bait the information from her with his earnestness.

"Piss off."

"You will not lose your abilities if you reveal this to me. You will not be changed or harmed in any way. I will let you go, right now, if you would only tell me the location of the Scholomance."

"I told you already, I don't know."

"A simple area in which to search, Valeria, that is all I need. Did he speak of the school's master, or of the fate of the tenth student? Was he the tenth student?" His voice rose in volume and intensity. "Is vampirism a curse placed upon the tenth student? Is this why it is believed they are chosen by the Devil as his due?"

"I do not know!" she shouted, ready to be stuffed back in the cage if it meant conversing with Arminius further.

"You must know!" he bellowed. His long hair was pulling out of its binding and beginning to string around his face, hot and damp with sweat. "He must have told you something!"

Valeria turned her head away from him, refusing to acknowledge his shouting with her attention.

"Tobias, would you light the lanterns please?" he asked calmly, choking down his anger as he smoothed his hair back into place. "I had

229

truly hoped it would not come to this, Countess. But I will have my answers, one way or another."

Tobias smiled smugly as he walked away, returning shortly with matches. Around her hung several lanterns, arranged in a circle of which she was placed in the middle. Tobias lifted the shield and lit the first one, which hung directly in front of her. He slid the shield back down and stepped back. Illuminated through the cutout in the lantern's shield, a blazing cross beamed onto her chest. Valeria pursed her lips, trying to hide the discomfort she was already feeling. Three more lanterns remained.

Part Seven:
The Unlikely Rescuer

Chapter Nineteen

Standing in a darkened room, Lamond was drawn to a large table in the middle of the room. He placed his hands on the rough tabletop and inspected the large map spread out on it. Starting in London and streaking across the breadth of Europe, was a single red line. He could smell the faint, metallic odor of dried blood. He followed the line to its finish, somewhere in Hungary. The final destination was hidden by a blot of blood that had dropped from the encrusted tip of dagger with an ivory handle. Lamond took the dagger and carefully scratched at the map to remove it. The city of Budapest was revealed. He laid the dagger down and felt a twinge of pain in his palm. Assuming he had somehow cut himself, he was surprised to see a cross branded into his flesh. Looking back at the dagger, he saw the intricately crafted silver inlay on the handle that he had somehow missed before.

Instantly becoming aware of a presence in the room, he saw Valeria standing in a doorway that he was certain had not been there before.

"Valeria!" he shouted, running to embrace her. She stood still as a statue, staring blankly ahead, arms at her sides. He released her and stepped back. She looked a mess, unlike anything he had ever seen from her before. What remained of her hair was matted and disheveled, her ragged clothing hung from her emaciated frame. Her face was gaunt, eyes sunken, skin grey. She could not see him, hear him, or feel him. She was nothing more than a sign, directing him further into the uncertainty beyond.

233

He walked down the cool stone hallways of the unfamiliar structure. He could smell the rich scent of the earthen floor being scuffed under his feet, see residue on the walls from torches and candles, and feel the smooth unevenness of the stonework on his fingertips. He did not know where he was going, but felt propelled forward. From darkened doorways, he would sometimes catch another glimpse of a signpost that was Valeria, silent and unblinking. The hallway curved and twisted, leading to stairs, and finally to a door coated in peeling red paint. He opened the door and his eyes were immediately stung by blinding white sunlight. As his nocturnal eyes struggled to refocus, he became aware of the smell of smoke, could taste it on his tongue.

In the center of the courtyard, a blaze was raging. The fire had been built high like a bonfire in what appeared to be a reflecting pool. The few inches of water that was present did not boil, despite the close proximity to the inferno. He squinted, his attention drawn to the center of the hungry fire. Trapped within the confines of stacked sticks and branches, he could see another effigy of Valeria. She stared at him, unflinching, either unaware or unable to react to the flames that encased her.

"Valeria! Valeria, wake up!" he screamed, desperately searching for a gap in the flames or the tender box that he could put his hands through, but the fire was too hot and the branches and boards were stacked tightly. He could feel the heat on his skin, irritating his eyes. He collapsed to his knees and cried, helpless to do anything to save the woman he loved. To his horror, he was unable to look away as her ragged dress suddenly combusted, her hair smoldering like dry straw. She did not blink, did not move as her skin began to blister and burn away. Lamond screamed. His chest ached like it would burst. He was too late. He had let her die.

For the second time, Lamond woke screaming at the stroke of noon. He slowly rolled to sit on the edge of the bed, the smooth hardwood flooring refreshingly cool beneath his feet. It was a relief to have the connection to the waking world, to be grounded to reality. He had dreamed of Valeria nearly every night since receiving the package of journals, but this had been the most terrifying of them all. He could feel his hands shake as he brushed his hair back from his face, his insides trembled. She felt so close to him, like she was looking over his shoulder, breathing on the back of his neck, yet he had never felt further from someone.

The image of Valeria wrapped in flames, allowing herself to burn, was stuck in his mind. He saw it every time he let his eyes to close. He forced himself to remember the entirety of the dream, beginning with the darkened room. He remembered the expansive table and the map. In his mind, he retraced the line that had been drawn from Paris to a city hidden by blood. Valeria's soulless eyes flashed before him, surrounded by flames. He shook his head, desperate to clear her image from his mind. Again he recalled the map, desperate to see the city beneath the dried blood. He rubbed his palm, remembering the burn from the silver cross in the handle. He searched his memory again, retracing his steps, country by country across Europe, until stopping in Hungary.

Budapest.

Somehow, across thousands of miles, she had answered his prayers and shown him where she was being held, but why had she been taken to Budapest? Why would anyone go to the trouble of transporting a dangerous and furious vampire across Europe? He deduced they were not slayers, or they would have simply disposed of her in London. No. Whoever had taken her had an agenda, a reason, which could buy him the time he needed to find her.

Lamond dropped his head, a feeling of defeat washed over him. His brief moment of elation was quickly tempered by the realization that she, much wiser and more powerful than he, had fallen victim to the very individuals he was now hoping to find. If she was unable to stand against them, how would he ever be successful? No. There was no way he could survive on his own. He needed help, someone to put the pieces into place, but whom? There was no one he could ask, no one he could

235

trust. As far as he knew, no one but himself knew she existed and aside from those who hunted them, no one who knew that vampires even existed, except one.

*****

A match was struck, flickering into burning life before floating in the darkness like a shooting star to rest on a waiting candle wick. Arminius gently puffed out the greedy little flame before it could reach his fingertips and lowered the shade on the lantern. A cross of light imprinted on Valeria's chest, her head dropped and shoulders slumped, still bound by the death sleep. Tobias lit the lantern directly behind her, before going to the one on her left, while Arminius attended the right. Vincent sulked outside the dim illumination of the lanterns, caressing his abbreviated left limb between his chest and right arm.

Arminius and Tobias stepped back and watched Valeria, waiting for her to wake. Impatiently Arminius consulted his pocket watch. At ten minutes after twelve, Valeria slowly lifted her head and tried to open her eyes, two minutes later than the day before. The lack of blood, numerous holy symbols, and abrading lanterns were without doubt taking their toll. Her perfect marble skin had been replaced by an ashen pallor and dark circles beneath her eyes, which has sunken back into their sockets. On her chest, back, and shoulders were etched the raw burns of the crosses that shone upon her from the lanterns.

For a week, they had watched the life drain away from her as she sat in the chair beneath the crosses. Like sand pouring from a cracked hourglass, Valeria was nearly spent, but Arminius still had not gained the answers he sought. He ventured closer and held a freshly cut clove of garlic beneath her nose like smelling salts. She recoiled as far as she could, her eyes widened and her face contorted with revulsion.

"Countess, can you hear me?" Arminius spoke in his calm, monotone voice. Valeria struggled to focus on him, her head wanting to collapse against her chest but the cross of light motivated her to keep her head up. Finally she locked eyes with him and waited for the endless string of questions to begin again. "Valeria, I only need a little information from you and this can all end. I will release you, I promise. Just tell me what I need to know."

"You won't let me go," Valeria whispered, her throat so dry it was difficult for her to vocalize. "You are going to kill me because I cannot tell you what you want to hear."

"You were closest to him of all his wives, his beloved. You were the only one who knew him while he was still human," Arminius began his routine of badgering. "Search your memories, Valeria. Go back across the centuries to the conversations you had with your husband after he returned from the Danube."

Valeria's eyes closed, her head nodded as she was being overtaken by sleep again, not due to her curse, but exhaustion. Tobias stepped up and slapped her sharply across the face. Arminius frowned at him, but did not scold him. Her head rolled back and slowly righted itself, her expression flat, as though in a trance.

"What did he say when he returned?" Arminius pleaded, leaning close to hear her fragile voice.

"He killed them all...even the children," Valeria whispered, her eyes rolling around of their own accord. "So many dead... can you hear their voices?"

"Is that what he asked you, if you could hear them?"

"No... Can *you* hear them, Arminius?" she whispered again, her lips nearly against his ear

"No. I cannot hear them, Valeria. What do they tell you?

"That you will be joining them... That I will kill you and then you can ask Vlad yourself." Valeria set her jaw and refused to sink within the darkness, not just yet. She straightened in her chair and stared them down, digging her fingernails into the wooden arms.

"Why do you mock me?" Arminius screamed, so close his nose nearly touched hers, finally broken by her stubbornness. "Just tell me

237

what I need to know! Where is the Scholomance? How did Count Dracula become a vampire? You will tell me, now!"

"Why do you think he told tell me?" she shouted back, calling up the last of her strength and courage for her last stand. "He never told me anything, never told any of us anything! For over four hundred years, he controlled my life, but never an answer, never a reason for being what I am. He just collected us, like objects, and pretended to love us only to abandon us. I have wished to know your answers a thousand times myself, but I do not. Only Vlad can tell you why he did the things he did, so you can kill me, or you can let me go. I do not care any longer."

Her remaining energy consumed, Valeria's chin fell against her chest, caring nothing for the light cross the burned the top of her head. Tobias approached her, and drew his hand to strike her again.

"No!" Arminius shouted. Tobias dropped his arm, unsure of what do since his only response had been taken from him. Vincent left the room, put off with his leader's patience. Arminius stepped back and looked at Valeria, perplexed. "Blow out the lanterns, Tobias. We are done for today."

***

Lamond woke at the strike of noon, the winter sun barely able to pierce the drapes of his sleeper car. He had dreamed of her again, the same dream for three days consecutively. It was as if they were both adrift in an endless ocean, in both width and depth. He was not aware of his own body, as he had been in dreams before, but only present in consciousness. He was looking down at Valeria as she sank further and further into the depths, her hand held overhead hoping someone would take it. The look of terror, of abandonment on her face was so intense, so sorrowful, that it stabbed his heart with a palpable pang. He did not take her hand, as he was only able to look and not interact, and slowly she drifted downward. Lost, absorbed into the darkness.

He rubbed his face with both hands and after a moment, he stood and shook the Parisian dust from his body, a precaution he had taken from reading Valeria's journals. Despite carefully sandwiching the soil between two layers of bedding, the gentle swaying of the train and restless slumber had resulted in waking the last two days a gritty mess. It was a minor inconvenience. Although she had seemed to overcome the need to slumber on the soil of her country, he had no way of knowing what would happen to him if he attempted it. It was simply a risk he was not willing to take at such a time.

By the itinerary, he knew he should only a couple hours outside of Brasov. His nerves began to scramble in his gut, increasing his thirst. Only the day before, he had passed through Hungary and left Budapest behind him. He had considered an early departure, gliding out a cracked window as a vapor on the wind, but he held firm to his plan. Even though he was a supernatural creature of the night, with strength far exceeding that of a mortal man and abilities that surpassed the imagination, he was afraid to attempt this rescue mission alone. He had pinned all his hope on Emil and hoped his plan was not in folly.

Lamond had just one day in Brasov to find and convince Emil to accompany him before leaving the next day for Budapest. He had made no plans for his return to Paris, leaving the house just as it stood. He had brought nothing with him, except for a single change of clothes for himself and Valeria, a small and tightly cinched bag of dirt from the garden, and the small package of journals, all carefully packed in a single overnight bag. It was optimistic thinking that he would be able to save her, but if he was successful, he knew her well enough to know she would appreciate his preparedness. A memory of her scent still lingered on her dress. Fading jasmine greeted him whenever he opened his bag, which he did often for no other reason. It gave him hope.

***

Finding a print shop belonging to a man named Mihai was easier than Lamond had anticipated, hindered only by his broken Romanian. The door to the shop was firmly closed against the winter cold, the windows fogged by the warmth inside. He anxiously stood outside and waited for an opportunity. When he saw a shadow pass the windows, he quickly grabbed the string and rang the doorbell. He shuffled from foot to foot, a thousand scenarios playing out in his mind. After a moment that seemed to last for hours, the door opened and released a gush of warm air onto the frozen street.

"Can I help you?" A man spoke, one who did not match the description of Emil in his mind.

Lamond paused, frozen. He pondered over what the man had said, hoping he understood him. He swallowed hard. "I need talk on Emil," Lamond said in his best, yet fractured, Romanian, thick with French accent.

The man studied him suspiciously. He rubbed his stubbly chin, nodded, and looked behind his shoulder. "Emil!" he called, motioning Lamond inside with a beckoning hand instead of words. Lamond walked cautiously into the shop, the smell of ink overwhelming his nostrils. The man he assumed to be Mihai, held his hand in front of him. Lamond froze in his tracks. "Stay here." Lamond nodded.

A few more anxious minutes passed and the young man he had only heard or read in story stood before him. Lamond's mind backpedaled for a second. Although he knew Emil was no longer a child, he had spent the entire waking hours of his trip to Brasov thinking of the many conversations he and Valeria had had concerning her godson, and the mental image he had created was far too young. This Emil was as tall as he, lean and lanky, but strong. His shirtsleeves were rolled up over his elbows, his apron and forearms stained with ink from the press. Sweat clumped his thick black hair against his forehead, his cheeks reddened from the frantic pace of his trade.

"I am Emil. Can I help you?" He introduced himself in fluent Romanian, much to Lamond's distress. He was only beginning to understand the language when Valeria left and had picked up a few additional words from reading through her journals. Ilona's Hungarian script had been a lost cause. Fleur's French journals had been greatly enlightening, portraying Valeria in a quite different light.

Lamond searched for the proper words, stuttering. "A place to talk?"

Emil nodded, Lamond followed.

Emil did not trust him. Lamond felt as though he could reach out and grab the tension between them. He was suspicious, could spot a vampire like none other. A shiver ran up his spine, what a slayer he could be. He prayed Emil never changed vocations. He followed him to a small area of the shop that was apparently used for storage where the noise was lessened and offered Lamond a seat on a stool. Emil chose to stand. He began to speak in a serious tone, one that let Lamond know he understood his nature and had no fear of him, but he spoke so quickly he could not follow.

Lamond searched for words, desperately inadequate for such important conversation. He wound his hands in his hair. "Français?"

Emil shook his head, disapprovingly.

"English?"

"Yes, I speak English," Emil answered, much to Lamond's relief. His English was sloppy, but much better than his Romanian. "And to repeat what I just told you, I know what you are, so don't bother trying to hide it. What do you want?"

"My name is Lamond Delaflote. I am a friend of your aunt," He stated carefully, unsure how Emil would react.

"That much I assumed." Emil bristled at the mention of her. "What business does a vampire have in my shop?"

"Emil, I believe... no... I know Valeria is in danger. She is being held somewhere in Budapest."

"If I may ask, how is it that you know this? My *Aunt* is quiet capable of taking care of herself."

Lamond considered the assortment of dreams, visions, emotions, and premonitions that had combined together to propel him to seek Emil's aid, but decided against revealing it to the skeptical young man just yet. "She was away on business and has not returned. I know she is in Budapest, where she had no plans of traveling. She was supposed to come back home to Paris."

"So that's it. You are the new man in Valeria's life and since she left you sitting back in Paris to go to Budapest, you automatically assume she is there against her will." Emil crossed his arms over his chest, rejecting Lamond's reasoning. "Go home, Monsieur Delaflote. Valeria can take care of herself. Good day."

Emil turned straightaway to leave, but Lamond reached out and grabbed his arm. Emil turned back with animosity, offended by his touch, disgusted by it. He yanked his wrist from Lamond's hand. "Keep your hands off me!" Emil shouted. "Valeria's business is her own, not mine. She is not my aunt, not anything to me anymore."

"You can discard her that easily? Valeria cared for you, kept you safe and warm your entire childhood, but now she is nothing to you?"

"I no longer consider your *kind* to be a part of my family," Emil spat, indignant, and started to leave once more.

"I know what happened to your mother." Lamond took the risk, regretting the words even before they finished slipping from his lips, but he had to stop him, think quickly before he rejected his invitation to the shop. "It is not Valeria's fault she died."

"How dare you speak of my mother, vampire!" Emil stomped close to him. Lamond could hear this heart pounding, his breath quick and hot like his temper. "I think it is time you should go."

Emil smiled victoriously, waiting for Lamond to be pushed from the shop just like Valeria had been ejected from their home, but he remained motionless.

"You did not invite me in, Mihai did. Your trick does not work on me, you little shit." Lamond smiled, hoping his plan worked.

"What did you call me?" Emil fumed, his forehead folded, hands trembling. He was so furious he wanted to punch him but he knew it would only hurt his own hand and would have no affect on him.

"You heard me, you spoiled little brat. I called you a little shit, le petit. Only a child would be so selfish," Lamond chided. Emil's face reddened, his eyes squinted narrow. He wanted to act out against Lamond more than he wanted to breathe but knew better. He knew Lamond could rip out his throat if he wished, regardless if the sun was up or set, before Mihai or anyone else could help him. "I never had a mother, but you were fortunate enough to have two, and an aunt who loves you like a mother. Yet you stand there and play the part of the victim, selfish, selfish boy."

Emil swallowed back his rage, gritted his teeth, and fumed. "Speak now or sit here until you rot, I do not care. But either way, in one minute, I am going back to work."

"Valeria is dying, somewhere in Budapest. I do not know who has taken her or why. All I know, without doubt, is I can feel a part of me dying as she dies and I fear she has little time left." Lamond had stopped gouging and now implored to Emil with the greatest sincerity. "I need you to help me find her, Emil, before it is too late. There is no one else who can help her."

Emil gritted his teeth. Lamond could hear he was holding his breath, struggling with himself. He obviously still loved Valeria, that much was evident, but his young pride was holding him back. "I apologize, Monsieur Delaflote, you have wasted your time. I cannot help you."

"Please!" Lamond begged, unashamed, as Emil walked away. "Please do not turn your back on her."

Emil did not turn around, but dropped his head shamefully. "I am sorry."

***

The distance from Mihai's warm shop to the house he had once shared with his aunt seemed to grow, stretched by the blustery winter wind. Emil pulled the collar of his coat high and his hat low, wishing he could hide from not only the wind but his conscience.

The wind reminded him of the cabin in the woods that had been their home for so many years. Valeria worked constantly to keep it insulated. She was always afraid he would catch a chill and get sick. He remembered so many nights waking to find her simply watching him sleep, but not the way a predator stares at prey. She was content and at peace, emotions that seemed to elude her the rest of her hours. Never, in all their years together, had he ever felt threatened by her. In fact it was the opposite. He slept soundly, knowing he was safe from any danger, the cub of the lioness. Now, if Lamond was to be believed, she was in danger. It was difficult for him to imagine, strong Valeria stricken weak and helpless.

Finally at home, the key turned in the frozen lock and he quickly went to build a fire. When Valeria lived there, the house was never cold. Several times he had come home to find she had made the house so stuffy and overheated he would have to open a window in the middle of winter. Living alone was far different and much colder. It was far too irresponsible to leave a fire burning while he was away, which meant the house was never fully warm. The fire grew slowly, casting an inviting glow across the now warmer part of the room. He pulled a stool close to the hearth and rubbed his hands, but the chill in his heart remained.

He stared at the fire until his eyes lost focus, lost in thought. She would have never abandoned him, would have never left him if he had not pushed her away, if he had not so deeply wounded her. She had wronged him by lying to him about his human mother, but she had given him far more and had never stopped trying to atone for it. Regardless of how deeply he had broken her heart, if he was in trouble, she would stop at nothing to come to his rescue. He stuck his finger to his lips and began to nibble at his fingernail, a nervous habit.

He looked around at the home she had given him, the home that he would have sworn she haunted although she still lived. A bit of her lingered in every room, in every darkened corner. He bit his fingernail too closely to the quick and jerked it out of his mouth. A residual taste of blood lingered on his tongue. "Well, damn…"

Chapter Twenty

It was nearly half past twelve before Valeria awoke, surprised to discover she was no longer in the chair, but back in the cage. She lifted her weary head from the bed of straw and squinted, trying to survey the room for any changes. Her vision was blurred, her eyes dried out. Every bone in her body ached with ancient pain, wounds from a century past had begun to reappear and ooze.

Since her dehydrated eyes offered her little assistance, she lay back down and listened. She felt out away from herself for any source of sound, like searching roots emanating from a tree. She listened for heartbeats, breathing, voices, and the scuffle of boots on the dirt floor. She felt the ground with her entire body for any vibrations or sounds that might be radiating through it. At first, she detected nothing but after a few minutes she began to hear approaching voices and could hear the armaments on their belts jingle as they walked. She laid perfectly still, eyes closed.

"She is still asleep, sir," Tobias said. Valeria could hear him nervously pulling his fingers through his wiry beard.

"She is weak. I suspect it will take longer and longer for her to awake until she is fully consumed by a catatonic state. It is the vampire mutations hoping to preserve itself, waiting patiently for its next victim," Arminius stated. She could feel their eyes on her.

"Just look at her laying there, a shriveled up tick, all dried up." A voice she had not heard in several days, Vincent. "I think you should kill the bloodsucking bitch."

247

"And then how will Mr. Arminius get his answers?" Tobias responded patronizingly.

"I don't know, Tobias. Maybe you can count ten ways to get her to talk, since I can only count to five!" he shouted back. "You would not be so happy to keep her alive if you only had one arm."

"Maybe we should feed her, just a little so she can talk again," Tobias said.

"Are you out of your mind?" Vincent exclaimed. "Should we just go grab someone off the street and throw them in there with her?"

"That's enough," Arminius said quietly, flatly. "She is very much aware of her condition. Soon her mind will be active and alive, but her body will be nothing but a husk. She will be trapped in a cage of her own design." Valeria could hear him cracking his knuckles as he spoke.

"But sir, what if she truly does not know?" Tobias asked. "What if this has been just another waste of time?"

"Then we will kill her and move on to the next. We will try again tonight, after sunset. If she does not know the secrets of the Scholomance, then she is of no use."

***

Disheartened at the waste of time, Lamond brushed through the busy train station to his gate. He had left a note with Mihai the night before, very simply stating where he was staying and the time his train was leaving the next day. It was the first to depart that afternoon. With no complications, he should arrive in Budapest by or just after sunset, which was to his best advantage.

Milling in and around the swarm of humanity, Lamond felt like he was inside a beehive. Everything buzzed, breathed, beat, or moved. He tried to keep his profile low, his head down, and get to the train and the safety of his own car as quickly as he could. Finally at his gate, he was thankful to be able to board early.

"Right this way, sir," the attendant said as he punched his ticket. Lamond nodded and stepped up into the train.

"Lamond, wait!" a voice called out, one that he recognized but did not expect to ever hear again. He stepped back down and saw Emil rushing toward him, waving his handkerchief overhead. Lamond could not help but smile, showing every pearly white and sharp tooth in his mouth. "Wait for me!"

Lamond met him with an extended hand and shook his heartily. "It is good to see you, Emil."

"She would come for me, without doubt," Emil said, nodding his head in reconciliation with himself.

Lamond nodded and boarded the train. "Follow me. There is much to discuss and so little time."

Once inside the privacy of his car, Lamond opened the overnight bag and was greeted instantly by the scent of Valeria and old books. He laid the journals out across the bed, the largest surface in the compact, yet comfortable, confines of the sleeper car.

"What is all this?" Emil asked, picking up the first and oldest book. He opened it and read for a moment, and then looked up at Lamond in astonishment. "It's Valeria's; when she was a human."

Lamond nodded. "I recognized her handwriting, but I could only read bits and pieces. My Romanian is horrible," he answered. He took another book, nearly as fragile as the first and offered it to Emil. "This was your mother's. I believe it is in Hungarian. I can't read any of it."

Emil laid Valeria's journal down as carefully as if he was placing a newborn infant in a crib and took Ilona's journal. His fingertips brushed the cover for a moment before he opened it. "She began writing this just before she was married to the Count, while she was still human, over four hundred years ago," he said in hushed tones, as if she could hear him and catch his snooping. "How did you ever acquire these?"

"Valeria got them from a man named Jonathan Harker. She mailed them to me just before she disappeared. She was going to England to

249

find him and Stoker after she finished with Van Helsing in Amsterdam."

"I do not understand. I recognize the names from Bram Stoker's book, *Dracula*. I read it, showed it to her…"Emil stopped, his words grinding to a halt, and then slowly the pieces began to fall into place. "What was she doing on this trip, Lamond?"

"Van Helsing killed your mother and Fleur, nearly killed Valeria. Harker killed Count Dracula, correct?" Lamond stated, recalling what he had read from the copy Valeria had shown him. Emil nodded. "She went to Amsterdam to avenge your mother's death, to kill Van Helsing. Then she went to England to find Stoker and Harker and learn who had sold off their stories. I know she succeeded in these because I received a telegraph from her just after Christmas."

"Yes… I did as well," Emil added. His voice and expression was tainted by what Lamond believed was shame. He was quiet for a moment before he revealed the cause, his head down, still holding Ilona's first journal. "This is all my fault."

"No one, certainly not Valeria, is blaming you for this," Lamond quickly added. The last thing he needed was an overly emotional human being dramatic. It was time for business, the rest could come later.

"But it *is* my fault. I think she would have left things alone, even with that book being published, if I had not sent her away like I did. She was happy in Brasov, and I ruined it for her," Emil said, voice cracking despite his effort to remain composed. He gently laid his mother's book back with the others and sat in the only chair just as the train began to pull out of the station. He propped his elbows on his knees and hid his face in his hands.

"This is no time for guilt or blame, Emil. Valeria is her own woman, makes her own decisions, you know that as well as I do. Everything will work itself out as soon as we get her back, safe and sound." Lamon ventured to place a hand of comfort on his new companion's shoulder. "You will have time to make this right. I promise. She is strong."

250

"That's what her name means in Romanian, to be strong. Did you know that?" Emil asked, hastily wiping his face.

"From the moment I met her," Lamond said with a hopeful smile.

"How did you meet her?" Emil asked, ever curious.

"Well…that is an interesting story," He stammered, a blush warming his cheeks. "She killed me. I can explain the rest later."

***

When her abductors finally left, Valeria attempted again to open her eyes, but found they were too dry to focus. Stranded in the darkness behind her eyelids, she remembered being trapped within her tomb the night Vlad, Ilona, and Fleur were murdered. She could feel the life-sapping power of the sacred wafer Van Helsing had placed atop it, muting her strength. She had meditated on Vlad's name and image, begging him for assistance, one last request. A flood of rats came and devoured the wafer, and allowed her to escape and save Emil. In the end, Vlad did not save her, or even save himself, but he did give her the chance to save herself.

She locked Lamond's image into her mind and repeated his name over and over, without giving her words voice, hoping the connection they shared was strong enough to transmit her emotions to him across the miles. She had deliberately kept Lamond and Emil out of her thoughts, afraid that somehow her captors would discover them. Now she knew they would stop at nothing to acquire the information they sought, that Lamond and Emil would never be safe as long as Arminius prowled. She chanted Lamond's name over and over until it became a subconscious act, like she was breathing in his image and exhaling his name. She hoped that somehow her focused energy would serve as a homing signal that, against all odds, he would be able to follow. She hoped he would come to her rescue, that her misguided rejections had not pushed him so far away that he was no longer willing to take such a risk. She prayed she would live long enough to see his face again and he did not die trying to save her.

***

For hours, Lamond and Emil poured over every piece of information they had at their disposal as the train sped toward Budapest. Lamond revealed everything, every dream and premonition. He laid his heart and feelings bare and hoped something within his thoughts and dreams would help them solve Valeria's riddle.

"I know how this must sound, how *I* must sound. I can't explain how I know these things. It is just there in my mind, like she is there telling me everything but I can only hear pieces of it."

"Well, this is what we know for fact. We know she left Paris for Amsterdam, killed Dr. Van Helsing. We know she was in London and met with Harker and Stoker before she was taken, we assume to Budapest," Emil said, laying out her steps. "What we don't know is who took her or why."

"What's in Budapest?" Lamond presented the question, hoping they could somehow find the answer together. "Anything important for vampires?"

"No, not to the best of my knowledge. It has the usual government buildings, historical landmarks, statues and parks, and a university," Emil said casually, but suddenly became quiet, like he was holding his breath. Lamond studied him, waiting for him to reveal the connection. "Budapest University."

Emil quickly grabbed his overnight bag and opened it, proudly revealing he had had the foresight to bring his own copy of *Dracula* along for the journey. Lamond's eyes brightened with hopeful anticipation as he watched Emil quickly flip through the pages, many of which were marked by dog-eared folded corners.

"What is it?" Lamond finally asked, as Emil continued to desperately search.

252

"Stoker said something about Budapest University. Van Helsing mentioned the name of a colleague at Budapest University." Emil scanned a few more pages before his face lit up with a successful smile. "Here it is! Arminius was a friend of Van Helsing's from Budapest University. He seems to be some sort of expert on Count Dracula, a historian."

"How much do you want to bet Van Helsing told this Arminius everything he had dug up over the last ten years on Count Dracula and his wives?" Lamond added.

"Exactly, and the best way to learn about a deceased husband is to ask his widow," Emil said triumphantly. Lamond stuck out his hand to shake with Emil, congratulating his work. "If we can find Arminius, we will find Valeria."

***

Valeria heard the door to the cage open, could feel the floor vibrating under her as they walked toward her. Only a few minutes had passed since the night had whispered to her, letting her know it had arrived but it had made no difference. A hand wrapped around each of her arms and she was lifted and pulled out of the cage and back under the hateful light of the lanterns. She was locked back into the chair, for what she knew would surely be the last time. She was defenseless, far too blood deprived to even present a threat to her careful captors.

"Countess, I know you can hear me. The time for games has passed." Arminius lifted her chin and forced her to look into his eyes. She could only see his blurry outline, partially eclipsing the lantern behind him. "I will have my answers tonight. Do you understand?"

He released her chin and her head fell limply against her shoulder. She thought of Lamond, the wonderful nights they had spent beneath the Paris stars. He had brought her so much happiness, given her such love and adoration, so much devotion, such an unexpected blessing that she had taken for granted, but now treasured. He had learned quickly,

253

had become a skilled and careful hunter. He was already charming, so that trait had only been amplified by his new chemistry. He would find his way without her.

Emil would only be safer. Freed from his connection to her and her famous husband, he would be able to continue his very human life in Brasov in relative safety. If she was careful, and did not reveal him to Arminius, he could live out his days in anonymity. He was strong, his mother's son. She knew he would succeed in whatever he attempted.

Snapping fingers in front of her face pulled her focus back to the present. She had not even noticed she had drifted away. Nothing Arminius had to say was important anymore, his threats all empty. Even if he did kill her as he had threatened, it was still just talk. Long ago, she had felt the cold, crushing maw of death enclose around her. She had felt the numbing, quiet of death, could hear it whispering to her even now. She no longer feared death. She had lived much too long for that.

"Valeria, I am going to ask you only once before I result to more… drastic measures. Where is the Scholomance?" Arminius said in his same, cold and dry tone.

"I do not know," she whispered, just as calm.

"Alright then… I have asked you politely, tried to keep this as civilized as you would allow me to do so. But I am out of patience and you are out of time," he said, holding his hand out to Tobias. He placed in it a small flask. Valeria could hear water sloshing around inside it. She knew what was coming. She dug her fingernails into the wooden chair arms and tried to steady herself for the pain that would bring the end of her long life. Lamond…. Lamond… Lamond... Her mind spoke over and over, her lips held tightly shut.

***

After dismounting the train in Budapest, Lamond and Emil stood in the middle of the street outside the station, unsure of which way to turn.

"How much longer until sunset?" Emil asked, consulting the unfamiliar skyline like an urban sundial.

"Only a few minutes now, I can already feel it," Lamond answered.

Emil turned a circle, looking all around him. "Where do we even begin?"

"Just a moment..." Lamond said, closing his eyes. Emil watched as he lifted his head to the sky, moonward, and inhaled deeply. He watched as the night invigorated Lamond, as its dark energy filled his veins and spread throughout his body. He remained silent for a moment, his head nodding gently, as if he was keeping beat with a song that only he could hear. He looked to Emil and smiled. "Follow me."

Emil had to remind Lamond on several occasions to slow his pace, to watch his step. His enthusiasm was leaving him behind and his speed was alerting the pedestrians they passed. The electric streetlamps flickered on and illuminated the city, elongating their shadows, as they sped down the sidewalks and through the narrow alleyways, twisting and turning.

"Where are you going?" Emil shouted, beginning to feel winded, legs fatigued. Lamond stopped and led him to an isolated corner of the darkest nearby alley.

"I can feel her, like she is in my brain," Lamond said, rhythmically tapping his finger against the side of his head. "She is close... I know that...but I can't..." He fidgeted, looking around uneasily. Finally he stopped, grabbed Emil by the shoulders, staring at him. "Don't scream."

Emil's eyes widened, his shoulders reflexively hunched. Lamond leapt skyward, his body shifting into a thick, rolling fog several feet off the ground before scaling the building and settling on the nearest rooftop with Emil in tow. "What are you doing?" Emil shouted, unable to see beyond the silvery haze, unable to move to stabilize himself, or even determine up from down.

"Shhh... You were slowing me down. This will be faster," Lamond whispered, although Emil could not tell where his voice had originated or if it simply surrounded him like the fog. He nodded his consent and tried not to dwell on the height or the gorge-like gaps between the buildings as they flew over them. Emil squint his eyes tight and tried to steady his stomach.

After several more minutes of what seemed to be mindless twists and turns and sudden changes in elevation, his ride came to an abrupt halt atop a roof. He shifted back and forth within the fog, as though he was trapped inside a wobbling gelatin dessert.

"Look at that," Lamond said as the fog began to thin and condense into a pillar before reforming into his fully dressed self. He directed Emil's attention to a courtyard in the distance. "Water and fire. That is what she was trying to tell me."

Emil squinted and could see the fountain topped by a flame and a large, complex building connecting to the courtyard in which it stood.

"She's in there?"

"Without doubt, I can feel her like a heartbeat, almost smell her," Lamond said, taking Emil by the shoulders again to deposit him softly on the sidewalk below. "She's in distress…dying."

"Then what are we waiting for?" Emil said and bolted forward. Lamond caught his hand and stopped him, nearly yanking him off his feet.

"You must be careful. We do not know how many people are in there with her. They have her trapped, so there must be something stronger than humans, something sapping her power…holy things, crucifixes, things that might not hurt you, but will make me weaker than a human. That is when I will need your help the most," Lamond cautioned. He had asked Emil to place himself in harm's way for Valeria's sake and he had accepted, but he did not want that compliance to be under the false illusion of guaranteed safety. "I want to save her more than anything, but if something should happen to you, she would never forgive me. She would kill me."

"She wouldn't kill you…" Emil said weakly.

"She would blame me for bringing you, so I am pretty sure she would kill me," Lamond stated again flatly, a hint of jest in his solemn tone. "She would probably regret it later though."

"Well good for you, I brought these." Emil opened his coat and proudly displayed his holstered dual revolvers. "No crucifix, garlic, or any other tricks they might have cooked up is going to make any difference to these."

"Are you a good shot?" Lamond asked. His excitement was quickly replaced by concern, doubting Valeria would have ever allowed him to touch a gun.

"Are you joking? I have been hunting and trapping since I was eight." Emil smiled and buttoned his coat again. "Aunt Veevee saw to it that I knew how to provide for myself, just in case she wasn't around. And while I might not take a hunting trip with these pretty little revolvers, I know how to use them."

"Alright then, we should not waste another minute," Lamond said, taking the lead as they approached the courtyard. "Stay behind me, unless I tell you to go ahead."

Only a short walk and a tall wrought iron fence stood between Lamond and Emil and the building where Valeria was being held. Fading and dispersing again into a blanket of fog, Lamond wrapped around Emil and lifted him over safely and silently. He only partially rematerialized as they crossed the cobblestone courtyard, reducing their noise to only one pair of feet. They passed the three tiered fountain, its trickling water the only sound in the quiet of the newly fallen night. The flame burned atop it, flicking and waving in the breeze that carried a few stray snow flurries, fed from an unseen fuel source beneath the cobblestone. Lamond pointed to it, reassuring Emil they were in the right location by its presence.

They huddled close to the door to reduce their visibility. Emil looked in both directions and then took a step back and aimed his boot at the doorknob.

"Wait!" Lamond whispered, spreading out across the door. Like a tendril on an octopus, he fed a wisp of fog through the keyhole. After only a moment, the lock unlatched. "Now, invite me in."

Emil placed one foot inside the doorway. "Come in, Lamond," he said, standing back so he could finish his work.

Lamond slipped back into the keyhole, congealing around the knob and lock like a mass of fog had clung to it. Another moment longer, and the lock was irreparably broken. The knob fell away from the door on both sides and into his fog before settling silently on the ground outside.

"Just securing a way back out," he whispered again. "Let's go."

Emil closed the door behind him and stayed close to the semi-transparent Lamond. He could do nothing but trust him and continue forward, almost blindly, down the winding and dark hallways. While he did his best to stay focused on the task before them, his heart swirled with so many emotions, with so much doubt and shame. He had dealt coldly with Valeria, broken her heart. She had set forth on this mission to avenge Ilona's death and hold those responsible for revealing their family's secrets to him and the rest of the world accountable. But he knew in his heart, which had never beat faster in his life, it was his rejection that had sent her to Amsterdam and beyond. While he had not abducted her or taken her to Budapest, the blame still rested on his shoulders. If she died, her blood would be on his hands. He would be far more accountable for her death than she had ever been for his human mother's death. For her sake and for his, she had to survive. He had to be able to right his wrongs. He had to have the chance to ask her to forgive him, a foolish boy, and tell her that she had done well for him. He had to tell her Ilona would be proud of her, and given the circumstances, even his human mother would appreciate what she had given him. He had to be able to tell her he loved her, his Aunt Veevee, one more time.

"Are you sure she is here?" Emil finally whispered as quietly as he could as still produce sound, sticking his head into the fog which was Lamond. "Is she alive?"

"She is here, beneath us. I bet she can feel us now," Lamond answered. Emil was unsure if he audibly spoke, from within his ear canal, or if he spoke directly to his mind. "I can feel something else, another kind of energy. It must be how they are containing her here. It makes me sick. Be on guard."

Lamond could feel the whisper of her life calling to him faintly, a mere shadow of what it once was. While in Paris, standing anywhere near Valeria was like standing on the shore of the ocean. She was alive with a cool, yet turbulent life force which hid the magnitude of its power beneath calm rolling waves. She radiated that energy and it soaked into him, like a plant absorbs sunlight to sustain itself. He could feel a diminished sensation of her, like a salty seaside breeze covering him, dangerously weak. But she was still alive. They were not too late and those who had hurt her, those who had so foolishly stolen the beautiful, explosive light from his evening star would pay dearly. He would offer their meager lives to her, a sacrifice to his goddess, her life restored from their deaths. He turned to look at Emil fully formed briefly.

"I can hear whispers, coming from down that hall somewhere, behind a few closed doors most likely. It is strange, but I can hear a male voice, but not his heartbeat. But I can hear her heart. She is still alive," Lamond whispered in the same quiet, almost telepathic manner.

Knowing they were close, Emil placed his hands on the handles of his guns, feeling the coolness kept within the metal. When the conflict began, it would happen quickly, almost in an instant. He had to be ready and not allow the slowness of his human reaction time and reflexes to compromise them.

"Hold on just a little longer, mon ange. I am coming for you," he said aloud, without fear of being heard while he slipped back into fog, surprising Emil with his boldness. He looked to Emil and nodded. The time had come. Emil drew his guns from their holsters, took in a deep breath, and nodded back, confirmation. There was no turning back.

***

"I cast you out, unclean spirit, along with every Satanic power of the enemy, every spectre from hell…" Arminius said, liberally dousing Valeria with holy water in the Sign of the Cross, from head to toe and across the shoulders. Although her need to sleep on Romanian soil to be rejuvenated had been dissolved by Vlad's death, she was still bound by other stipulations of her husband's curse. She was still reduced to a near catatonic state from sunrise to midday, still needed an introduction to cross a threshold, and the same affront for holy items and sacraments that afflicted Vlad also held power over her. Every drop of the simple holy water that Arminius threw on her felt like miniature daggers digging into her flesh. At first she thought that invoking the ancient rite of exorcism against her was foolish, but slowly, over the course of hours, it felt as though the cells of her body were struggling to stay fused. The combination of her weakened state, the lanterns, the words he spoke, the motions he repeated, and the holy water were working to separate the human and inhuman elements within her, not to her cure but most certainly to her death. She cried out in pain, writhed in agony, which only encouraged Arminius to continue. "Tell me Valeria, where is the Scholomance? Who is the tenth student?

"I do not know!" she shouted, louder than she realized she had ability left.

Arminius screamed in frustration, pulling his hair. "I cast you out, unclean spirit, along with every Satanic power of the enemy, every spectre from hell, and all your fell companions; in the name of our Lord Jesus Christ. Begone and stay far from this creature of God," Arminius growled, lashing her with the water. Tobias stood nearby, but in the shadows, close at hand for his master. Valeria screamed out again as she was being torn asunder at the molecular level. Her body had assimilated with the vampire's curse when it conquered her at the moment of her mortal death and then rewrote her into a new creature immortal. It was the virus that had taken over her body, had allowed her to regenerate, and had replicated and spread to Lamond. Now it was being undone from what remained of her humanity. She could feel darkness closing in around her, a silent blackness from which she did not expect to wake. It was the same comforting darkness, the familiar caress from a friend she had met long ago on the banks of the Arges River. It welcomed her back again, to rest from her toil. She closed her eyes and sank.

"Mon ange... I am coming for you..." A familiar voice broke the perfect stillness of Sheol, like a ray of light piercing the clouded sky. Lamond. Had she truly heard his voice or had her mind played a trick on her? She concentrated her remaining energy to only listening, ignoring the rest of the world in search of a heartbeat, a signature in sound. Then as surely as she still lived, she heard the quiet, elongated beat of her lover's heart, slow and strong, unmistakably his. He had heard her plea and had come to her, to save her again. She could not help but smile, could not keep a whispery breath of laughter from escaping her lips. Sheol would have to wait for another day.

"What is it?" Arminius demanded, hoping she had slipped into delusions and would finally reveal his answers.

"You will see... soon." She smiled and rested her head back against the back of the chair. If he had made it this far, she knew nothing would stop him from getting to her. She just had to be patient. Searing thirst scalded her throat, a sensation that had given up on being quenched weeks ago returned with the promise of satisfaction. She looked at Arminius through partially opened eyes. She had already gotten a taste of his friend, but she knew his blood, his red hot life, would only be that much sweeter.

"Tobias, have a look around. See if anything is off," he instructed. Tobias dutifully departed, like a watchdog sent out to patrol his yard.

Arminius stepped back and looked at the Countess Dracula, stubbornly resisting him. She *had* to know. He could accept nothing else. She was the only link to the answers he sought, the only key to unlock the secrets of the Scholomance.

Chapter Twenty- one

Emil felt as though his footsteps sounded as loud as an elephant's, walking behind the silently floating Lamond. He held the grips of the guns tightly, perspiration misted the inside of his palms, crossed his forehead, and the small of his back. As powerful a team as they made, both he and Lamond had their share of weaknesses. Lamond was subject to every defense that held Valeria captive and, if their rescue somehow became a standoff, he would be incapacitated at dawn. He was all too aware of his own flaws. He was mortal, a soft, living, breathing, bleeding, human man who could be killed in a hundred easier ways than a vampire. Fortunately for him, the holy traps and weaponry invoked against vampires did nothing to him. Valeria's captors were humans too, just as fragile as he, but by no means helpless. They would be armed, no doubt, against human and vampire kind.

They had heard her shouting, defiant and strong, at her captor. They had wanted to rush in with guns blazing and fangs bared, ready for blood, but their better sense had prevented it. Lamond had not been able to detect a human pulse to match with the voice. They knew there was at least one enemy lurking within the darkness and they had to assume there were more.

Lamond's confidence was bolstered when he realized he had walked down the hallway in which they stood in his dream, despite having never set foot in Budapest before that day. He knew where to find her, but he also knew there were multiple rooms, attaching hallways, and alcoves from which they could be ambushed. A noise stopped him as still as a statue, a raised hand signaling for Emil to stop as well.

"Footsteps, no heartbeat," Lamond whispered. Emil pulled the hammers back on his revolvers. "Wait... let's see where he goes." Lamond spun around Emil like a spider wrapping its prey in a cocoon of silk and lifted him to the ceiling. Hovering there, they watched a man in white robes with a lengthy beard walk beneath them and disappear down the way they had just come.

"Is he a vampire?" Emil asked, so quietly he could not hear his own voice.

"No. He is certainly human, a sneaky human at that," Lamond whispered against his ear drum. "No way of knowing how many might be down here."

Before Emil could prevent it, one of his revolvers slipped from his moist palm, though the fogginess of Lamond, and crashed against the hard packed earthen floor, firing a single shot. The noise erupted from the gun like a shockwave from an explosion, concussive. Reflexively, Lamond and Emil dropped from the ceiling, retrieved the fallen gun, and rushed forward.

* * *

Arminius dropped the bottle of holy water when he heard the shot, quickly extinguishing the lanterns. He left Valeria trapped in her chair, smiling like a cat that had just caught a mouse in her claws. He closed the door behind him and headed down the hallway to investigate, stopping to concur with Vincent.

"I heard a shot. What is happening?" he asked, holding his wounded arm against his chest, still early into his recovery.

"It appears someone has come to rescue the Countess. Tobias is already looking into it. Stay with her, out of sight," Arminius said. His usually calm tone was ruffled, his back stiffened with tension. He turned and headed down the adjoining hall, retracing Tobias' steps.

264

***

Lamond yanked Emil around the corner of an adjoining hallway just as gun was fired behind them, the bullet grazing the plaster beside them. The man who passed under them had backtracked when he heard the shot from Emil's fallen gun and now they were under fire. Emil hastily checked doors that lined the hallway, only to find them locked. At the dead end of the hall, he slammed his shoulder against the last door, once, twice, three times before the lock splintered away from the frame.

"Get in here, Lamond!" he shouted, holding the door open a crack. Another shot echoed through the network of hallways and a bullet dug into the wall behind where they had just been standing. Emil slammed the door shut, nearly closing it on Lamond in the process. "Why are you solid now, when we are getting shot at?"

"It just went away and I can't change back. We must be getting close to something," he answered, quickly moving away from the door. In the darkness, behind Emil, Lamond caught the outline of a person. "Look out!"

He reflexively sprang forward, pushing Emil out of the way, only to realize it was a large statue of the Virgin Mary holding the infant Jesus in her arms standing alongside numerous statues of revered priests and nuns. Emil spun around but was nearly blind in the blackness of the windowless room.

"There are statues of saints, crucifixes, shelves full of books, this place used to be a church, or a convent, something like that."

"Whatever it is, we have to get out of here without getting shot full of holes," Emil stated while nervously pacing. "He knows where we are. He's out there, just waiting for us to stick our heads out to blow them off."

"Maybe not," Lamond said, pushing a large statue of a very pious monk toward the door. "You just have to see him first. Open the door."

Emil stood with his back flat against the wall and stretched his leg out. He caught the edge of the door with the toe of his boot and pushed it open. It swung back and smacked the wall.

"Now get behind me, low to the ground. See if you can get a shot off," Lamond said, rocking the heavy statue out into the hallway and crouching down with his back turned, hiding Emil with the statue and his own body. Emil took aim around the plaster hem of the monk's robe and waited for a sign from their assailant.

With an explosive shatter, the statue's fragile head burst from its shoulders, raining down shards of plaster and dust on them. Emil fired back instantly and they heard a man cry out with pain.

"Move!" Emil shouted, running down the hallway with Lamond in tow, sliding along the wall and as he turned the corner he shot again, but his target had already retreated.

"He's bleeding," Lamond said, noting the thick scent of freshly drawn blood.

"He will be back, just grazed his arm. We got to keep moving."

Rushing down the hallway, running at full speed, Lamond led Emil down the last hallway he remembered from his dream. He could hear Valeria's heart, could feel the tingle on his skin that only being close to her gave him. Her energy was so frail, just a sliver of her former self. More than ever before, he needed to find her, needed to hold her in his arms, hold her close and never let her go again. He was so overcome with emotion, so distracted by his aching heart, that he nearly missed seeing a man at the far end of the long hallway turn on his heels and run.

"Stop!" Lamond shouted, running as fast as he could while under the oppression of the surrounding holy items. Emil drew a gun and prepared to fire at the first sight of the man again.

"Where did he go?" Emil shouted, desperately looking for a hint as to which door he had entered in.

Suddenly a door behind Emil swung open and Arminius leapt out, wildly swinging a knife. Emil jumped back, but not before the razor sharp blade caught his forearm. The scent of his blood instantly spiked the air. Lamond turned, enraged, placing himself between his human companion and Arminius. Retaining reflexes fractionally faster than that of a human, Lamond dodged Arminius' lunges and swipes, the blade flashing in the dim light. Lamond took aim and landed a thunderous punch to his attacker's face, knocking him to the ground flat of his back.

"I can smell her on you, you son of a bitch!" Lamond screamed, kicking the knife from his hand. He knelt over him and lifted him by the collar of his white coat and punched him again. Blood splattered Arminius' face, blemished the snowy white purity of his uniform, and smeared across Lamond's knuckles. "Where is she?"

A shot rang from the hallway and Lamond's back arched in pain. Tobias stood leaning against the doorway to steady his aim. Lamond turned and growled like a wild animal, enraged and wounded. He leapt from Arminius and dove into Tobias. Emil stood over Arminius, a gun pointed at his face, trying to convince himself not to kill him where he laid. He looked at his tarnished coat, his chest emblazoned by the large silver cross.

"So that's how you keep your heartbeat so quiet," he said, tapping his finger on Arminius' chest. "Clever but not clever enough, you should have never laid a finger on her, Arminius."

His eyes grew wide in disbelief that Emil knew his identity. "Who are you?"

"My name is Emil, son of Ilona Szilagyi- Dracula," he said proudly, an overdue confirmation. "Valeria is my aunt. You will regret what you have done before this night is over."

While Emil introduced himself to Arminius, Lamond and Tobias rolled in the hallway, each struggling to gain an advantage. The bullet lodged behind Lamond's shoulder blade dug deeper with every movement as he struggled to take the gun from Tobias. Finally overtaking him, he flattened Tobias to the ground, digging his fingers into the wound to his arm that Emil had given him earlier. Tobias howled in pain as Lamond's fingers sank into his flesh. He finally released the gun and Lamond grabbed it and shoved it into the waistband of his pants at the small of his back. He grabbed his hand, pinned it to the floor and pushed with a knee into his gut to keep him still. Lamond pulled his fingers out of the wound on Tobias' arm and pushed his head over, exposing his throat. He could see his pulse, his blood pumping just under the thin skin of his throat.

Lamond opened wide and then sank his fangs deep beneath Tobias's flesh, slicing deeper and longer than necessary. Adrenaline soaked blood flooded into his mouth, so potent, so full of fear and life, that it began to heal his wounds in spite of the prevalence of holy objects and the even the cross etched on his victim's coat. He could feel the wound surrounding the bullet shrink, pushing it out of his flesh like a splinter. Another mouthful and the bullet erupted from the skin and fell out of his back, caught inside his shirt. Tobias struggled, but Lamond held firm, ensuring that he inflicted enough damage and took enough blood that he would not survive.

Once last mouthful, and Lamond stood victorious and rejuvenated, wiping his mouth on his sleeve. He took the gun from his waistband and fired a single shot, aimed directly between Tobias' eyes just to be certain.

Lamond returned to Arminius and yanked him to his feet. "Take us to her, or we will kill you and then find her. You choose," he said with his face so close to Arminius that would have no choice but to smell Tobias' blood on his breath.

Arminius glared at him silently and then began to walk with Lamond holding him firmly by one arm, while Emil walked close behind with a gun pushed against the back of his head. Just as the dream had foretold, they entered a large, dark room, but instead of finding a map lying on a table there was a single chair, with an emaciated body draped across it.

"Valeria!" Lamond shouted, leaving Arminius to Emil's safekeeping. He fell to his knees in front of her, almost afraid to touch her. Her wrists and ankles were cuffed to the chair, her remaining hair obscuring most of her sunken face. She looked like death, like they were already too late. Tears welled up in his eyes at the sight of her, despite hearing her tired heart still beating. He lifted her face, gently brushed the hair from her face and kissed her parched lips. "Valeria, I am here. It's your Lamond, mon amour."

She slowly opened her eyes, just a crack, and the hint of a smile hid at the corner of her mouth. "You came for me..." she whispered, her dry eyes trying to focus on his face. "He left me...but you...you came for *me*..."

"Of course, I came for you, mon petite étoile..." he whispered, lightly kissing her cracked and tender lips again. "My little star."

Emil stood silently, allowing them to have a private moment. The barrel of his gun ensured that Arminius was watching, taking in his own defeat in the remaining moments of his life. Lamond pulled the pins from the cuffs on her ankles and wrists, gently rubbing them.

"Bring him here," Lamond shouted, motioning Emil closer.

"Who's here?" Valeria panicked, instantly becoming aware of a human heartbeat. Her eyes searched desperately to find the source.

"It's me, Aunt Veevee. Don't be afraid," Emil whispered, choking back tears. Rage boiled up his chest, almost instantly exploding. He pushed Arminius to his knees in front of the withered Valeria. He grabbed his head, under the chin and across the forehead, forcing him to look at her. "Look what you did to her, you bastard, you damn bastard. Look at her!"

Lamond moved to Valeria's side, never taking his hand from hers. He understood why Emil needed to make Arminius accountable for her condition. He had seen his guilt on the train, how he blamed himself for Valeria's situation. Emil was transferring a measure of his own guilt and blame onto Arminius, forcing himself to look at the destruction his selfish words had wrought. He yanked the coat from Arminus' shoulders, removing the power of the cross, and tore away the neck of his shirt.

He took a knife from his boot and gave it to Lamond, holding the gun against the back of Arminius' head again. Lamond grabbed Arminius' wrist and slashed across it, quick and deep, and pushed it against Valeria's mouth. When the first drops of blood fell across her tongue, her eyes widened, and she bit into his flesh without hesitation. He attempted to struggle, to pull away from her, but stopped when he heard the hammer of Emil's gun draw back and click into place, ready to fire.

Life began to spark within Valeria's body once again, igniting with a fire that demanded fuel faster than she could glean from his wrist. Having regained just enough energy to move, she struck out at his throat and dug her fangs in to blood gorged artery. Arminius' eyes widened with fear, knowing she would be his death. Emil and Lamond held his arms, restraining him, as she drained the life from him and made it her own.

She could feel his blood spreading through her, refreshing her mummy-like body, healing wounds, old and new. Her hair began to replenish itself, her skin returning to its alabaster perfection. Her vision cleared, the fog lifted from her mind.

"Wait!" he cried out, begging, nearly breathless. "Please! Before I die, please, tell me…. Tell me where the Scholomance is…"

Valeria paused, released his throat and stared at him with a puzzled face. Even now, his desire to know her secrets overwhelmed him, even in the face of death.

"You wish to know my husband's secrets?" Valeria said, watching the blood bubble from his throat each time his slowing heart beat. He nodded his head, no longer able to speak, his eyes setting cold and fading. "Ask him yourself," she answered dryly. She smiled at him devilishly, licked her lips, and continued her meal.

Part Eight:
Begin Again

Chapter Twenty- two

With the last beat of Arminius heart, Valeria rose and stood over his corpse, strong and whole. Lamond pulled her into his arms, gently lifted her face in his hands, and brushed her lustrous golden hair behind her ear. He kissed her again, her lips finally feeling as they should against his, as he remembered them. He pulled her against him as tightly as he could, and felt the strength that had returned to her body and the softness of her curves. Electricity washed over his body, static charging the fine hairs of his arms to stand on end. She gently pulled his bottom lip between hers with just the lightest tension. He caressed her head against his chest, rested his cheek against her hair and breathed her in, absorbing her, living within her energy.

Emil shuffled uneasily, clearing his throat, out of place.

"Emil…" she said. Lamond gingerly released her and she slowly slipped from his embrace. She walked toward her nephew with outstretched arms, her eyes already becoming misty. "I heard your voice. I thought my ears were deceiving me."

Movement within the shadows caught Lamond's eye, but a fraction of a second too late. Vincent sprang from the shadows with a knife that matched Arminius' drawn back. Before he could call out to them, Vincent struck, sinking his knife deep within Emil's back.

"Emil!" she screamed and rushed to him as he began to crumble. She caught him up in her arms, easing him to the ground. Lamond rushed past them and overtook Vincent before he had a moment to act again. He flattened the coward against the ground, grabbed his head in his hands, and twisted it to the left, and then quickly to the right, feeling the bones within his spine snap and fracture with each turn of his head. He dropped his head and his neck folded and contorted into an unnatural position from the unsupported weight.

Valeria rolled Emil onto his side and reflexively pulled the knife from his back, which was followed by a sudden gush of blood. "Oh God! I should not have done that! Lamond, help me! Please!" she screamed, rocking Emil back and forth like a small child, desperately trying to hold pressure against his wound at the same time.

"Emil, what are you doing here?" she said, pushing her hand under his back to apply pressure to the gaping gash, instantly painting her hand slick with his blood.

"Aunt Veevee, I am sorry I made you go..." Emil said with a sick gurgle prominent in his voice. "I am... I'm sorry."

"Shhh... don't worry about any of that right now. We are going to get you to a doctor, get you taken care of, and then we can talk," she said, tears falling from her eyes and onto his face, despite her efforts to hide the severity of his condition from him. "Damn it, Lamond. Help me get him up!"

"I can't move, Veevee," Emil said, with a voice little more than a whisper. "He got me good."

"Oh God!" Valeria cried out, knowing he would bleed out before they could find a doctor. Lamond sat behind her, supporting her as she cradled Emil.

Emil struggled to touch her face, unable to reach her on his own. She placed his hand against her face and held it there, time passing much too quickly for her to know what to do, to know what to say. He smiled weakly, eyes heavy.

"He is dying, Valeria. Save him," Lamond whispered in her ear. She shook her head defiantly, glaring hatefully at him. Emil gasped raggedly and coughed, blood mixed with spittle settling back on his pallid face. "He is running out of time, Valeria. *You* are running out of time." Lamond urged.

"I will not put my curse on him!" she shouted.

"You are cursing him to death if you do not save him!" Lamond shouted back.

Valeria squint her eyes, tears thick with stolen blood streaked down her cheeks. She could hear his heart struggling to produce even one more beat, and then it suddenly began pounding erratically, racing out of control. His chest rose and fell, shallow and violent, convulsing. Her mind flashed back to the first time she ever laid eyes on Ilona's borrowed son, his wounded neck still weeping from Vlad's bite, wrapped within the safety of her arms. It was almost as though he survived because of Ilona's unwavering faith, as though her will had been enough to give him strength.

"Ilona, please forgive me..." Valeria whispered before biting into her own wrist, tearing a deep gash that quickly bubbled and poured forth. She placed it against Emil's colorless lips and allowed it to flow into his upturned mouth, insuring it drained down his throat. He choked and coughed, but seemed to swallow at least a portion of her dark gift. She held him against her chest, rocking him as she had done some many times as a child, listening to the life escape his body. She cursed herself under her breath, cried, and prayed she had not waited too long. The desperate fluttering of his heart suddenly stopped. His chest fell flat.

Emil was dead.

Valeria fell back onto Lamond and wailed out, holding her nephew/son's lifeless body in her arms so tight, it was as though she was trying to keep the life from escaping his body, covered in his blood.

"Please, baby... Please come back..." she cried desperately as Lamond held her up. "You can't die, too..."

***

Somewhere in muffled darkness, Emil thought he could hear someone calling his name, a familiar voice, but so far away. He felt weightless, as carefree as a child. Valeria was safe. He and Lamond had saved her. An overwhelming feeling of happiness washed over him. He had done well, redeemed himself. A warm, welcoming light began to unfold from a single pinpoint in the darkness. Like stepping into the sun on a chilly day, the light soaked into him, chasing away the darkness. He could see several figures moving within the light, their bodies in silhouette against the glaring backdrop.

As he approached the light, two figures stood out from the others, both distinctly feminine.

"Such a handsome man you have become," a gentle voice said. Ilona's loving face came into focus, her smile as warm as the light that surrounded them.

"So tall, just like his father." The other woman spoke. Although he did not recognize this woman, his heart told him that she was his human mother.

Emil looked at them both, astonished to see them, to see them together. He understood that all had been forgiven, that the two halves of his identity had been unified.

"Valeria got herself into trouble, didn't she?" Ilona asked in a tone that told Emil she already knew the answer. "I thought she was going to get here before you did."

Emil was speechless, taking each woman by the hand, ready to follow wherever they led.

"Oh no my dear, you are not staying. It is not your time," His human mother said, without even a hint of sadness, as though the next time they met would be only moments away, instead of a lifetime.

"You have far too much living to do." Ilona kissed his forehead. "Take care of Valeria. She needs you more than she knows."

Their moment between worlds having passed, the light folded in atop itself and disappeared back into the darkness, stealing his mothers away. Again he heard another familiar voice, Valeria, begging him to come back. He turned away from the direction of the light and toward her voice.

Suddenly Emil felt himself entombed in red haze, overwhelming him, engulfing and infusing him. Then it was though he was falling, his life crashing back into his body. He could feel every pain, every ache, his life spreading out through every fraction of his body. His eyes popped open, wide and terrified, his body straining to move in every direction at once for reasons he could not understand. Pounding filled his ears, Valeria and Lamond's heartbeats crashing in his ears like thunder, along with his own slow, steady pulse. He could smell a hundred distinct scents at once, but first of all he could smell was blood, his own blood soaked into his clothes and all over Valeria.

He desperately clawed at his back to find his wound, which had already healed.

"Do not be afraid, Emil," Valeria said crouching down to look into his eyes. We brought you outside, away from all the relics so you could recover faster."

Emil looked to Valeria, eyes open as far as they could stretch. "I died, didn't I?" he asked to reaffirm what he already knew was true. She nodded in agreement, knowing words were not necessary. He had been stabbed by Arminius' henchman, bled to death in Valeria's arms, and returned from death. He was now a vampire. "Now what? We cannot stay here."

"No, we are leaving just as soon as you are ready to travel. I think Arminius and his goons were just the nail of a finger on a much larger hand, possibly rouge members of a larger group." "You are special Emil, created from two different vampires," Lamond spoke up, standing close to Valeria. "The Solomonari will be back. They will want to know what happened here."

"What are we going to do? Wherever we go, they will be chasing us," Emil said, panic setting into his voice.

"We begin again, Emil, far away from here, in a new country with new names." Valeria walked to him, took one of his hands in each of hers and helped him to his feet. For the first time, he looked upon the night with his new eyes, clearly and unhindered. The world had been reborn with him. The night whispered to him, called to him, just like it called to Valeria and Lamond. It was evident on his face. She recognized it and smiled, hoping to comfort him with her calmness. With Emil's help, Lamond had brought her back from the brink of death, had overcome seemly insurmountable odds to save her. She would never doubt his love or loyalty again. Again death had been denied its due when she stole her nephew from its very claws and had given him a new, darker lease on life. Lamond smiled as well, his chest filled with pride and his heart with joy and relief. Nothing could stand against them and prosper. Valeria and Lamond were certain that together, the three of them would survive, no matter what the future held. "We will begin again together, in America."

The End

Acknowledgement:

Heartfelt thanks to you, the reader, for choosing to spend your precious time with my work. I am so thankful to be able to continue Valeria's journey with you. Thank you to the wonderful Rue Volley for giving my book a beautiful face and to the amazing Elizabeth Anne Lance for making her sound as good as she looks. And a very special thank you to SJ Davis and everyone at Crushing Hearts and Black Butterfly Publishing for your support and guidance and for making this house a home. We are onehouseunited!

Made in the USA
Middletown, DE
30 November 2014